# HURRICANE HILL ROAD

CHERRY KING

*Judy,
I hope you enjoy
my story. Blessings!
Cherry King*

11/19/2014

HURRICANE HILL ROAD

TATE PUBLISHING
AND ENTERPRISES, LLC

*Hurricane Hill Road*
Copyright © 2014 by Cherry King. All rights reserved.

No part of this publication may be reproduced, stored in a retrieval system or transmitted in any way by any means, electronic, mechanical, photocopy, recording or otherwise without the prior permission of the author except as provided by USA copyright law.

The opinions expressed by the author are not necessarily those of Tate Publishing, LLC.

Published by Tate Publishing & Enterprises, LLC
127 E. Trade Center Terrace | Mustang, Oklahoma 73064 USA
1.888.361.9473 | www.tatepublishing.com

Tate Publishing is committed to excellence in the publishing industry. The company reflects the philosophy established by the founders, based on Psalm 68:11,
*"The Lord gave the word and great was the company of those who published it."*

Book design copyright © 2014 by Tate Publishing, LLC. All rights reserved.
*Cover design by Jan Sunday Quilaquil*
*Interior design by Jomel Pepito*

Published in the United States of America
ISBN: 978-1-63185-390-6
1. Fiction / Christian / Historical
2. Fiction / Christian / General
14.08.06

To the memory of my late mother whose story is loosely depicted in this narrative. She led a life of dedication to her family and to anyone else who needed a helping hand or a loving touch, accepting anyone, never taking into account that person's race, gender, or station in life. This is the legacy she passed on to her children and grandchildren.

To my friend of over forty years, Wilmer Bishop. Her perspective as an African American who has lived in the South and her validation as to the authenticity of parts of the story led me to have the courage to publish.

# ACKNOWLEDGMENT

My husband, Bob, was a tremendous help in editing, making suggestions and supporting me on the whole project.

My Aunt Ibbie Ledford, who has experience in publishing three books, gave me valuable insight and strong encouragement.

My son-in-law Tim Ledford and my daughter Tami edited several times and suggested improvements.

JoAnn Taylor, my closest friend, gave me pride in my work and kept me going on the writing.

JoAnn's daughter Kelly Guseman worked tirelessly on the old photos to get them ready for publication.

Cynthia Ballenger, my friend and prayer partner, gave me ideas for the title and a dream of big possibilities for my story.

My eight children and twenty-two grandchildren and my many friends have been a blessing to me in this process.

# CONTENTS

Prologue ............................................................. 11
Voice from the Past ............................................ 15
Beginning Again ................................................. 21
Starting with Hope ............................................. 31
Memphis ............................................................. 42
Letters ................................................................. 52
War's Tentacles Reach Out ................................. 64
Peggy's Diagnosis ............................................... 76
Robert ................................................................. 88
The Accident ....................................................... 93
Love Creeps In ................................................. 109
Complications ................................................... 119
Terror in the Night ........................................... 131
Fighting Loneliness .......................................... 140
Molly ................................................................. 146
Angel ................................................................. 152
Trying to Start Again ....................................... 163
Jim Moves On ................................................... 169

Family Reaction .................................................................. 173
Catching Up ...................................................................... 180
Looking Back .................................................................... 187
Coping .............................................................................. 193
Laundry Business ............................................................. 202
Regrets .............................................................................. 209
Fighting Old Battles ......................................................... 215
Disaster ............................................................................ 226
A Different Path ............................................................... 231
Getting Better .................................................................. 240
Young Marion .................................................................. 245
Marion and William ........................................................ 255
Life Changes .................................................................... 262
Running for Office .......................................................... 267
Searching .......................................................................... 273
Together Again ................................................................ 278
Book Club Questions ...................................................... 285

# PROLOGUE

Early in 1942, soon after the bombing of Pearl Harbor, a site thirteen miles south of Dyersburg, Tennessee, was chosen for an Army air base, which became the home of the B-17 bomber. The people in the rural area around the base soon saw their skies filled with the sights and sounds of these large planes swooping and maneuvering through the skies as pilots trained for bombing missions in World War II. These planes were an ominous sight, especially frightening to children who were hearing bits and pieces of stories about war, and it wasn't unusual to hear of accidents in flight. Seventy thousand pilots were trained with twenty-two accidents occurring. They sometimes flew so low that a person looking up could get a glimpse of the pilot.

Sam and Maud Lane were raising their family of ten children on a small cotton farm in the fertile soil of the Mississippi River bottomland in the tiny community of Millsfield, near Dyersburg. Papa, as they all called Sam, had been head of a household since he was thirteen years old. When his father died of tuberculosis, leaving his mother with five small children, Sam quit school and went to work, doing anything that would provide for survival of his mother and siblings. This forced apprenticeship and his keen mind made him one of the best farmers and business partners in the area. He felt blessed that their first three children were boys. The four of them became a working team that many of the farmers in the area envied.

Sam and Maud were complete opposites: Mama, tall and thin with dark hair and eyes, ran a tight ship. She was stern and stoic. Papa could have easily passed as Santa Claus's brother with his twinkling blue eyes and jolly, easy-going way with family and acquaintances; but this laidback personality had resulted in his dream of providing handsomely for the twelve of them to be crushed by an unscrupulous land owner.

Mr. Wilson, who owned most of the land in the valley, made a deal with Sam and his three boys to pasture and care for his very large herd of cattle, promising to share the profits when they were taken to market, and also to give Sam enough of the choice herd to start his own cattle farm. As with all Sam's business dealings, there was nothing in writing, only a handshake, so when all was done, Mr. Wilson made excuses, refusing to honor his agreement, and Sam ended up with little money for all their work and no cattle. Since there was no signed contract for proof, Sam took what he was offered and went back to cotton farming on his small parcel of land.

The whole family worked hard and Maud was frugal to a fault. An environmentalist before the word was even invented, never allowing anything to be wasted no matter how much work it took to make it usable. Her oldest daughter, Margaret, born after the three sons, found that out the hard way when she made an offhand remark about saving chitterlings.

Most families threw away the intestines of the hogs that were slaughtered in the fall each year, but Maud insisted they be saved to make chitterlings. She fried them into crisp snacks for the family and gave many of them away to neighbors. A long, tedious process went into making them edible. They were placed in a large bucket of freezing cold water to soak, and Maud picked and cleaned them several times a day, removing any intestinal residue that remained. Fifteen-year-old Margaret didn't think it was worth it. Observing her Mama's hands turn red from the cold, she made her thinking known.

"Mama, I wouldn't go to all that trouble if I was starving just to save them old chitterlings! Look at your poor hands. I bet you can't even feel anything they are so cold!"

Maud lifted her head, turning her dark eyes on her daughter. As they stared at each other, Margaret immediately knew she had said the wrong thing. Standing up, tall and thin, Maud dried her hands gingerly on her apron, trying to warm them enough to get the blood flowing and the feeling back into her fingers.

"Well, Missy," she chided her daughter. "I think this job will be just the thing for you. You are not too good to pick chitterlings. We never know when we, or somebody we know, will need a little extra food. It'd be a sin to waste them over a little laziness. This is now your job. Sit down here and get at it."

She pointed to the stool she had now vacated and Margaret spent many hours with her hands in the cold water, crying and repenting of her rash comment, and learning one of the many valuable life lessons Maud and Sam taught their children day by day.

Their little farmhouse sat back off Hurricane Hill Road, white frame with a porch across the front where porch-sittin' was a favorite pastime for family and neighbors. They had moved to this house soon after their little Tom had died. He was only six months old when Maud laid him on the daybed for his nap while she went quickly to the garden to pick beans for dinner. When Peggy yelled, "Mama, this old baby is crying," she hurriedly finished her job, then rushed to tend to her son. It was too late. She found him where he had fallen between the bed and the wall. He had suffocated. After that, Maud became so distraught every time she went near that room that Papa decided to move them to the little white house on Hurricane Hill Road where he had a few acres to grow good cotton and corn, and Mama could try to deal with the nightmare. With the birth of two more babies, she moved on with life, but she always told her children, "Watch your babies carefully. I didn't do that and I let my sweet little Tom die."

When Peggy was born, Margaret was glad to have another girl three years younger than she was, then Samuel and Little Tom. Jenny, Abby, and Frank came along after the older boys and Margaret were nearly grown. They were a typical West Tennessee farm family, eking out a living off the land they loved until Japan devastated the United States Naval Fleet in Pearl Harbor and war began to permeate everything.

# VOICE FROM THE PAST

## FEBRUARY 1984

Margaret was heading from the kitchen down the hallway toward her front porch when the sudden loud ring of the phone sitting in a niche in the wall startled her so that she jostled her second cup of coffee, spilling a few drops on her hand. Wiping the hot liquid on her shirt and checking for redness, she picked up the receiver.

"Hello."

"Hello. Is this Margaret Corwin?"

"Yes," she sighed.

Not recognizing the voice, she immediately concluded it was another loose end needing to be tied up since the death of her husband Carl. It had been almost a year, but things still kept coming up that she hadn't been aware of. His illness and alcoholism had made him do some strange things in almost forty-five years of marriage. She braced for what was next.

"Margaret, this is a voice from your past. You may not even remember me. We were really young when we accidentally met."

Then she heard the laugh! Knew the voice! It couldn't be! The sound of her shattered cup of hot coffee crashing on the hardwood floor echoed down the hall.

"Margaret, are you okay? Margaret?"

"Jim? Is this Jim Hayes?"

Silence.

What made her jump so quickly to that conclusion? She was seriously starting to worry about what the loneliness was doing to her. It must be one of those "loose ends" after all.

"I'm sorry! I…"

"How did you ever recognize my voice after forty years? That's incredible! I surely don't sound like I did when I was twenty!"

Silence.

"Margaret? Are you still there?"

"Y–Yes! I just can't believe it's you!"

Laughter welled up from somewhere deep inside her and entwined with his, bringing back a familiarity that took her breath away.

Silence.

Breathe!

*Ask! Ask! Be sure!*

"Is this really Jim Hayes who fell into the tree in my pasture way back in 1944?"

"Yes, it is. I'm sorry to startle you so. If this is a bad time, I'll call back. I heard that you lost your husband recently and I just wanted to express my sympathy. I'm sure that was a difficult thing to go through."

There was no way for her to express the feelings that were washing over her. She fought the dizzy feeling that threatened to send her to the floor along with the shattered coffee cup.

"Thank you so much," she managed to whisper.

"It must be hard after all those years of being together to try to go on alone." His voice brought her back.

"It's lonely," was all she could manage to say and not lose control. The years of enduring Carl's abuse made it hard to deal with her emotions now that he was gone. When she wanted to feel relieved, guilt flooded in, and she searched her soul for what part she might have played in their stormy marriage.

"I think I know how you feel. I lost my wife five years ago. Breast cancer. It was hard to see her go through so much pain. Was Carl ill for long?"

"I'm sorry...about your wife. No, not very long."

Shaking her head to clear her mind, she suddenly knew she had to see him, touch him, to know it was really Jim. Unless she could see him, she would wonder whether she had talked to him at all. Lately, she had been on the edge of believing that she may be losing her mind. Was this just another indication of that?

"Where are you? Where are you calling from, Jim?"

"I'm right here in Dyersburg. I had to come to Memphis on business from my home in Michigan and decided to stop here on my way just to see if I could talk with you. I've subscribed to the State Gazette for years, so I read Carl's obituary. Found you right in the phone book."

She smiled at how familiar his laugh sounded. It was beginning to sink into her consciousness that she was really talking to Jim Hayes. How many times had she thought about him all these years?

Though she knew then and now that they could have made no other choice, she'd vowed never to forget his voice, his laugh, his touch. It had been her secret for all these years, but could she bear to bring it out into the light now?

His voice cut into that thought. "I wonder if we could meet somewhere for lunch today? Do you have plans already?"

He seemed to have read her mind.

Plans? Margaret almost laughed aloud. Dear God, if she could only focus on a plan!

"No! No plans. That will be great!"

"You'll have to name a place. I'm new here."

She quickly told him how to find her favorite Tennessee barbeque restaurant.

"Okay, I'll see you there at noon."

The line went dead, but she hung on to the receiver for a while, and then slowly laid it back on its cradle. Memories of forty years ago came flooding in. She was a wife, mother of three babies when he came crashing into her life, needing her help, and changing her forever. What they had longed for and allowed themselves to experience left her with a lifetime of secret guilt that she kept bottled inside. The pain those memories brought back made her double over, and, sitting right down in the floor in the puddle of coffee, she hugged her knees and tried to breathe deeply, but the pain only increased.

She wanted to see him—had to see him. *But it's been so long. What will he think of me now?* Pulling herself up, she stumbled into the bedroom, catching a glimpse of herself in the mirror. The image that stared back at her shouted of neglect and grief. "Pathetic!" Several strands of gray hair strung out from around a bandana. A pale face streaked with worry lines looked too small for the body above one of Carl's oversized T-shirts which half covered the old polyester pants she had worn to work at the coat factory for years. Staring at her feet, she tried to remember where those floppy slippers came from, deciding that her daughter Janie must have left them.

"How could I have neglected myself so much? What can I do to keep him from regretting that call? What if he takes one look and heads back to Michigan?" She was talking aloud to the mirror. "Well, of course, that's what he's going to do anyway, isn't it?" She had to chuckle at how much she sounded like a teenager getting ready for her first date.

A long soak in the tub gave her time to relax and think. Think—that's what she hadn't been able to do for almost a year now. She wanted to, and knew she had to, but it was just too painful. Her mind had refused. However, suddenly it seemed to be opening up just a crack where the old optimistic Margaret Lane Corwin could peek out.

*I'm so glad I didn't sell the house and move to Memphis with Carla. He wouldn't have been able to find me in the phone book.* Then she had to laugh at herself. *He said he was just passing through on business. This is only a quick lunch, don't go off on a romantic fantasy!*

Wrapped in a towel, she stood in front of the closet. "I have nothing to wear," she moaned, finally settling on a pair of white pants that still fit and a rose-colored blouse that Carl Jr. had given her for her birthday. Her hair, dried and fluffed, didn't look so bad, but she reminded herself she hadn't had a decent haircut in a long time.

There was still an hour before she needed to leave for lunch. She had time to do some more of that thinking she so wanted to do, but found it more confusing and painful than she had anticipated. Her mind drifted back to the thoughts she had harbored in her dreams for forty years. She could imagine Jim and her together hand in hand walking down the beach...

*What am I doing? I can't keep thinking this way! There are things I would have to tell him that I can't ever reveal!* She jumped to her feet and headed out to the front porch swing, which was a refuge she had sought many times when life seemed to overwhelm her. Moving the swing softly back and forth with one foot, she looked through the screen her son Junior had tacked up from pillar to pillar to keep out mosquitoes on sultry Tennessee evenings. Her eyes scanned the grassy lawn out toward the small brick homes across the busy highway.

*I'm not ready for this. Why did I choose Boyd's? Half the people there will know me. There may be people there from the church. What will they think? Maybe I should just not show up. Do I need to complicate my life anymore right now?*

Just on the edge of panic, she took a deep breath and calmed her nerves. Closing her eyes, she prayed earnestly. *Lead me to do the right thing, Lord.*

Thinking more clearly, she reasoned. *Maybe it won't complicate things. I've been waiting for that phone call for forty years and now*

*God has sent it when I need it most. I won't let what people think keep me in this pit of despair. It's time to face how forty years has changed things.*

# BEGINNING AGAIN

### 1984

Margaret was almost ready to turn into Boyd's parking lot when it suddenly occurred to her that she and Jim might not even recognize each other.

*Why didn't I ask what he'd be wearing?* she fretted, while glancing anxiously around the parking lot, not knowing what to look for. *I didn't even ask what kind of car he was driving!*

There he was! Leaning against his car, legs crossed, arms folded. Dark jeans and a soft blue shirt enhanced his graying, curly hair. She would have recognized him anywhere! Parking behind him, she gave a little wave as he smiled and headed toward her. They met in front of her car, and she quickly stuck her hand out to him for a handshake. He took it in both his and leaned over, planting a gentle kiss on her cheek.

"You look wonderful!" he was saying, but her rapidly beating heart almost drowned out his voice.

"So do you!" she replied as she gained her composure. "You still look as young as you did the last day I saw you forty years ago."

His robust laugh was one of the many things she had loved about him then, and it hadn't changed. "Maybe I do. I was in pretty bad shape that day."

"And I was too," she sighed. "But I'm in worse shape now. I guess I've just neglected myself lately."

"You're a wonderful sight for these old eyes." He gave her hand a warm squeeze. "It's so good to see you again. Let's go in and order lunch. We have so much to catch up on. I can't wait to hear how life's been for you."

She took her hand back. "Yes, it's almost been a lifetime, hasn't it?" *But now it seems like only yesterday*, she thought to herself.

He followed her to the door, held it open for her, and they stepped inside.

"How many, Mrs. Corwin?" Patsy Bender, the hostess, looked from Margaret to the tall man behind her and back to Margaret. She had known Margaret all her life and stared at her with a questioning look, as if she expected Margaret to say this man was not with her.

"Two," Margaret replied.

Patsy hesitated, then grabbed two menus and led them across the dining room to a small table in the corner. Margaret felt many curious eyes on her and Jim as they followed Patsy. Some belonged to people she knew and she acknowledged them with a smile. Most returned the smile with a shocked look.

"Tell me all about your life, Jim," she begged after they had ordered. "I've wondered so many times how things went for you after you left here. Did you still have a long recuperation? Your injuries were so bad."

"I was taken back home to my mother who put my recovery as her top priority, of course. I spent a few months in the hospital rehabilitating my arm and leg. It was a year before I could get back to any halfway normal life. I stayed in the service, but wasn't able to fly for a while. I was put on office duty until the war was over, then helped muster returning soldiers back into civilian life, but I eventually got back to flying which, of course, I loved. I finally got to see what flying in wartime was like in Korea. It wasn't the glamorous life I had thought it would be when I was a young man."

"I'm glad you could fly again. I remember how much you loved it."

"Except for dealing with Juanita's illness and death, life has been good, Margaret." He smiled. "I have two daughters. They have wonderful husbands and I have three grandchildren who are the light of my life. Here are some pictures."

He pulled out his wallet and proudly displayed three photos. Two of them showed his daughters' families while the third one was of him and Juanita. Margaret looked at them a long time, drinking in the beauty and happiness that smiled back at her.

"They're beautiful. You must be so proud!"

"Yes, I am." He laughed, putting them back carefully. "I spent twenty more years in the Air Force, moving all over the world, then settled in Michigan near Juanita's family and went to work for Ford Motor Company. I'm retired now."

"Well, how did you ever have business all the way down here from Michigan?" It was an innocent question meant to move the conversation along, but she noticed his obvious hesitation and discomfort in answering. Did she ask the wrong question? Maybe that was prying.

He smiled, looking down at the tablecloth in front of him for a few seconds, and then looked into her eyes. "I'm just going to tell you the truth, Margaret, since we're face to face now. I don't have business in Memphis. I came here to see if I could find you. After I read about Carl's death, I wanted to see if you were okay. I hope that's not too much for you to think about right now. I didn't want to blurt it out over the phone."

It's what she had wanted to hear, but didn't dare hope for. "That's the nicest thing I've heard in a long time." Warm happiness swept over her, a feeling she had almost forgotten.

"It's your turn now. Tell me all about your life the last forty years. I know you're still grieving Carl's death. I've had more time than you've had since losing Juanita, but I know how that feels."

The food arrived and they began to eat as Margaret pondered how to answer his request. It wouldn't be as easy as his was to answer. Her life had not gone well and she just didn't know how to explain that. He might blame himself, and she certainly couldn't tell him about her most heart-wrenching secret—some time, but not yet. Where could she even begin to explain how complicated things had become after he left? Well, it was better to start with something positive.

"I don't want to complain about my life, Jim. There are some wonderful things about it. My five children and seven grandchildren are great, but life with Carl turned out to be very hard for all of us. He drank more and more after coming home from the war, and interacted less and less with the family. I don't think the children ever really knew him. I don't know if I ever did either. I could never influence him to let the Lord in his life. I'm sure I didn't do a very good job of that." She smiled into his sympathetic eyes. "I'm so glad you found Juanita and had a good life."

"I loved Juanita dearly, Margaret, but you were always in my mind and heart. I told you I could never forget you and it was the truth. I didn't marry until several years after I was torn away from you. I guess I just hoped one day I'd hear from you. I know that I might have died without your care back then, but it wasn't gratitude that kept you in my heart. After I met Juanita, I discovered I could love again, but I think if we're lucky we find only one true soul mate, and no matter what happens, that one is always with us even if we never get together. You were that soul mate for me. I didn't fool myself into thinking we'd ever even see each other again, but I couldn't let go of the memories."

"It was the same with me, Jim. I cried to God many nights just to be able to unburden my heavy heart to you like I did so many times sitting by the fireplace in the old Wilson house when you were injured and I was trying to take care of you, and many times I felt as if you were there with me. I took myself back to our time together, wondering about what would happen if you showed up and rescued me. That soothed my soul and I could drift off to sleep, trying to recover from Carl's criticism of something I had done that he didn't like or if I were worrying about where he was and if he was safe, knowing he was out with his buddies and drinking too much. I often worried that holding on to the memory of you was part of what was wrong with my marriage, but I just couldn't forget."

"What happened to that promise you made to me? Why didn't you contact me?"

"I wanted to, but it just wasn't that easy. I couldn't put you and my family through what it would have taken to change things, and despite what you and I had together, I believe that marriage is for life and I thought I had no right to just give up on it. Carl needed me despite how he treated me, and I believed God wanted me to stay with him. I feel I could have done better if Carl had indicated that he wanted things to be different. Besides, I told myself you had probably moved on. I couldn't take a chance on disrupting your chance at a good life. Hearing now about you and Juanita tells me I made the right decision."

As it had been from the first time they met, they found themselves able to talk easily, expressing their innermost feelings knowing the other would understand completely.

Jim chuckled. "To hear us talk, you'd think we spent years together, when the truth is it was only a few months, we never left your house, and I could hardly move. Most of the time, you had to care for your children, your sister and her child, and me. I don't know how you did it."

"Caring for people you love is never a burden," she reminded him. "I loved all of you so much. It was what I wanted to do, what I felt God wanted me to do."

"That's the main thing that drew me to you. Not everyone would look at it that way. Most would have resented it. I knew I would never meet such a special person again. I always held our time together in my heart."

A blush spread across her face at such a compliment. She was more used to hearing Carl tell her how she had failed to do things right, not how good she had done. She couldn't remember a time when he praised her for being herself. She tried to remember why Carl had been attracted to her when they were young. He was her brother Chuck's best friend, and worked on Papa's farm with her brothers. Maybe he was more attracted to her family than to her.

"Let's go out to my house, Jim, where we can talk privately. We have so much to talk about. You can follow me. It's not far from here. Do you have time?"

He laughed. "I am retired. I have nothing but time, and I am here because I wanted to spend time with you. Lead the way, I'll follow."

Carl had bought this house twelve years ago out on the highway to get away from any close neighbors. He seemed to have an unreasonable fear of being associated with anyone other than his fishing or hunting buddies. Like his mother, feelings of inferiority had permeated his life to the point that he felt he could never measure up—to what? Maybe the horrors of the war he had to endure made it impossible for him to cope with everyday life. She could hardly remember how he had been when they were growing up together before he was drafted into World War II, but they had loved each other then and planned a very different life together than it turned out to be.

All of this added to Carl's drinking, smoking, and depression, which he often took out in anger at Margaret's optimism and friendliness. Their marriage took on a pattern in which Carl was helpless to solve any problem, even one as small as getting the car repaired, so he'd go to bed and let Margaret handle it, then belittle her about how she did it and how much it cost.

Thinking back on all this, she wondered: *Maybe guilt and fear made me think I deserved that treatment after Jim came into my life.*

The house that had been home to her for so many years now left Margaret feeling so alone and isolated. She had even thought of taking Carla, her youngest daughter, up on her invitation to move to Memphis and live with her and her two daughters. Carla's divorce had almost devastated the whole family at first, but with Margaret's help, she had finished college and landed a demanding corporate job in the city. However, for some reason, Margaret wasn't yet ready to let go of the home she'd known for so long. *Maybe this was the reason,* she thought, gripping the steering wheel of her car as she pulled into the long driveway, glancing back to make sure Jim was behind her.

She walked quickly into the house, wanting to get there before Jim did so that she could straighten a few things if necessary. Looking around, she saw the dust of neglect, but everything else was okay in the living room, which she felt sure was the only room he would be in. She took a deep breath, tried to relax, opened the door, and invited him in, knowing her life would never be the same from this day forward.

She was wrong about staying in the living room, as they decided to sit on the cool screened back porch drinking iced tea, watching the lovely summer afternoon swim by. Only the two of them existed on a bridge that spanned forty years of time and distance, taking only a puff of remembrance to leap back into the warmth they had once felt for each other. They had shared heartache and happiness before, but now perhaps it could go forward rather than end in hopelessness as it had the first time. They knew there would still be obstacles to overcome, but hopefully, not so much as when they first met.

They didn't hear the car pull in the drive but were suddenly aware of footsteps coming down the hall, past the bedrooms and through the kitchen toward the back door.

"Mom, are you here?"

Margaret recognized Janie's voice just as her daughter stepped through the door and out onto the porch. Startled, Janie stood with mouth agape while Margaret hastened to introduce her.

"Janie! Hi! I want you to meet a good friend of mine from way back in the 1940s. This is Jim Hayes."

Jim thought about putting his hand out for a handshake, but could see Janie seemed shocked, so he made a different approach. He told himself he had to be prepared for this kind of reaction from Margaret's children.

"Janie, you were too young to remember me when we saw each other last, but I remember you. You still have that beautiful curly hair that you had as a baby."

Margaret was smiling broadly at him in a way that made Janie feel uncomfortable. What was going on here? Janie finally put out her hand limply. "H–Hi," was all that she could manage to say. Jim shook her hand and patted it gently.

"Would you like a glass of tea?" Margaret could see her daughter was grappling to understand what she was seeing—her mother with this man. Margaret hoped she would stay a while and get to know Jim.

"N–No, I can't stay. I came by for the papers you have from the Veteran's Administration. Mr. Harrington needs them to finish the gravestone. I told him I would bring them to him today."

"Okay, I'll get them. I'll be right back, Jim. Come on, Janie, they're on the desk."

As soon as they were in the hallway, Janie hissed in a coarse whisper, "Mom, who is that man?"

"I told you, Janie. He's an old friend—a very nice, old friend. Don't be so obviously jumping to conclusions you know nothing about. I need friends right now. His friendship means a lot to me."

"Did he know Daddy?" Margaret could see she was trying to make sense of what she was observing. "Did he work with Daddy or with Grandpa on the farm?"

"No, but he knew Grandpa—back then. Here are the papers. Is this all you need?"

She looked them over. "Yes, yes it's all here. I'll just take them over there so they can get the stone finished. They'll let us know when it is done."

Looking closely at her mother, she saw something different about her—very different. "Are you okay, Mom?"

Margaret gave her daughter a warm hug, which she realized she hadn't done in a long time. Things seemed so much clearer to her now.

"I'm great!" She laughed.

"Do you want me to stay?" She was doing the whispering again.

"No, Janie. You go do what you have to do. I'll talk to you later when I don't have company."

She turned and left her daughter in the hallway. Returning to the porch, she stopped to gaze at Jim standing with his back to her, looking out over the field behind the house. It was one of those fields covered with wild plants lying fallow through some government subsidy. She slipped under his arm and they stood still for a while enjoying the sunset and the closeness, feeling at home at last with each other. All that had happened in those years since they parted seemed to melt away.

"Janie was upset, wasn't she? I don't want to cause trouble in your family, Margaret. This might be too much for your kids, especially so soon after Carl's death."

She looked into his worried eyes. "Jim, you won't cause trouble in my family. The kids just think they have to be protective of me, that's all. We'll talk to them and give them a chance to know you. It won't be a problem." She felt the other kids would be fine, but she wasn't sure this was true of Janie and her husband.

"They'll need time, I know, and you probably need time too. I forget it's been less than a year since Carl died. I just rushed in here as if we could take up where we left off. Maybe I should go back to Michigan for a while. We can keep in touch."

"No, Jim, I don't need time. Time almost ran out for us, but God has given us a second chance. Please don't leave again."

He stood up and stretched, then took her hand. "That's what I was hoping to hear. I've looked into renting a little apartment above the grocery store in town. I'll go ahead with that tomorrow and we can see how things go from there. I have your number. I'll call in a couple of days when I get settled. This still won't be easy for us, Margaret, but we have a chance to start again now without so much against us as we had before."

She watched his car pull out of her driveway and onto the highway. Everything came back to her as if it had happened only yesterday, even though it had been forty years since she had wrenched her heart away from him.

Too excited for sleep, she sat down on the couch and picked up a photograph from the end table. She and Carl were smiling at her on their wedding day. They had started as a happy couple, but things turned out to be so different.

# STARTING WITH HOPE

## JUNE 1940

### DYERSBURG, TENNESSEE

An off-key chorus of "Lady in Red" surprised Margaret and Carl as they stepped out of Russell and Sarah's car onto the sidewalk. They were headed for the large red brick courthouse sitting majestically in the middle of town square. The green lawn all around it was lined with sidewalks and across the streets were businesses frequented by townspeople and local farmers and their families: Rexall Drug Store was on the corner, Frances Theater next to it. On another corner, Woolworth's Dime Store, Biggs Furniture, and two dry goods stores. Manners Men's Shop, two banks, a pool hall, and various other establishments thrived as the commercial center of small town Dyersburg, Tennessee.

Margaret and Carl thought they had kept their marriage date a secret, but someone had alerted other friends and family, and they were all on hand to witness the event.

"Sarah! You told!" Margaret cried. She could see the sheepish look on her best friend's face.

The laughter drowned out Margaret's protest as a small army of footsteps headed toward the office of the Justice of the Peace, crowding into the small space, and already celebrating. Sarah and

Margaret had been friends since childhood and Sarah was almost as happy as Margaret to have her best friend marry her older brother. The red dress Margaret had made for the occasion didn't meet her mother's approval, but she knew Carl liked her in red and had thought it would only be a simple ceremony with Sarah and Russell as witnesses. However, she was happy now that they had loved ones around to share their momentous occasion.

Flustered by the number of mildly rowdy guests, the magistrate made short work of the union. Later, Margaret could barely remember what was said. She had wanted a small church wedding, but Carl's shy nature and his aversion to Margaret's "religion" just wouldn't allow him to agree to such a formality. She lovingly agreed to his wishes, praying daily that the Lord would change his heart.

Afterward, there was the usual tradition of driving around the town square blowing their horns and yelling, followed by a convoy to Russell and Sarah's small home out on the West Tennessee cotton farm where the family band played and Mama's teacakes and iced tea enhanced the sweetness of the happy occasion. Mama would have been appalled had she seen Carl and several of his friends sneak to their cars for gulps of whiskey. At midnight, the newlyweds drove back to their two-room apartment in town, a duplex with a large living room and bedroom combined and a tiny kitchen in the back. Off the back porch was a small bathroom shared with the two men who lived in the other side of the house.

Carl, Margaret, Russell, and Sarah

Anna Rose Corwin came screaming into the world in the early morning hours of one of the hottest July days on record in West Tennessee. Born at home with Margaret's Mama and old Doc Turner's assistance, she was a perfect baby that filled Margaret's life with more love than she had ever imagined and was only five months old when the Japanese bombed Pearl Harbor and the US entered World War II.

Margaret hugged her little one close while listening to news of the devastation. The horror of it all seemed to reach out from the radio, grabbing her heart with chilling fingers. What kind of world had she brought her baby into? Being one of the oldest of ten siblings, Margaret had helped Mama with babies ever since she was barely out of babyhood herself, but having her own child felt different. She wanted everything to be perfect for Anna Rose.

Carl's job at a local machine shop was hard work twelve hours a day, six days a week. At 6:30 each evening, he came dragging in, grumbling about wanting to quit, but there just weren't any other jobs in this small town, and when did he have time to look for another job?

Leaning into the icebox, he downed his nightly swigs of Old Charter Whiskey and Coke, then napped on the divan. Margaret learned to take Anna Rose outside to play, making sure he wasn't disturbed before dinner. She had experienced his anger several times when Anna Rose was fussy after his long workday.

"Can't you keep her quiet? I have a headache. I've had to listen to noise at that shop all day, and I need some peace and quiet at home," he yelled. It was a side of him she hadn't seen before they married, and it frightened her a little, but she blamed his foul mood on how hard and long he worked every day.

Sunday mornings, Carl was up before daylight and off with his buddies hunting whatever was in season, or fishing when there was nothing to hunt. Her heart was broken when he wouldn't go to church with her, or even spend his day off with her and Anna Rose.

Many Sunday afternoons, Sarah would come to visit. Sarah and Russell had no children in their three-year marriage, so she loved to play with Anna Rose. The two women would sit in the small two-room apartment, sewing dresses or undergarments for the baby or crocheting hats and sweaters, laughing at the superstition about sewing on Sunday.

Maud always cautioned them, "You girls will have to pick those stitches out with your nose when you get to heaven! Sunday is a day of rest."

On most Sunday mornings, Margaret's father would come chugging by in his old truck. Knocking at the door, he'd yell, "Come on, Anna Rose. Let's go to church and see your grandma and the young'uns."

Margaret would grab up the baby and climb in beside Papa, anxious to feel the comfort of the familiar hymns and an inspiring sermon in the little church where she had grown up. After church, she and Anna Rose spent the afternoon with Mama and

Margaret's five younger siblings. There wasn't much work going on, since Mama insisted only "necessary" work could be done on Sunday. Mama did the cooking on Saturday, but assured them that cleaning up the kitchen was necessary on Sunday.

"Miss Maud," as Papa always called his wife, "I'm going down to the store and do some resting." He chuckled as he came through the kitchen. Doing nothing was very hard for Papa. Cranking up the old truck, which he always had trouble starting, he chugged down the road to his cousin TC's country store for an afternoon of playing checkers and telling stories around the potbellied stove.

Margaret tried to confide in her mother. "I'm worried about Carl. He works twelve hours a day, six days a week, and then goes off hunting or fishing with Lyle or Will all day on Sunday. They all drink too much too."

She got no sympathy from Mama, whose strong philosophy was that a woman's job was to make life as easy as possible for the man she married because he provided for the family, even though Margaret could plainly see that the women worked just as hard as the men.

"Now, Carl's a good man, Margaret. He works hard all week, so he's got a right to spend one day resting. Don't be nagging at him."

Margaret couldn't see how hunting and fishing were resting, but she guessed that was a way of resting for Carl. That was what he loved to do and he did work so hard during the week.

"I don't nag him, Mama. I just worry he's wearing himself out, and Anna Rose hardly knows her daddy."

Margaret longed for her baby to have a fun-loving, attentive father like Papa. Carl just wasn't like Papa. In fact, he was just the opposite, shy and reserved, feeling awkward in the company of people he didn't know. Carl was very much like his mother, Clara Jane.

Mama retorted. "Anna Rose will appreciate him if she sees that you do. Just take good care of both of 'em. That's your job."

Clyde Corwin had four sons, but felt closest to Carl, his firstborn, whom he had always called "Son." Margaret and Anna Rose looked forward to his visits. He worked as a night watchman at a local factory, which left his afternoons free for his favorite pastimes: hunting and fishing.

At times, he would burst through the door without knocking, setting Margaret and Anna Rose to giggling. He was the complete opposite of his quiet, reclusive wife—his dark hair and sharp nose standing out amongst her family of Irish descent who were all blue-eyed blonds.

"Where's that baby girl? She needs some of Grandpap's squirrel stew!" Holding up two squirrels he'd shot that very morning, he continued, "Help me dress these, Margaret, and we'll get the pot ready. There'll be hot stew by the time Son gets home."

"Let me put Anna Rose down for her nap and I'll help you skin them," she replied. That wasn't Margaret's favorite job, but she did it often for Carl and Clyde, holding the back legs while they cut and pulled the skin from the animals they'd shot. Meat rationing had made it a treat for them to have what the hunters brought in. Clyde enjoyed cooking and the two of them took pride in the delicious meals they concocted together in the kitchen. Margaret often wished Carl had inherited a little of his father's fun-loving personality.

"When will Son be home? I got something to talk to him about. How would you like to live in Memphis?"

Margaret was taken aback. *Where did that come from?* She laughed nervously. "Why are you asking me that?"

He waited until Carl came in to explain, leaving Margaret in suspense.

As soon as they were sitting down to eat, he told Carl the news. "I've been to Memphis to apply for a watchman job at the Humko plant. I saw the job in the Want Ads of a Commercial

Appeal that was laying around at the store. I've got the job starting in two weeks and they said they could probably use you too. If you'll take the day off Monday, I'll take you there to apply."

Carl was hesitant. Putting himself in new circumstances was hard for him, but Clyde would not take "no" for an answer and the two men made plans to leave early Monday morning. Margaret was a little overwhelmed, but welcomed the opportunity for change. Carl came back with the news that he would start work in Memphis the same day as his dad. The men had rented a sleeping room temporarily, but promised to look for an apartment when they had time so their families could move there with them.

The Corwins had never traveled very far from their hometown, but Margaret hoped the move would change things for Carl. Clyde quickly learned that finding a home for him and his six other children was impossible. It was wartime, people had flocked to the cities for jobs in the factories and places to live were scarce, especially for anyone with children.

As often as possible, Margaret and Anna Rose would take the two-hour ride on the Greyhound bus to stay with Clyde and Carl for a few days and spend time looking for an apartment for the four of them. The sleeping room was cramped, but at least she and Anna Rose had some time with Carl. Clyde had to sleep during the morning since his watchman job was at night, so Margaret needed to take Anna Rose out. She perused the newspapers and rode the city buses, carrying Anna Rose in her arms, begging any prospective landlord to rent to three adults and one very quiet baby, but she was becoming really discouraged. Carl told her to give up and he would just commute a few times a month, but Margaret persisted. With gas rationing and only his father's truck for transportation, she felt sure they would rarely see him if they didn't find some place in Memphis to live. Besides, they couldn't afford to pay for two rentals, and Mama and Papa didn't have room for Margaret and Anna Rose to move in with them. She was determined to find a place in Memphis.

Once again, Margaret wearily adjusted Anna Rose on her hip, and climbed down the bus steps. An apartment she had seen advertised for rent was just one block down from the bus stop across from a little park. Looking up from the sidewalk, she double-checked the address and walked across the large front porch. The old two-story frame house needed some paint, but the porch was swept clean and obviously someone loved the well-groomed yard. Margaret knocked and heard footsteps coming down the hall.

Mrs. Wyatt stood looking through the screen door at the small, weary young woman with a baby on her hip and a newspaper in her hand. The baby laughed, waving her arms at this stranger as if she knew her.

"I'm looking for an apartment to rent. I read your AD in the paper. Could I talk to you about it?"

Mrs. Wyatt hesitated, watching the arms of the little girl reach out toward her.

Margaret explained, "You look a little like my husband's mother. She must think you're her grandma."

Mrs. Wyatt opened the screen door, took Anna Rose in her arms and invited Margaret in, introducing herself while pointing to a chair near the fireplace.

"You look tired. Why don't you rest awhile?" Mrs. Wyatt remarked as she took off Anna Rose's hat and coat and placed the baby on the floor with a roll of yarn to play with from her sewing basket.

Margaret smiled and leaned back in the easy chair with a sigh. "Thank you. This is nice. Anna Rose and I have been riding that bus and walking the streets for weeks looking for a place to live. Nobody will rent to anyone with children. What do people have against one little girl?" Her frustration suddenly came out and she hid her face with her hands to keep back the tears.

"Oh, we don't have anything against her, honey!" Mrs. Wyatt smiled fondly at Anna Rose. "We just have one small three-room apartment for rent with a shared bathroom. There's no place for a little one to move around and play. Mr. Wyatt is particular about his yard." Then she asked, hesitating, "Does she have a daddy?"

Margaret sat up quickly. "Yes, oh, yes. I'm looking for a place for me and my husband and his dad. They both work at Humko. We're from Dyersburg, but Carl couldn't get a good job there. He works days, and his dad is a night watchman who sleeps days so Anna Rose is used to being quiet. Didn't I see a park just across the street? I could take her there a lot. We need a place so badly." Margaret was begging now. "Please consider us, Mrs. Wyatt. I see you have a phone. I could call the boarding house where Carl is staying and leave word for him and his dad to come by and meet you and Mr. Wyatt after work."

Mrs. Wyatt smiled and looked at the little girl chasing after the ball. She thought of her son who was now serving overseas in the Army and how she prayed everyday for him to return home safely and someday give her a grandchild like this little girl. She turned back to Margaret. "You haven't even seen the apartment. How do you know you'd even want to live here?"

Margaret sighed, "I'm about ready to accept anything. But you're right, I do need to look at it." She pulled herself up from the chair, hope creeping into her heart. Maybe this meant they would finally find a home.

"Come, I'll show you what we have and we'll see. It'll be up to Mr. Wyatt. He makes the final decisions."

Margaret picked up Anna Rose and followed the tall, thin lady with gray-streaked hair and a plain housedress down the hallway to the back of the house. Mrs. Wyatt unlocked the door and opened it into a large living room with a small kitchen on one end. Two doors opened off that room. One was a large bedroom with a bed and dresser.

"I suppose you could put a baby bed in here," Mrs. Wyatt said softly as if she were thinking out loud.

Margaret was sure of that. This room was bigger than the one they had back home. The other bedroom was very small with a single bed, a dresser, and a chair.

"This would be perfect for Grandpap," she cried. She could already see them living in this apartment.

Back in the hallway, Mrs. Wyatt opened a door to a small bathroom. "This has to be shared with Mr. Wyatt and me. Five adults and a baby with one bathroom may get cramped," she warned. "We have two bedrooms upstairs. One is my son's. He is in the Army. I'm not sure where he is right now." A dark shadow seemed to come over her face, and her eyes took on a far-away look.

Margaret laid her hand on Mrs. Wyatt's arm. "I will pray for his safety."

"Thank you. Prayer is certainly what we need in these times."

She saw the look of gratitude as Mrs. Wyatt pulled herself back to the business at hand.

"We've been used to an outdoor toilet most of our lives and we share a bathroom in our present apartment. I promise we won't crowd you in the bathroom. We can bathe in a tub in the kitchen," Margaret offered.

Carl and Grandpap came by soon after Carl was off his shift at work, and the adults felt immediately comfortable with each other. Mr. Wyatt and Clyde shared a love for gardening and had lots of stories to tell.

The Corwins were invited to stay for supper, which Margaret helped prepare while Anna Rose took her nap on a quilt spread on the floor near the fireplace. The AD had said "No children" but it turned out to be Anna Rose who secured the home for the Corwins.

Clyde and Margaret went back to Dyersburg on the weekend and moved all they could pile on his truck back to the little apartment at the Wyatt's. Margaret loved it so much. Sarah followed along with her car loaded with odds and ends that wouldn't fit on the truck. The two friends spent several happy days getting everything arranged. Margaret felt a little lost when Sarah had to leave, but she stayed busy with her new home, and was comforted by the miracle of having found such a perfect place to live. She spent her days working around the house, taking care of Anna Rose and visiting with Mrs. Wyatt who was fast becoming a second mother to her.

The Wyatt House, Mrs. Wyatt and Anna Rose

# MEMPHIS

## 1942

Life in Memphis turned out to be a much-needed change for Margaret as well as for Carl. Mrs. Wyatt treated her like a daughter. The Wyatts invited the Corwins to attend church with them on Sundays, which Margaret was so happy to do, but, though he didn't have his buddies to hunt and fish with, Carl wouldn't go to church. He read the newspaper and dozed in his chair most of the day.

Carl seemed more relaxed after work and paid more attention to Anna Rose. While he and his father still had their evening drink, Carl would often come home from work, put his newspaper under his arm, and head for the park with Anna Rose in the stroller saying he would keep her out of the house so Clyde could get plenty of rest. Anna Rose played while her dad read and Margaret finished supper. The evening meal had to be done precisely at 6:00 so Clyde could eat and get to work by 7:30. While she washed dishes, Margaret chatted about her day with an occasional "uh-huh" from Carl.

"Carl," she began one cold February evening. Turning from the sink, she saw that he was dozing in his chair. She gazed at him for a while with her hands suspended in the warm sudsy dishwater. He looked peaceful and handsome with his dark curly hair and soft pale face. Drying her hands on her apron, Margaret knelt beside him placing a hand gently on his arm. When she was sure he was awake, she told him her good news. "Carl, I think we're going to have another baby. I haven't seen a doctor, but I'm pretty sure," she announced with a happy giggle.

As usual, Carl's negative nature kicked in. He said nothing for a few seconds, then sighed and started folding his paper in a way that made Margaret think he was angry.

"Well, I sure hope I can get a raise soon. We'll have to start saving for the doctor bills." He got to his feet, allowing the newspaper to drop to the floor, and then added. "Don't tell the Wyatts yet. They might want to kick us out of the apartment with two babies. They didn't even want one at first."

Margaret was incredulous. "Oh, Carl, they wouldn't do that! We're friends. I have to talk to Mrs. Wyatt. She's like a mother to me. I can't keep quiet about it."

"Okay, but don't say I didn't warn you. I don't know where we'll find another place or the money." He stalked off to bed leaving her kneeling by the chair.

Taken off guard by Carl's attitude, she felt he was blaming her for being pregnant. "I guess he's just tired," she sighed.

Mrs. Wyatt was almost as excited as Margaret and said nothing about "kicking them out." However, Carl was obviously brooding about their situation, and became quieter and more worried. In April, as they sat over their modest meal of navy beans and cornbread, Clyde, as usual, presented them with a solution to the crowding apartment.

"Son, tomorrow, I'm going across the river to Arkansas with another fellow at work to look into a job over there. This fellow says Mohawk Rubber in West Helena needs a night watchman. If I could get in there, I could rent a house in Helena and move your maw and the kids with me. Helena is a smaller town and has a lot more available houses. That would be better for all of us."

Margaret knew Clyde missed the rest of his family back in Dyersburg. He only saw them occasionally on Sundays when he could get enough gas to go back for the day. Margaret and Anna Rose would sometimes ride with him to visit with her family. Gasoline rationing had severely cut down on their trips.

Later, Margaret sat down by Carl to discuss what Clyde had presented to them. "Carl, that would work out good if your dad gets that job. We'd have that extra bedroom for Anna Rose!"

"Yeah, but we'll have to come up with Daddy's part of the rent and groceries, and what are you going to do if I get drafted?"

Margaret was worried about the draft too, not even wanting to think about what she would do when she was left alone with two babies. They both knew Carl's notice would be coming soon. At first it had been mainly the unmarried young men who were drafted to go to war, but the new wave of conscriptions were taking young married men like Carl. Sarah's husband Russell had a back problem and was classified 4f so he didn't have to go, but Carl and Margaret knew this horrible war would soon make havoc of their lives.

They took each day without a draft notice in the mail as one more day to try to live a normal life, but sometimes felt it would be better just to find out and get it over with. Margaret kept praying the war would end and he'd not have to go at all, but the truth was that even if there was no war, there would still be the draft.

Margaret, Anna Rose, and Carl

## 1943

The Wyatts reduced the rent since there was one less adult using the bathroom after Clyde got the job in Arkansas where he was able to find a large, old house on a shady street in Helena and move his family there. Margaret helped the Wyatts with the "victory garden" for a share in the produce. Still, Carl was so bogged down with worry that he wasn't much of a companion to her or Anna Rose. Being left alone with two small children when the draft notice came haunted Margaret. She prayed daily that God would provide a way for them to live when Carl had to leave them and that he would come back safely.

She waited until late in her pregnancy to see a doctor, not wanting to spend the money until absolutely necessary, knowing it would give Carl something else to worry about. Mrs. Wyatt finally convinced her to see Dr. Shores who had an office in his home down the street. She liked him, and he set her due date as early in September. However, on her third visit, he sorrowfully told her he'd have to refer her to another doctor because he had been drafted into the Army and would be headed overseas to care for wounded soldiers. He wouldn't be around for her baby's delivery. Seeing the doctor he referred her to would require a long bus ride downtown, or she'd have to take a taxi, which was expensive. Carl worked all day, Mrs. Wyatt didn't drive, evening hours were impossible because of blackouts due to the war. She stared at the card the nurse had handed her wondering what she could do.

She had fretted for hours by the time Carl walked in the door. After listening to her story, he decided he had an answer. "All that sniffling and crying won't do any good. Pack up yours and Anna Rose's bags. This weekend I'll take you over to stay with Mama and Daddy in Arkansas for a while. You can have the baby there. They've got a doctor and a hospital right close to them." He sounded almost angry, but Margaret had become accustomed to the tone. He was so worried about going to war, and when he was worried, he always sounded mean and angry, but she felt he was trying to make things easier for her.

"I'll call them tomorrow from work and see what they say," he assured her.

This sounded wonderful. The baby might come any day and she needed help. Sarah and Russell had moved to Arkansas right after Carl's parents had. Sarah had gone to work as a telephone operator.

"It looks like we're not going to have a baby, so I might as well do something," she told Margaret sadly.

Of course, Carl's family was looking forward to their coming. Anna Rose was the only grandchild on Carl's side of the family and they all doted on her. Carl's mother and younger sister Hannah would take good care of them all. Margaret hugged Carl tightly and thanked him for understanding. He smiled and seemed to relax a little, knowing that he wouldn't have to worry about Margaret for a while and she could concentrate on having the baby with help from his family. He could manage alone until they came back.

The three of them took the train to Arkansas. Carl stayed until Margaret and Anna Rose could get settled and see the doctor for the first time.

Carl's sister Hannah and his three younger brothers, Mack, Don, and Harold, lived at home with his parents, Clyde and Clara Jane. They all helped Margaret get unpacked and had set up a baby bed for Anna Rose in Hannah's room and a bassinet for the new baby in with Margaret.

Carl's mother, Clara Jane, was a generous, kind person, but she had become somewhat of a recluse, due in part to her husband's gregarious, take-charge nature. Being naturally shy, it was easy for her to let Clyde take care of everything while she did her at-home duties with the house and children. Other than going to church, she stayed at home.

Clyde, like his son, wanted nothing to do with church. He hadn't been raised going to church and he associated Clara Jane's church with her family who had rejected him, indicating he wasn't good enough for their daughter. While he was somewhat of a crude vagabond when she met him, Clara Jane loved him dearly and he was very good to her and the children.

Clara Jane, as a young, sheltered beauty from a respected middle class family, had been swept off her feet by the handsome Clyde, who worked at a sawmill owned by her father. Clyde was an orphan, living by any means he could, sleeping wherever anyone would take him in. Clara Jane now seemed disappointed in the life she had chosen. The passion and glamour of their forbidden romance wore off quickly as she ended up taking care of her six children with whatever little Clyde could scrape together from odd jobs. Clyde's job in Arkansas was the best he had ever had and gave Clara Jane hope that things would be changed for the better from now on.

Carl had inherited his mother's shy nature and his father's love of the outdoors along with his taste for whiskey. Clara's sweet nature and Clyde's outgoing personality had eluded him. Margaret worried about Carl and knew she would miss him as he left to go back to his job in Memphis, but the welcome from his family lifted a great burden off her mind.

Her new doctor was kind and put her at ease. She had been there three weeks when Mary Jane, her second daughter, was born. The delivery was easy, but she wished Carl could be with her. It seemed luxurious to have the baby in a hospital. Margaret was in the hospital for five days, being cared for by friendly nurses and enjoying Mary Jane when the baby was brought to her room.

Back at the Corwin's after the hospital stay, Margaret was pampered, and the whole family doted on Anna Rose and Mary Jane, whom they immediately decided to call "Janie." Sarah came by every day after work to hold the new baby while Margaret napped. They had been best friends before they were sisters-in-law and enjoyed being together again. Sarah confessed her disappointment that she and Russell hadn't been able to have a child.

"Maybe it's just not time yet, Sarah. It may happen soon."

Margaret confided her growing anxiety about the war and the possibility of Carl's being drafted. "Sarah, what will we do when he's gone? He could even be killed! I don't want to think about the danger he'll be in. I don't know how much more time we'll have together when I get back home. He might have no time at all with Mary Jane, and he hasn't even seen her."

Sarah hugged her friend close and tried to reassure her, but she too was worried about her brother. However, Margaret was almost sad when the doctor said she was well enough to go home. Sarah volunteered to take a few days off work and drive them back to Memphis. She could stay a few days to get them settled. Mrs. Wyatt was glad to have Margaret and the babies back home, and Carl had already put Anna Rose's crib in the small bedroom.

"Sarah, it's great that you will be in there with her for a few nights so she can get used to sleeping in another room." Margaret sighed gratefully.

"She'll be fine, Margaret. She's a sound sleeper. You just get your rest. You'll have your hands full with two babies."

That was certainly true, but Mrs. Wyatt was always around to lend a hand or take Anna Rose in the stroller to the park so Margaret and Janie could rest in the afternoon.

The tension of waiting for the draft notice to arrive stretched tighter and tighter each day, making Margaret apprehensive and tearful and Carl more moody. One evening, he came in from work with an alternative that seemed to ease his mind somewhat.

"My notice will be coming any day now, Margaret. I'm tired of the waiting." She felt this was his usual pessimism, but she had to admit she was as worried as he was. "I don't want to be drafted and end up on the front lines, so I'm going to try to join the Navy. I went with another man from work today to see a recruiter, and he said I could work as a machinist on a ship if I joined. They give you a few weeks to report after you get your notice so I can join then. I've made up my mind that's what I'm going to do. It's the lesser of two evils, I think. I might not even see any combat. What do you think?"

"That sounds fine." She sighed. None of it sounded "fine" to her really. She knew ships were being blown up too, but if it eased his mind some, it was "the lesser of two evils," as he put it.

The notice came the next week and Carl immediately took it to the recruiter. He was signed up to report to Millington Naval Base just before Thanksgiving.

Suddenly, things were changing too fast. Their fears became reality and Margaret was overwhelmed. Carl wrote a letter to his parents telling them what was happening. Mrs. Wyatt wanted Margaret and the children to stay in the apartment. "Mr. Wyatt and I will help you any way we can. Carl won't have to worry about you at all," she assured them.

However, in just a few days, Margaret heard a knock at the front door and opened her door to see Mrs. Wyatt escorting Clyde down the hall toward her.

She ran into his arms crying. "What are we going to do, Grandpap? What if he never comes back?"

"Now just don't think like that, Margaret. We'll all do fine. Let's get some stew going for Son when he comes in."

Carl was glad to see his father, and after a hot meal of squirrel stew, the two men settled down in the living room for their usual drink.

"Son, your maw and I have talked it over and there's just one thing to do. Bring Margaret and the young'uns over to our house. They can stay with us while you're gone. We got plenty of room in that big old house and you won't have to worry about them. You can just take care of yourself."

"Thanks, Dad." Carl shook his father's hand and Margaret thought she almost saw tears come to his eyes. She knew there were tears in hers. He looked across the room toward Margaret. "Does that sound okay with you?"

"Yes, of course!" Margaret answered. While her heart was gripped with despair, she knew this was the answer to her prayers for her and the children, and for Carl's peace of mind. She didn't want to be alone at such a time, living day-by-day not knowing if she would ever see him again. Would the girls ever get to know their dad?

The Corwins had lived in the Wyatt's apartment for over a year. It was hard for Margaret to leave them. The two women hugged fondly and Margaret promised to visit soon.

"Those girls will be so big I won't recognize them when I see them again." Mrs. Wyatt stroked their hair and kissed each little face as they headed out the door to the train station.

It was like seeing members of her family leave.

# LETTERS

## 1944

Margaret and her girls were happy with Carl's family back in Arkansas while Carl was in basic training. The familiarity of life with a big family, busy days, and her best friend close by gave her little time to think about the danger Carl would soon be thrust into.

She'd grown up with all those familiar things, but now there was the added convenience of indoor plumbing, a phone, and sidewalks that made it easy to take the children for walks in the stroller. Only when she finally got Janie to sleep and her head hit the pillow at night did thoughts of what lay ahead overwhelm her, and she prayed earnestly for Carl's safety and that he would come to trust in God.

Both Sarah and Hannah had jobs as telephone operators and they had persuaded Clyde to install a phone in the house, so while in basic training, Carl was able to call home once a week. He had always been a man of few words and the calls had to be short because of the cost, but hearing his voice settled Margaret's nerves. She would often put Anna Rose on for a few seconds.

"Say hi to Daddy, Anna Rose," Margaret would instruct as she held the large black receiver to the little ear.

"Hi to Daddy," Anna Rose would mimic, which gave Carl and Margaret a much-needed laugh.

After the six-week training, Carl had a week at home before being shipped out. His parents and siblings all tried to make his time with them special, knowing it would be a long time before they saw him again. His and Margaret's time together was exuberant and passionate with an underlying dread and desperation that was barely spoken until the night before he boarded the train.

"I may not be able to call for a long time," Carl whispered as they lay next to each other. Margaret held him as tightly as she could, wanting to remember this feeling of his body next to hers. "I'll write as soon as I can, and I'll look forward to letters from you."

She was determined not to have his last picture of her be that of a whimpering, helpless creature, even though that's how she felt inside.

"Carl, I know you'll have to go through some horrible times, and I'll miss you every minute, but God will keep you safe and when this is over, your family will be here waiting to get on with the rest of our lives together. That's a promise."

She made him that promise and vowed to God to keep it whatever it took, not knowing at the time how hard it would really be to do that.

He smiled in the dark at her usual optimism, but it sent him off thinking she was probably right. He'd hold onto that thought no matter what happened. She and the girls would be there for him when he'd done his duty for his country.

Six weeks went by before Margaret heard anymore from her husband. She tried to imagine where he was and what he was doing, but knowing that that reality was impossible, she chose to think of him, handsome in his uniform, out on the blue Pacific looking over the side of a ship or in his work clothes concentrating on a piece of machinery that needed to be repaired. Enemy submarines, Kamikazes, and guns crossed her mind briefly but she wouldn't allow them to stay there.

His first communication was only a brief postcard dated March 1944.

> Doing fine. Kiss the girls for me. You can write me at this address.
>
> Love, Carl.

A naval station address in San Francisco was at the bottom of the card.

"Is that where he is?" she wondered aloud to Sarah when she came by after work.

"Probably not. That'll just be where his mail goes, then they'll forward it on to the ship where he is. Let me write that address down. I'll write him too. I have to run home now and make supper for Russell. He'll be home from work soon." She gave Margaret a warm hug and rushed out the door.

Margaret waited until everyone was settled that night before she pulled out pencil and paper from a drawer and began her letter.

> Dear Carl,
>
> I got your card today and I was so happy to hear from you. I know you can't tell me where you are or what you're doing but I picture you in my mind every day—so handsome in your uniform like the last time I saw you.

She smiled, knowing that would make him blush.

> Janie's cutting teeth and being a little fussy, but your mom rubs her gums with some concoction she mixed up and it seems to help. She's cooing and laughing and crawling all over the place now. Anna Rose is getting spoiled rotten. She loves to romp and play with your brothers, and she's always begging them to play "Boogie Woogie" on the piano. She dances and claps when they play.
>
> Mama writes once a week about how they're doing in Tennessee. Papa isn't doing very well since Chuck and

Dave left the farm. Chuck has taken his family to Detroit where Dave got him a job in a defense plant. That only leaves Sam and Frankie and the girls around to help Papa, but Sam says he's going to join the Marines as soon as he's old enough which will be in two months. Joe's busy with his own little farm, but he helps Papa when he can. Jenny and Abby help out a lot too. Peggy and Robert and their little Bobby are doing fine, but they expect Robert to be getting his draft notice soon too.

Hannah is working at the telephone company now with Sarah. When they are not working, the two of them are helping me make some clothes for the girls.

I miss you so much and I pray, pray, pray for you all the time. Don't worry about us, we're doing fine, just waiting for this war to be over and you to be back with us soon.

All my love,
Margaret

She mailed this first letter the next day, then wrote a little each night after that, and mailed a letter to him every fourth day. It was another month before she heard from him again. It was a real letter this time, but with several lines blocked out. She had forgotten about censorship.

April 1944

Dear Margaret,

I'm getting some of your letters here on the _____ but I can tell by a few gaps in what you say that some aren't making it to me. I don't care about that; just keep writing.

I'm making it okay. I like my job as a _____ and am working with a fine group of men here in _____. I think your papa will do fine. Jenny works as hard as a man on the farm.

I love you and the girls. Kiss them for me. I wish I could do it myself and especially that I could kiss and hold you.

I think about you all the time. See you soon, I hope. Tell Mama and Daddy and all "Hi" for me. I love you all.

Carl

Dear Carl,

I have some wonderful news to tell you this time. I haven't seen the doctor yet, but I'm pretty sure we're going to have another baby. I haven't told anybody. I wanted you to know first. I have a feeling this will be a boy. When you get home, maybe you'll see your new son. Isn't that great?! I'll let you know soon what the doctor says. I am going to see the same doctor who delivered Janie if I can.

Well, Sam joined the Marines last week. I didn't get to see him before he left, but Sarah and Russell said they'd try to drive me over to see him when he comes home from basic training before he ships out. That should be sometime next month.

Spring is finally here. It's rainy but warm, and I'm helping your dad get the ground ready to start the garden. Anna Rose thinks she's big enough to help. It's hard to believe she'll soon be three years old. Janie's pulling herself up on her feet and trying to walk. I think she'll walk early.

I love getting your letters. It helps me feel closer to you no matter where you are. Write soon. I love and miss you.

All my love,<br>Margaret

July 1944

Dear Margaret,

The news about my "son" is really good, but if it's another girl that will be okay too. Go to the doctor soon and let me know when it's due. I'll try to get a leave to be there, but I don't know if that will be possible or not.

    I'm learning a lot in my job and it's good to know I'm helping my country so we can have a good life when I come home. I wish I could tell you more but I know it would just be blacked out.

    I hope things are better with your folks in Tennessee. Tell Jenny to keep on plowing. Has Sam been home yet? Tell him to get a Jap for me. He'll be okay. Don't worry about him.

    I love you all. I miss you and dream about being with you every night.

Carl

The baby was indeed the son they had looked forward to. Born in early October, he was only thirteen months younger than Janie. Margaret wasn't prepared for how this new situation would send her into an emotional storm. Carl was right, he couldn't get a leave to come. He had to be informed by telegram of Carl Junior's birth. Though Margaret had said she wouldn't name a son Junior, she changed her mind with Carl in such a dangerous situation. In case something terrible happened, his son would carry his name.

"Carl should be here," she cried. "This is his son. He should be here! Why doesn't God hear my prayers anymore? Isn't he even listening?"

Sarah tried to console Margaret but she continued to be distraught. "Don't be so discouraged, Margaret. This war isn't God's fault. I'm sure he wouldn't want it to continue either. He'll take care of Carl."

A telegram from Carl arrived at the hospital when he had heard the news.

> Take good care of yourself and Junior STOP I will be with you as soon as I can STOP Proud dad STOP Carl

Margaret held it to her lips and anguished for her husband, her feelings of inadequacy, and her sheer weariness. She needed him. They needed to be together and be a family. How could she go on? The faith that had always been her anchor was slipping away from her.

"I can tell Carl's just trying to sound positive for my sake. It's not even like him. He wants to be here, not where he is!"

Tears came to Sarah's eyes too. She patted her friend's hand. This was so unlike Margaret, usually so optimistic, but having the two babies so close together without her husband here and not knowing what danger he might be in seemed to be her breaking point.

"You're tired, Margaret. Just get some rest. Things will look better soon." She fluffed Margaret's pillow and called the nurse. "She may need something to calm her down," Sarah whispered as she left.

Two weeks later, back home with Carl's family, she did feel better. Junior was a good baby who slept and ate regularly. There was lots of help with the children and a letter from Carl.

> Dear Margaret,
>
> I hope you and the kids are doing okay. I can't wait until I can be at home and see how they've grown. I know they're getting big. Does Anna Rose still remember me? I'll have

to get acquainted with Janie and Junior, but we'll have the rest of our lives to do that.

I'm sending a package to you with something special in it. Let me know how you like it.

Keep the letters coming. I know you're busy with three babies now, but I really look forward to the mail. I've gotten some from Sarah and, of course, Mother.

It's been almost ten months since we saw each other, but I keep a picture in my heart of the way you looked when I left.

Carl

Margaret had never been one to allow herself to become despondent, taking pride in not being whiney or helpless like her sister, Peggy, who had used what Margaret termed "being spoiled rotten" since she was a child, making her life and those around her miserable at times. Margaret had always said she would not allow herself to be that way. She was the big sister—the one who fought the bullies at school that picked on her younger sister, but things seemed all wrong now. She couldn't seem to pull herself out of the black hole of despair. Thinking of Peggy, Margaret had to admit that maybe she had judged her sister too harshly. Some circumstances could make a person despair—even a strong person. She went through her days barely able to do what she had to, unable to pull herself out of this helpless feeling. It even seemed her prayers went as high as the ceiling and fell back down around her.

The next letter Margaret received was not from Carl. It was from her mother in Tennessee.

Dear Margaret,

I hope you and the kids are doing good. I'd love to see that new little boy. I bet Anna Rose and Janie are getting big. We're just trying to hang on here.

As I told you, Sam's joined the Marines and your Papa is pretty sick. He coughs so hard it scares me. The doctor thinks he may have asthma. Jenny is doing the farm work and still trying to go to high school. Abby and Frankie help her out and we get along, but that's not the main problem, it's Peggy. Like Carl, Robert got his draft notice and joined the Navy. When he left last week, he brought Peggy and Bobby here because she had gotten so weak she couldn't take care of the baby. We've had the doctor out to see her, but he don't know what's wrong. I'm writing to ask if you could come and help us out for a while. I'm getting worn out trying to take care of everybody, and you and Peggy were always so close. Maybe she'd perk up with a visit from you. I don't know if she's seriously sick or if she just can't handle Robert's being gone and thinking about what danger he is in.

I know this is a lot to ask because you have your own family and a new baby, but we just need you so. Let me know if you can come and we'll try to help you get here somehow. Give the babies a big hug for us.

Mama

It took a few minutes for her to take in what Mama was saying. When it finally sank in, she sat down in the middle of the floor and sobbed. How could they ask this of her? She had her problems too, which she hadn't been coping with so well lately. Mama had nine kids, couldn't one of the others help her now? Didn't Mama know what it was like to have a one-month-old and two other little ones? What good could she be to them? She'd just be bringing in more chaos!

When Carl's mother kept asking what was wrong, she just handed her the letter. Clara Jane held her daughter-in-law close and let her have her cry. When Margaret was calm enough, Clara Jane asked, "Do you have to go? We were hoping to keep you and the kids until Carl gets home."

"I know Clara Jane. I just can't go into all of that now. I have to take care of myself and my kids. I just can't do it!" She felt so hopeless.

"Well, you'll just have to write and tell her you can't come right now. She'll understand. She knows what it's like to have little ones to take care of. Besides, Carl wanted you to stay here while he is gone."

That night, she sat on her bed trying to write a letter to her mother. How could she refuse her, but how could she have the strength to take on such a task? It overwhelmed her just to think about it.

Dear Mama,

I was so sorry to hear about all the trouble you and Papa and Peggy are having. These are such hard times for us all with the war taking away all our menfolks. I hate to tell you this, but I just can't come right now. I can't seem to get over the birth of the baby and I need to be here where I can have help with the other kids. I think I would just add to the problem with three more babies. Maybe Papa could get Izzy to help with Peggy and Bobby. Let me know how things are going. I wish I felt better so I could help you. I sure wish Sam hadn't left. I am so scared for him and Papa needs him right now. Maybe I can come for a while when Sam gets a furlough after his basic training. I want to see him before he leaves for overseas.

Love,
Margaret

After the letter was mailed the next day, she wanted it back. Why did I tell her I couldn't come? I've never told Mama no, but what could I do? I'd have to spend all my time taking care of my own kids. How could I help them? She argued with herself. Mama's answer made her anguish even more.

Dear Margaret,

I was so disappointed to get your letter saying you couldn't come. I guess that was too much to ask of you at this time when you just had the baby, but I am just frantic as to what to do. I get so tired every day trying to deal with Peggy's sickness and Papa's too, and then take care of little Bobby. Abby and Jennie try to help, but with school and doing most of the farming, they don't have much time. I hope you get better soon. We will make it somehow. We always do.

Love,<br>Mama

Margaret stared at the letter then began to pray, asking God to give her an answer and the strength to carry it out. The answer came to her clearly—as clearly as if God were speaking to her right there in the room. What am I doing feeling so sorry for myself? Look at what Mama is dealing with! I need to get hold of myself and remember I'm not the only one that's having a hard time. I've at least got to go see how things are.

She went to talk to Clara Jane. "I've been thinking about Mama, Clara Jane. She doesn't deserve to have to handle all this by herself. I've always been there for her, so I can't abandon her now. And Peggy! Something very bad is happening with her." It suddenly hit her hard that her sister may be dealing with a terrible disease. "She's never been very strong. Her condition may be more serious than we know. I have to go. I don't know for how long. You know I want to stay here with all of you. It would be much easier for me, but I've got to think about my family now. I don't know how I could make the trip on the bus with all three kids, though."

"Okay, if you think you must go, write your Mama and tell her you'll come. We will miss you so much but we have a surprise for you."

Clara Jane explained to her that she and Clyde and Sarah and Russell had been saving their gasoline ration stamps to surprise her with a trip to visit her folks for the holidays, so they could just do it earlier. Sarah and Russell would drive her there. When Sarah came by after work, Margaret hugged her friend close.

"You're the best friend in the world," she whispered. "You always come through when I need you."

"We're family too, remember? We'll drive you over, then come and get you as soon as you feel you can come back. I hope that will be soon," Sarah lamented.

Just two days before they left, Margaret received Carl's package—a beautiful light-blue Japanese housecoat with lovely embroidery. She put it on, and Sarah took her picture.

"You can send this to Carl and some pictures of the children too," Sarah promised.

"I wonder if he is in Japan or has been there!" That sounded very scary.

"I doubt if any of our soldiers have been in Japan yet. I don't think anyone can get in there now. He probably picked it up in a port somewhere." Sara shrugged her shoulders and hoped this wasn't something else for Margaret to worry about.

# WAR'S TENTACLES REACH OUT

## 1944

The despair that had overtaken Margaret's family when she walked back into it after having been away for a year startled her. Papa didn't look well. His face was gray, and coughing spasms often racked his body. The first night in the house was a nightmare. She lay on the couch with Junior sleeping fitfully in a dresser drawer Mama had placed on the floor near her. Anna Rose and Janie slept on a quilt nearby. Papa's coughing kept everybody on edge all night. Sometimes, she held her breath wondering if he was going to breathe his last or if he was going to be able to take his next breath.

Peggy was worse than Mama had indicated in her letter. Robert had moved her and two-year-old Bobby in with Mama and Papa when he had to leave for the Navy. He didn't know what else to do. She just lay in a small bed in the tiny back room she shared with Jenny and Abby. Hardly able to raise her head, only eating a few bites each day, she was lethargic and losing weight. She had become hysterical when Robert left. Papa went for Dr. Turner and he had to give her a shot to calm her down. Bobby had become the responsibility of Mama, Jenny, and Abby. He was confused and unhappy missing both his parents. Mama was trying to hold everything together but seemed frantic and constantly worried.

"We sent Sam money to come home after his basic training, but he didn't get to come. They shipped him straight out," Mama reported sadly as she and Margaret worked in the kitchen the next day. "I pray every day he'll be safe, but I don't have much hope that he'll ever come back alive." The hopelessness in Mama's voice broke Margaret's heart.

She couldn't answer. She knew it was true, and couldn't bear to think about it. Why did Sam insist on joining the Marines? Those young men were being sent in waves onto the Pacific Islands to be mowed down with gunfire as they tried to flush out the Japanese.

"What can we do about Peggy? She can't go on this way." Margaret wanted to change the subject.

"The doctor doesn't really know what's wrong with her. He wants her to be tested to find out, but he doesn't have the equipment, so it'll have to be done at the hospital in Memphis. He'll make the arrangements after Thanksgiving. Meanwhile, we need to keep her quiet and try to get her to eat more, but it is impossible in this house with all that is going on and Sam coughing all the time."

Very early the next morning, having endured two sleepless nights, Margaret stood on the front porch contemplating what was ahead of them all, trying to think of how she could help relieve the chaotic situation. So far she felt she was just adding to it with herself and her three babies in the small house.

She looked out at the serene landscape before her. Fields of dead plants, having been stripped of their snowy cotton caps, lay on each side of the house. After that stood woods of tall oaks with a few brown leaves left on their branches surrounded by dark green cedars hugging their trunks.

Thoughts that she fought to suppress began to flash into her mind. Peggy and Bobby need to be out of the house. What if she could move out with them and take care of them, but how could she? The thought overwhelmed her. Why was this her responsibility? No, I can't. I've got to go back to Arkansas. I've always jumped in and saved everybody in this family, but I can't do it this time. I can't!

Her eyes traveled across the front lawn down to Hurricane Hill Road, covered with a new layer of red gravel, then up the hill on the other side where an old abandoned house stood between two pastures. A large unpainted barn sat on one side, a horse and her colt grazing nearby and a fenced pasture with a large oak tree in the middle on the other. She was eyeing them with interest, sipping her first cup of coffee when Papa joined her. He put his arm around her. She laid her head on his shoulder. A plan was slowly forming in her mind. Even as she resisted the thought, she heard herself cautiously voicing it.

"Papa, who owns that house across the road there?"

"It's on part of Mr. Wilson's land, but we've been using the barn and pasture. He said we could use whatever we needed. He don't need it right now. Nobody's lived there for a long time. I think the coons and squirrels have claimed it."

"Do you think it could be fixed up to be lived in again?"

"I don't know, why?"

"I was wondering if we might could fix it up good enough for me and my kids and Peggy and Bobby to live in while our husbands are away?"

He jumped back and looked at her with dismay for several seconds.

"Are you seriously considering that?" he asked finally.

"Papa, somebody has to help Peggy. You and Mama have your hands full already and if we're right across the road, maybe we can help each other without being crowded into one little house. Do you think it's a good idea?"

She thought she saw tears leap to his eyes, but he turned and leaned his elbows on the porch rail quickly, staring out across the road.

"Papa, do you think it would work?"

"Yes," he answered, hesitating at first. "Yes, I do. I think we can fix up that house. It won't be great, but it's only for a little while until the boys get back from the war." He looked into her eyes then, not even trying to hide the tears. "Margaret, you'll be taking on a big job. Are you sure?"

She leaned on the porch rail next to him and decided to be honest. "No, I'm not sure, but I am willing to look at it. It may be good for me. Keep me busy so the time will pass faster. Let's go over and take a look at the house before everyone gets up." She had just nursed Junior and he was finally sleeping peacefully, so she felt she had a little time.

The Old Wilson House

Up close, the house looked worse than it had seemed from across the road. The door, which hung on one hinge, opened into a large room with a fireplace. Behind that was a small room that she supposed had been used as a kitchen. On the left of the living room was a hallway. Two large bedrooms opened into the hall. She could see outside through cracks between the boards of some of the walls. A door beside the fireplace led up a narrow stairway to a large attic. It was pretty discouraging.

"I can get Joe and one of Mr. Wilson's farm hands to nail some metal pieces on the holes in the roof so it won't leak, and they could clean the bird nests out of the chimney." Papa was already planning on this solution.

Watching him, Margaret could see how much he wanted this to work. He had been the proud head of his household since he was a boy. Now he was desperately looking for a way to deal with the illness that was causing him to spiral out of control. Seeing him so hopeful, she forced herself to look at the possibility more objectively.

She took some mental notes of what she'd need to do to the inside. In spite of its age, the house was sturdy and she could see that it could probably be made to feel cozy. She began to form some ideas.

Being the first girl in the family in the 1920s had molded her into becoming the "go-to" person for all of them. By age five, she had taken charge of Peggy and her baby brother at the end of the cotton patch while the older boys and her parents chopped the weeds from the cotton in the spring or picked it by hand in the fall. When baby Tom died, Peggy started school, and babies kept coming, Mama depended more and more on her oldest daughter. This was what she did, and taking charge of things now made her feel in her element more than being pampered by Carl's family back in Arkansas. The depression that had gripped her when Carl Junior was born took a backseat to fitting into the place she had always taken in the family. This began to feel right. She sighed, knowing that she had to try, but wondering where she would get the strength.

"Papa, I need to tell Sarah what I'm going to do, and let her know they won't need to come back for us. Do you think TC will let me call her from the store?"

"Of course, I'll take you there this afternoon." The relief she saw on his face made her feel she had to make this work.

She also needed to catch Carl up on this new decision. She was sure he would want her to help her family, but she also knew he thought she and the children would stay with his family in Arkansas. She hoped he would understand. After everyone was in bed that night, she poured out her heart to him.

Nov. 10, 1944

Dear Carl,

Well, things have really changed since I last wrote you. I'm at Mama and Papa's now, and I think this is where I'm going to have to stay, at least for a while. Papa is so sick and Peggy needs me to help her. She can't even get out of bed. We don't know yet what's wrong with her. She will have to go to Memphis for some tests.

We're going to fix up Mr. Wilson's old house across the road. Peggy and the kids and I will move into it. It's not the greatest, but I think it will be comfortable enough for us and close enough to Mama and Papa for all of us to help each other out. I know it's not what we thought we'd be doing, but these war times have made things so hard. I just wish so much there wasn't a war and you could be back here with us, but we have to make do with what's handed to us, I guess, until it's over.

I'm proud of what you're doing and pray for you every day. I hate to say it, but I was feeling sorry for myself after Junior was born and you couldn't be here, but I'm getting over it now. I think knowing I can help Mama and Papa and Peggy has made me more able to forget about my problems a little. I feel this is where God wants me to be.

I'm sending some pictures of the kids that Sarah took and one of me in the beautiful housecoat you sent me. I love it. I hope you get the pictures soon. The kids are so cute, Carl. I wish you could see them in person. Maybe soon.

All my love,
Margaret

Pictures of Margaret and the children for Carl

She wanted to just scream and cry and beg him to come back home, but she knew it was futile and would make things harder for him (and probably not get by the censors). She sighed as she looked through the pictures she was sending him. Closely observing herself in the pictures, she was suddenly struck with how worried and tired she looked. I hope Carl doesn't notice that! She worried more, but sent them off with a prayer. *Lord, let him get them, but don't let them be a cause for more worry for him.*

In the next few days, Joe repaired the roof and front door and cleaned out the chimney. Papa covered a few broken windowpanes with cardboard. Margaret decided to just lock the door that led to the upstairs attic. Except for storage, they would use only the four rooms downstairs. There was no way to heat the upstairs, and keeping enough wood handy for the fireplace was going to be a big job anyway. She surely didn't want to take a chance on the children trying to climb those stairs.

Tomorrow she would pick up the cardboard boxes her cousin TC had saved for her to nail on the inside walls to keep out the cold air that whistled through the cracks. She'd ordered heavy wallpaper to go over that and linoleum for the floors. It wouldn't be fancy, but she hoped they'd be comfortable even with no indoor plumbing and a fireplace to constantly feed. The challenge loomed larger for her as the days passed and more work for her kept cropping up.

She sat back on her heels and pushed a string of hair out of her face. Getting this house ready to live in was a big job, but she was making headway. With the help of her two sisters and her little brother, she had covered the walls and cleaned most everything. She could tell by the fullness in her breasts that it was time to go back across the road and nurse Junior. Getting up off her knees and grabbing the bucket of dirty water, she looked around and observed the progress.

"I can do this, Lord, with your help. I have to do it for Peggy and Mama and Papa."

This challenge was bringing her out of the grip of depression she had suffered after Junior's birth. Feeling a warm surge of milk on her chest and seeing spots form on the front of her dress reminded her again that Junior would be ready for his morning feeding. She had gotten into a routine of getting up very early, working by the light of a kerosene lamp to clean the old house before the children awoke, then tackling the task again in the afternoon when Jenny and Abby were home from school to help Mama.

Mama and Papa's five rooms were filled to overflowing. Margaret was anxious to get Peggy, Bobby, and her three little ones over to the Wilson house where she could take away some of the work and worry from Mama and they could all be a little more relaxed.

Walking out onto the porch, she looked across the road at her parent's house. Her heart leapt into her throat at what she saw. Flinging the bucket away, she ran down the hill calling out to God with frightened gasps, "No! No! Dear God, NO!"

Two cars had driven up the driveway. She recognized her cousin TC and his wife getting out of the front car. The other looked like some sort of official car from the government. TC, Louise, and two uniformed officers were standing on the porch as Margaret ran up the steps. Mama was already crying hysterically as Papa opened the door wide and motioned them to come in, though he couldn't say a word.

One officer asked if they would like to sit down, but they shook their heads, as Mama cried, "No, I can't. What do you want? It's Sam, isn't it?" Louise was at her side, trying to comfort her as the officer read the cable he took from his coat pocket.

WESTERN UNION

WASHINGTON DC

MR. & MRS. SAMUEL LANE-

DEEPLY REGRET TO INFORM YOU THAT YOUR SON PRIVATE FIRST CLASS SAMUEL W

LANE USMCR WAS KILLED IN ACTION IN THE PERFORMANCE OF HIS DUTY AND SERVICE OF HIS COUNTRY. NO INFORMATION AVAILABLE AT PRESENT REGARDING DISPOSITION OF REMAINS. TEMPORARY BURIAL IN LOCALITY WHERE DEATH OCCURRED PROBABLE. YOU WILL BE PROMPTLY FURNISHED ANY ADDITIONAL INFORMATION RECEIVED. TO PREVENT POSSIBLE AID TO OUR ENEMIES DO NOT DIVULGE THE NAME OF HIS SHIP OR STATION. PLEASE ACCEPT MY HEARTFELT SYMPATHY. LETTER FOLLOWS -

A. A. VANDERGRIFT LIEUT GENERAL USMC COMMANDANT OF THE MARINE CORPS

"Margaret! Margaret! What's happening? What's wrong?" Peggy was screaming from her bed in the back room. Margaret ran to her sister's side.

Taking Peggy in her arms, Margaret sobbed out the terrible news. "It's Sam! He's been killed. Oh, Peggy, he's been killed!"

It took a while for Margaret to settle Peggy down. She was bordering on hysteria until the sedative Dr. Turner had left for her began to work and she finally drifted off to sleep rolling her head on the pillow and moaning, "What next? What next?"

The baby was crying to be nursed and the children were hungry and confused seeing the adults so upset. Mama and Papa had retreated to their bedroom, while Jenny and Abby sat sobbing on the sofa. Frankie had run out to the barn followed by his dog, Old Sport.

Margaret forced her mind to think about what to do next. She took out biscuits, butter, and jelly, setting a place at the table for each of the three small children. She poured milk for them, and then sat in the rocker near the table, nursing Junior and helping Janie with her food, barely able to see through her tears.

After a while, Frankie came back in the back door. Margaret hugged him close then had him sit down at the table with a plate of food, which he picked at sadly. He and Sam had been close, now his big brother was gone. It was hard for a seven-year-old to grasp.

That evening, after the children were asleep, the adults, with Jenny and Abby, sat sadly in the living room contemplating what had happened.

"I knew this would happen," Mama cried. "Why did he have to go? I begged him to wait. He was too young!"

Papa just patted her hand and was too grieved to say anything.

"I had a nightmare last night. I saw his face all covered in blood. I knew something had happened to him," Mama continued. "I think he was trying to say goodbye." She collapsed into sobs again.

"What do we do now?" Abby moaned. "Do we have a funeral? How do we know for sure he's really dead? Maybe they're just telling us that. Maybe it's a big mistake!"

Papa got his voice. "They had his dog tags. He was buried there, but when the area is secured, they'll bring his remains back and we'll have a service. Meanwhile, we just have to go on living without him." He put his head in his hands and his shoulders shook with grief.

Margaret knew now that no matter how hard this would be, she was where God had placed her. She had to somehow find strength to help keep the family going. She worried that Sam's death would be the final circumstance that would bring Papa's health to a point of no recovery. The dark cloud that hovered over the entire country at this time seemed concentrated over the grief-stricken family group huddled together in the living room of this tiny Tennessee farmhouse.

# PEGGY'S DIAGNOSIS

## 1944

The day after Thanksgiving, Margaret, her brother Joe, and Papa moved Margaret and Peggy's meager belongings into the house across Hurricane Hill Road. Sarah and Russell came from Arkansas in Granpap's truck filled with baby furniture and helped with the move. The front bedroom was set up for Peggy with her own bedroom furniture that had been stored when Robert left and Mama's rollaway bed for Bobby.

Russell put up the two cribs in the back bedroom for Junior and Janie. Anna Rose would sleep with Margaret in the large front room, which would double as a living room with Peggy and Robert's sofa and chairs in one corner and, at the other end of the room, Margaret's cherished bedroom set she bought when she was sixteen.

She remembered so well how she had begged Papa to give her the small cotton patch at the corner of his land nearest the house. She promised she would chop the weeds by herself in the spring and pick all the cotton in the fall. However, she soon found she had made a rash promise, not realizing how hard that would turn out to be for one person alone. Papa, as usual, seeing she was working long hours but getting behind, pitched in to help with the picking, but still kept his promise. She took the one hundred dollars he sold her cotton for and bought the beautiful bedroom set she had seen in the window of Biggs Furniture Store. It had gone with her to the tiny apartment where she and Carl first lived, to the apartment at the Wyatt house, and to Arkansas. Now it held a place of honor in this old house, giving her a sense of belonging that she so needed.

A table and chairs and a coal oil cook stove were crammed into the small kitchen with a washstand by the door on which was placed a bucket filled with drinking water from Mama and Papa's well. Papa brought over a large barrel of water, which he and Frankie set on the porch for extra water. The well at this old house had long dried up.

Frankie helped pile cut firewood in the tiny lean-to room that opened into the backyard so Margaret would have it handy for the fireplace.

Mama brought over a big pot of white beans, corn bread, and stewed tomatoes for supper. That night, Margaret and Anna Rose slept in Peggy's room, giving their bed to Russell and Sarah. Tomorrow they would bring Peggy and Bobby to their new home. The lamps were extinguished early and all fell into bed exhausted.

The next morning, over coffee and hot cakes, Sarah had a proposal for Margaret. Sarah could see that Margaret was extremely tired and weary at this point and felt her suggestion would be a great help even if Margaret couldn't see it right away.

"Why don't you let me and Russell take Janie and Anna Rose home with us for a few weeks? It'll give you and your mama a break. You'll have time to get settled in with Peggy and maybe get her to the hospital in Memphis for those tests that will give you a better idea about what to do for her. All of your family can have a breather and try to deal with Sam's death with fewer distractions. Mother and Hannah and I would love taking care of them for a while. We miss them since you had to leave us. We have more time to give to them right now than any of you do."

Margaret paused for a moment to think about this. Her first reaction was, "No, I can't do that, Sarah! I would miss them too much. Sometimes they're the brightest spot in my day."

"I know, Margaret, but you've got your hands more than full here, and it would only be for a few weeks. You probably won't even have time to miss them that much. Try to think about what is best for them."

In the end, Margaret relented and waved with tears streaming down as her two little girls went happily to Arkansas with Uncle Russ and Aunt Sarah.

When they had gone, she took Junior in her arms, rocking and cradling him in front of the large fireplace while she cried for want of her husband, loss of her brother, and already missing her little girls. It had been a long time since she was able to sit alone and think about what she was doing. This was not going to be easy.

"Oh, why, why can't this terrible war be over?" she pleaded with God. "We need our men," she whispered in despair. In the warmth of the fire and the closeness of her small son, she seemed to hear God answer.

*"It's okay. My grace is sufficient. Don't lean on yourself, lean on my strength and I will direct your ways."*

By the time she had laid the sleeping baby in his crib and returned to put another log on the fire, she saw Papa drive up the hill with Peggy and Bobby in the seat beside him. Frankie and Old Sport were in the back of the truck. She ran to help Peggy inside and proudly showed her to her new room.

Peggy's countenance changed. Seeing her furniture and the quiet neatness of the sunny room that was hers seemed to soothe her nerves and renew her spirit. She hugged Margaret gratefully.

"Thank you, sister." She smiled.

"It wasn't just me," Margaret protested. "The whole family helped. We all just want to see you get better."

Margaret helped her remove her slippers and fluffed the pillows around her. Taking a brush she had found among Peggy's stored personal things, she began to brush her sister's hair.

Peggy took her by the hand. "I don't just mean fixing up this house and this room, Margaret. I know you're giving up a lot more. You were having a nice life with Carl's family and had lots of help there. Thank you."

"You're welcome!" Margaret tried to lighten the mood. "You rest now, and I'll fix some lunch. Dr. Turner will be here this afternoon to see you again. Maybe he'll have some answers for us."

Dr. Turner did have some answers. He had made arrangements for Peggy to be taken to Memphis on Monday. An ambulance from the funeral home had been hired to take an older man to the hospital there and Peggy could go in the same vehicle, saving gasoline. The man's wife would be riding along with him, and one person could go with Peggy to help get her settled into a room. The ambulance would come by at 8:00 a.m. and return by 4:00 p.m. The family member who went with Peggy could ride back in the ambulance.

Mama had come over to hear what the doctor had to say. When he left, they began to make plans for the trip.

"Mama, you can go with her. I'll take care of things here and you'll be back before dark," Margaret offered, but she was shocked by Maud's answer.

"No, Margaret, I can't go. I wouldn't know what to do. You've lived in Memphis, you know your way around, and besides, Peggy would feel better with you. Wouldn't you, Peggy?" She turned with her question toward her second daughter, but Margaret didn't give Peggy time to answer.

"But Mama, how can I go? What about Junior? I can't take him, but he has to be nursed. He's only two months old!" She was becoming exasperated with her mother's seeming unreasonableness.

"You can pump and fill some bottles. I can feed him while you're gone. It's only for a few hours. He'll sleep most of that time."

Maud Lane had rarely been out of Dyer County and the thought of a trip to a big city to conduct business she knew nothing about overwhelmed her.

"Please go with me, Margaret," Peggy added. Margaret began to see her sister as that same child she had protected from being bullied by Nadine and Sybil Block when she first started school. This was a new and frightening experience for her, and Margaret, always the dependable "fixer" of her family's problems, came to the rescue again.

"Okay, Peggy, we'll work it out. You get some rest now."

They closed her door and went to the kitchen for coffee.

"Mama, I don't know if Junior will even take a bottle. He's never had one. You may have a hard time with him if I'm gone very long."

"We'll be fine, Margaret. Maybe he wouldn't take a bottle from you, but if you're not around and he's hungry, he'll take it, especially if it's your milk. I had to wean Bobby onto a bottle when Peggy's milk dried up. He did okay."

Maud, the mother of ten who'd lived on a farm all her life, knew how to solve almost any problem that had to do with babies or making a good life for her family with very scant resources, but couldn't even imagine herself trying to get through the maze of a big city hospital.

"I just can't go, Margaret. I would be lost and I can't help her like you can. I promise I'll take good care of Junior."

Margaret saw desperation in her mother's eyes. With Sam's death and Papa and Peggy's illnesses, she was reaching her breaking point. Margaret knew she would have to go with Peggy and just trust that Junior would be okay.

"I know you will, Mama." She laid her hand on her mother's trembling one. "He's a tough little boy, and you're a miracle worker when it comes to babies. We're all going to be just fine."

Maud's grateful smile was enough to make Margaret glad she had consented in spite of her apprehension over leaving Junior.

Their first night alone in the old house turned out to be a little disconcerting for Margaret. She had never given any thought to being afraid, but sitting by the fire with her cup of coffee after Peggy had taken her sedative and Bobby and Junior were tucked into bed, she felt the darkness close in on her. The kerosene lamp beside the bed flickered across the paper as she tried to write a few lines to Carl. Moving shadows danced about the room from the lamp on the mantle.

She suddenly realized she had never lived in a home without Papa or her husband. She got up slowly and locked the front door with the skeleton key, but there was no way to lock the back door except with the small piece of wood that had been nailed to the door frame and turned horizontally to keep the wind from blowing it open. She prayed for God's protection and piled several pieces of firewood against the door, so at least she could hear them fall if someone tried to get in, but she slept fitfully after extinguishing the lamps.

The next day, she nailed more pieces of wood to the back door frame. Each night over the weekend, she felt more at home and began to laugh at her fear. *Who in their right mind would bother two women with no money and a house full of kids,* she mused. Well, "in their right mind" could be the key.

Margaret pumped as much breast milk as she could without short-changing Junior's feedings and stored it in a quart jar in Mama's icebox. It was almost full by Monday morning. Maud boiled a bottle and nipple she had used for Bobby. Still, Margaret was reluctant to leave him when the car arrived.

Peggy was placed on a cot stretched down the middle of the long black limousine. Her head lay between the driver and Margaret, her feet between Mr. Moore and his wife in the back seat. Mr. Moore looked pale and weak as he leaned with his head on a pillow in the corner of the window. Mrs. Moore looked strained and worried, so the ride was quiet, with each person deep in his or her own thoughts or too weak to engage in a conversation.

Margaret thought about Carl—wondering when she would hear from him again. She hadn't heard if he'd received the letter with the pictures she'd sent. She decided she needed to write him another long letter as soon as she got back home. She had to tell him about Sam's death and their move into the old Wilson house. It was hard not hearing from him—not knowing if he was okay. Sam's death heightened her fear for Carl.

Once they arrived at the hospital, there was no time for thinking. Margaret had expected a hospital to be quiet and sterile, but this one was almost chaotic, a sea of overworked doctors and nurses and desperately sick people trying to get the care they needed.

Peggy was placed on a cot in the hallway while Margaret filled out papers and held them close for Peggy to sign.

"We don't have a room ready for her yet, Mrs. Corwin. We're trying our best. We'll get her one as soon as possible." The nurse was kind but abrupt, taking the papers quickly and moving on to the next patient in the hallway.

Margaret pulled up a chair from down the hall and opened the bag Mama had packed for their lunch. She devoured a biscuit sandwich of butter and fried salt pork. Peggy nibbled on a biscuit, but ate little. Margaret went to the water cooler and got two cone-shaped cups of water for them to drink.

Peggy was getting more exhausted and agitated by the hustle and bustle around her as the afternoon wore on. Margaret asked every nurse who came by how long it would be before she could be moved to a room.

"Soon," was usually the only answer.

"I can't take this anymore," Peggy cried. "Let's go home. All this noise is driving me crazy." She grabbed Margaret's hand and tried to sit up.

Margaret brought her another sip of water and tried to calm her.

"We can't, Peggy. We have to get you better and this is the only way. You'll be in a room soon where it's quiet and you'll feel better. Here, take this pill Dr. Turner gave you." She looked up to see a nurse helping Mr. Moore down the hall.

"See, there goes Mr. Moore. He's getting a room now. You should be next. You both came in at the same time."

As she tried to soothe Peggy, the ambulance driver came down the hall. "Mrs. Corwin, we have to leave now. Are you ready to go?"

Peggy grabbed her hand. "Please don't leave me here this way, Margaret. I can't stand it!" she begged.

Mrs. Moore came by and stood waiting by the driver. Margaret looked at the tears streaming down her sister's face and knew she couldn't leave her.

"I'll catch a bus back later," she decided. "Please leave a message at Lane's Grocery for me. I'll write it out."

She borrowed a pencil and paper from the nurses' desk and scribbled a quick note.

> Mama and Papa,
>
> They don't have a room ready yet for Peggy. I can't leave her here until they do. I'll take a bus to Dyersburg, then a taxi out to the house. It shouldn't be much longer now. I hope the baby isn't giving you a hard time.
>
> Margaret

She folded it and gave it to the driver who promised to get it to TC at the store. She knew TC would take it to Mama. Now, she was really glad it was her that was here with Peggy. Mama never would have been able to stay and take a bus later.

At five o'clock, a nurse came with a wheelchair for Peggy. She made Peggy comfortable in a private room and brought her a bowl of soup. When Margaret was sure Peggy was settled, she gave her a hug and rushed out the door hoping to get a bus quickly. Hailing a taxi, she hurried to the Greyhound bus station with which she was familiar. She and Anna Rose had taken a bus back to Dyersburg for several visits when they lived in the Wyatt house.

The station was crowded with soldiers and sailors trying to get home for a last visit before shipping out or for a furlough after basic training. The ticket she purchased would be for the last bus out to Dyersburg that day. She took the only seat she could find in a corner of the station and tried to relax, but kept thinking about Mama and Junior wondering how they were doing with her being so late.

When the bus pulled up to the door, there was almost a stampede. Margaret quickly got in line as it loaded, but she was too far back. Just as she stepped up to the door, the driver began to pull the lever that would close it, leaving everyone else to wait until morning.

"No! No! No!" she cried as she pounded on the door with her body halfway inside. "I have to get home to my baby tonight! I have to! Please! I'll stand if I have to!" She kept pounding and pleading.

The driver looked at her, then stood up and walked back into the bus, returning soon with good news.

"You're in luck, lady. A nice young sailor has volunteered to stand until he gets off at Millington so you can have his seat. Come on."

Sinking into the seat she gave a tired, but heartfelt thanks to the sailor. Looking down, she saw what the bus driver must have seen that prompted him to find her a seat. The front of her blouse was soaked and the smell of sour milk permeated the warm, close space around her. She pulled her coat across her chest and dozed off, thanking the Lord for getting her back home tonight.

Troubled dreams floated in and out of her consciousness—Peggy screaming while doctors stood over her with huge probes and scalpels, Junior lying on top of a mountain while she clawed her way up, unable to reach him, Carl floating face down in the ocean while his ship sailed away without him.

Suddenly, she was jolted awake as the bus came to a stop.

"Dyersburg!" the driver announced.

"What time is it?" she asked as she stepped to the front of the almost empty bus.

"Nine o'clock."

She rushed around the side of the station and climbed in the back seat of a waiting taxi.

"Where to, ma'am?"

She couldn't think straight. Leaning back on the seat, she tried to gather her thoughts out of the fog of exhaustion and still half-asleep. The man turned to look at her with concern.

"Ma'am? You okay?"

"Yeah. Uh, Uh, head out toward Hurricane Hill. I'll be able to tell you in a minute."

She sat up, shook her head, and finally was able to tell him what road and which way to turn and where to stop.

Home! Weariness overtook her as she dragged up the steps where Mama was holding the door open for her.

"The baby is fine, Margaret. I ran out of breast milk but gave him some boiled cow's milk and water. He loved it. He's sound asleep now."

"I've got to pump some milk, Mama, if he's not ready to nurse. My breasts are so full and sore, and I've leaked all over my clothes. All this sour milk makes me smell like a drunk. I bet that taxi driver thought I was drunk!"

"How is Peggy?" Mama wanted to know, as she poured a pan of warm water for Margaret to wash up in, and warmed up the leftover soup from supper for her.

"I don't know," she answered wearily. "I hated to leave her, but the nurse said she'd be fine. I just hope we hear something soon. They said they'd keep in touch with us through Dr. Turner's office."

After washing up and getting into one of Mama's gowns, she collapsed on the sofa and slept soundly until Junior awoke early for his morning feeding.

Dr. Turner kept in touch with the hospital in Memphis by phone about Peggy's progress and relayed it to the family. She was diagnosed with tuberculosis and after two weeks of treatment there, she'd need to be on strict bed rest for several months at home.

When the ambulance brought her back two weeks later, Margaret tried to be ready. She moved Bobby's bed in with Janie and Junior to make sure Peggy wasn't disturbed during the night and gathered equipment Dr. Turner told her she would need to clean and sterilize everything Peggy used to keep the rest of the family from contacting the disease. He left small containers self-addressed to the lab in Memphis that Peggy would have to cough and spit into once a week.

"Do you have a goat on the farm, Margaret? They say goat's milk might be very good for her."

So Papa bought a goat and tied it to a tree in the front yard and Margaret milked it twice a day, often having to catch it first, since its favorite thing to do was chew the rope apart and head for the greener grass along the fence row.

Soon after Peggy came home, Russell and Sarah brought Janie and Anna Rose back. They'd been away for three weeks and Margaret had missed them so, but she had to admit it had been a great blessing to know they were well taken care of and not an extra burden on Mama as they had to deal with Peggy's hospital stay.

Russell brought in a big mysterious box full of gifts that weren't to be opened until Christmas. Margaret stashed it in the stairway and locked the door again.

The next night after Russell and Sarah left and the children were tucked into bed, Margaret sat by the fireplace with her cup of coffee smiling at Anna Rose's steady breathing which seemed to mirror her life now. Finally, she could settle into the way things were going to be while Carl was gone.

Carl and Robert had signed up for three years in the Navy. One year had gone by for Carl—had it really? Yes, yes, it went fast, so maybe the next two would go just as fast since she knew now what she'd do—live across from Mama and Papa, taking care of Peggy and the children, not an easy job, but steady and predictable and one she felt now that she could handle with her family's help. She sighed resolutely and fell asleep in the chair.

The steadiness and predictability would last only for a little while.

# ROBERT

## 1944–45

Christmas was sad for the adults still grieving from Sam's death, but brightened for the children by the gifts in the box Russell and Sarah had left. Abby and Frankie cut a small cedar tree from the woods and strung popcorn to circle around it, and Margaret set it in a bucket of rocks in front of the window. Anna Rose and Frankie cut out brightly colored pictures from the Sears and Roebuck catalog to hang on it.

Mama, still reeling from Sam's death, refused to use any decorations other than the star in her window representing her son who gave his life.

"This is not a time to celebrate," she insisted.

After the holiday, Peggy became ecstatic when a letter arrived from Robert saying he would be home for a few days before being shipped out.

Margaret helped her shampoo her hair and reluctantly pulled out a beautiful lace bed jacket she had tucked away in her dresser after her honeymoon.

Margaret was worried. She never liked the way Robert treated Peggy, and now she wasn't sure he would respect the fact that she was very ill. He ran with a wild crowd of friends and drank too much. She tried to approach the subject with her sister.

"Peggy, you and Robert need to be careful," she warned. "You know you're very sick and strenuous activity could set you back."

"That's none of your business," Peggy snapped.

"It is my business," she cried. "I have to take care of you and Bobby! I don't want to see you get worse."

"Is that the way you look at it?" Peggy pouted. "You have to take care of us?"

"I didn't mean it that way, Peggy. I mean you're my sister and I don't like to see you suffer so. Does Robert know how sick you are? Have you told him what the doctors said?" It was as if they were children again and Margaret was still protecting her little sister.

"He knows I'm sick." She evaded Margaret's eyes.

"Does he know you need complete rest? Does he know you have tuberculosis and that he could even catch it from you?"

"I don't want to worry him with all the details when he's going into war. It wouldn't be right!"

Margaret was furious.

"Well, if you don't tell him, I will. He has a right to know. Maybe he could even get a deferment because you're sick."

Peggy was beginning to get upset, which made her start coughing violently.

"Margaret, don't! I couldn't stand it. Please!"

The look of anger which had flickered across Margaret's face quickly changed to sympathy. She began to regret being so blunt with Peggy.

"Okay! Okay! I won't say anything!" She fluffed Peggy's pillow and gave her a sedative. "Just rest now."

The day Robert was to arrive, Peggy insisted on putting on her nicest dress and sitting in a chair in the living room. She was so thin and her dark eyes were sunken, but they had a sparkle in them that Margaret hadn't seen since Robert left. Perhaps this would be a good thing—if only Robert would act like a responsible adult.

He came bursting in the door in the late afternoon. Picking Peggy up from the chair, he whirled her around as she laughed weakly.

"How's my sweetheart?" He asked loudly.

"Fine," she lied.

"Where's that boy of mine?" He grabbed Bobby up, but Bobby, not being used to the gregarious loudness of his father, began to cry. Margaret could smell the liquor, but tried to be friendly for Peggy's sake.

"Hi, Robert," she smiled. "Are you hungry? I have dinner ready."

"Hungry as a bear," he cried, hugging Margaret tightly. "Thank you for taking care of my family. Peggy looks like she's doing good under your care." He went over and kissed Peggy.

Margaret excused herself to go to the kitchen, angrily dishing up the food and setting the table. Dinner was filled with stories of his experiences in basic training, with lots of colorful language. When Peggy meekly reminded him of the children's presence, he would apologize, but slip back into it again.

After dinner, the rest of the family came over for a visit. He repeated many of the stories, but tempered his language knowing Mama would not approve and would tell him so. When the family left, Peggy and Robert took Bobby and went to her room, closing the door.

Margaret fumed and worried as she cleaned the kitchen and readied the children for bed. She had just finished nursing Junior and was tucking him into his crib when she thought she heard the front door open and close. Going to the window, she saw a car backing down the hill into the road.

She rushed to Peggy's room. "Where is Robert? Who was in that car"?

"Shh! You'll wake Bobby. Here, take him to his bed."

Margaret took the sleeping child from beside his mother and put him in his bed, but she wasn't done speaking her mind about what she considered Robert's horrible behavior. How dare he take off with his friends after having been with his family only a few hours! They hadn't seen him in months!

Peggy had changed clothes, climbed into bed and turned her face toward the wall pretending to be asleep, but Margaret knew she was trying to avoid talking about Robert.

"I know you're not asleep. Where did he go?"

"He's had a very hard time for months. He deserves a little fun with his friends before he puts his life in danger for us." She still faced the wall and Margaret could tell she was deeply disappointed even while she defended him.

"You–You're crazy to let him get away with that!" Margaret sputtered.

"Leave me alone, I'm tired," Peggy moaned.

Rage turned to pity for her sister. She patted her back, then locked the front door, stomped into the living room, and sat before the fire with her evening cup of coffee, determined to stay up until Robert came home —if he came home. She was not going to keep her promise to Peggy. He needed someone to straighten him out, and she was going to do it.

Loud knocking on the front door just before dawn aroused Margaret from the chair where she had fallen into a deep sleep. Jumping up, she fumbled with the lock, then faced Robert angrily, though he was barely able to stand and leaned groggily against the door.

"Be quiet, you'll wake the kids up, you fool," she hissed, trying to be sure he heard her, but trying not to awaken Peggy and the children. "Don't you know your wife is very sick and needs you by her side every minute you can be here? What do you think your drunken antics will do to her? She has tuberculosis and is very weak. She could be contagious. You need to be careful for yourself that you don't get sick too. She needs lots of rest, not the aggravation you're giving her!"

Tears of anger were streaming down her face, but she doubted he even grasped what she was saying. She grabbed the front of his coat and forced him to look at her. He stared for a few seconds, and then brushed her aside. Stumbling in through the door of Peggy's room, he slammed it tight and she heard him put a chair in front of it.

Lying in bed next to her sleeping daughter, Margaret sobbed as she listened to their muffled voices.

She was glad the next day when Robert slept until noon, then got up and left with one of his fellow Navy buddies. She went to check on Peggy when he was gone. Peggy was huddled in the corner of her bed, crying softly.

"He's gone back to that horrible war," Peggy whispered. "He only had three days. I probably will never see him again."

Taking Peggy in her arms, Margaret tried to console her. "Don't think that way, Peggy. He will come back and you three will have your whole life together." She held her sister and soothed her until she finally fell asleep. A new, deeper sadness crept into Margaret's soul. Robert had only been home two days. She wondered if he really had to go so soon or if he didn't want to face the embarrassment of how he had acted.

# THE ACCIDENT

1945

Anna Rose and Frankie

Frankie and Anna Rose, as young as they were, became the runners back and forth across the red gravel road carrying mountains of diapers to Maud for washing, then back to Margaret for the three babies. Pulling and pushing Frankie's little wagon or swinging a flour sack full of diapers between them, they sang, "Dinga-Dinga-Dinga-Dinga Didy-A" and made a game of the chore. Once in a while, when Frankie was in school, Anna Rose made the trip across the road alone under Margaret's watchful eye, especially when she ran out of clean diapers for three babies

"Anna Rose, Junior is asleep and I can't leave. Frankie's still at school, so could you go over and get a few of the clean diapers that Grandma Lane washed for the babies? Junior will be soaking wet when he wakes up. I'll stand here on the porch and watch you until you get inside the door, then Grandma will do the same when you come back, or maybe someone will be there to help you bring them back."

Margaret put her small daughter's coat on her and tied a scarf under her chin. Though not quite five years old, Anna Rose went eagerly, feeling like a big girl helping her mother.

Margaret smiled, shielding her eyes from the sun, watching her little daughter skip down the hill, look both ways, cross the gravel road, then start up the dusty driveway toward her grandparents' house. Hearing the familiar sound of a plane approaching, flying very low, she looked up.

Quickly looking back at Anna Rose, she saw her fall into the dust, covering her head with her arms. Forgetting the sleeping baby in the house and the two toddlers playing in the living room, Margaret ran to Anna Rose, gathering her in her arms, trying to calm the screaming child.

"Mommy! Mommy! The Japs are coming to bomb us. Help! Help! Mommy!" she cried hysterically.

Trying to wipe away the dust mingled with tears streaming down Anna Rose's cheeks and into her mouth, Margaret kept talking softly to her frightened child, holding her close to her heart.

"No, honey, no. It was only one of our planes training to go get the bad men so they won't hurt us. It's okay. They're gone now. You're okay."

They sat in the dust as she cradled Anna Rose in her lap. Maud heard the screaming and came running to them.

"Take her back home, Margaret. Here are a few diapers. I'll send the rest with Frankie when he gets home from school." She patted Anna Rose on the head as Margaret stood with the little one in her arms.

"Thanks, Mama, I need to get back to the other kids. I guess she's heard too much war talk."

"This war is gonna be the death of us all," Mama muttered as she turned to go slowly back to her work.

It was only a few days later that the accident happened. January 24, 1945.

Margaret, busy with Peggy and the children, soon paid little attention to the large planes that daily flew through the skies over their home, training pilots to go to war. The airbase nearby had become the main training base for B-17 bombers. She had so many other things on her mind that she rarely thought about the reports that there were several crashes as the pilots trained for wartime flying.

She had just stepped out on the back step to empty her dishwater when she heard planes approaching again. She turned to go back inside, but noticed that the two seemed unusually low and close together. Shock and horror gripped her as she witnessed one plane clip the other, then both burst into flames. The thunderous sound and spreading plume of fire and smoke sent a stab of dread to her heart, as she immediately worried that the planes might be carrying a bomb. Soon, an acrid smell of melting metal and debris made her nose burn and her eyes water. Sensing how close this was to her home, Margaret pulled herself away from where she had been standing mesmerized on the back step, and ran back in the house.

Rushing into the living room, she gathered all the children, placed them by the front door, and helped Peggy into a chair near them, so that they would be ready to run if something hit that might set the house afire. In the woods, she could see a huge plume of smoke rise into the air as if the whole forest was on fire. She whispered a prayer of thankfulness that it was obviously too far away from them to do any damage to their home.

Stepping onto the front porch, she could see Mama and Papa, Jenny, Abby, and Frankie across the road standing on their porch gazing into the sky where a lone parachute was drifting toward the ground. It came closer and closer, finally slamming into a large oak tree at the end of the pasture beside Margaret's house.

Papa, Frankie, and the two girls came running. Margaret met them and yelled to Jenny and Abby, "Go inside and watch the children and help Peggy back to bed," as she headed toward the tree with Papa and Frankie close behind.

They could see only two boot-clad feet dangling from the end of the ropes attached to the huge mass of cloth that nearly covered the branches of the tree.

"Frankie, go tell Jenny to jump in the truck and go down to the store and call somebody from the airbase," Papa directed. "She needs to tell them we have an injured pilot on our property."

As Margaret began to climb into the tree pushing through all the cloth, she heard a soft moan.

"He's alive," she reported. "I heard him moan, but I haven't seen him yet."

Frankie was running back up the hill as Jenny took off toward the store in the truck. "Frankie, go get that pair of wire cutters we used to fix the fence last week. We may need to cut some of these cords to get him down. Margaret, see if you can see how bad he's hurt. I'll go hitch up the horses to the wagon and bring it over under the tree so we can lower him into it." Papa was organizing everyone to try to rescue this soldier that they knew must be badly hurt.

The two of them ran to their tasks leaving Margaret by herself, pushing through the cloth, trying to make her way to the man.

"Oh, my," she cried as she lifted a fold that revealed his full form. Blood streamed from under his helmet across his face, making him unrecognizable, and his left arm dangled limply at his side. His uniform was ripped, revealing bloody gashes all over his body. "This doesn't look good." She touched his arm and he groaned with pain. He was alive, but she wasn't sure for how long. Time might be a factor.

Papa soon returned, directing the two horses to pull the wagon underneath the man's feet. He helped Frankie up into the tree, and he climbed above where Margaret sat on a branch near the man's head. They passed the wire cutters up to him. Slowly, he cut the lines that held the man in the tree as Margaret and Papa lowered him into the wagon that Mama had lined with a quilt. Margaret placed another quilt over him and removed his goggles, then she began to wipe away some of the blood from his face with a dishcloth she had tucked into her apron. She and Papa looked at him, then at each other several times, not knowing what to say or do.

Frankie climbed into the wagon, looked into the man's face and blurted out what Papa and Margaret had thought, but were afraid to say.

"He looks like a colored man to me."

Getting no answer, he stared at the shocked looks on the faces of Margaret and Papa and decided he was right.

Finally, Papa answered, "I think you're right, and he sure is in bad shape." Looking at Margaret, he asked, "Do you think we can help him? What can we do?"

Here she was, faced with another challenge, but knowing that she would never shrink from helping a helpless human being no matter what the circumstances. It was obvious this man might die without some immediate care.

"Drive the wagon slowly over to our back door, Papa. Frankie, there's a kettle of warm water on back of the stove. Pour some in a pan and put a washcloth in it. Bring it to the wagon, and then get me two more quilts from the quilt box. We need to keep him warm."

"Margaret, do you know what you're doing? Should we wait for help from somebody?" Papa was trying to process a way through a situation they'd never before faced. Margaret knew it had nothing to do with the discovery that this was a black soldier. She had learned from his example a respect for all people, no matter what their race or circumstances. He had grown up with his best friend Clarence. They played together as children, worked side by side pushing a little wagon through the community selling produce to keep their families together after Papa's father died and Clarence's father left his family. They picked cotton together and took on any odd job they could find, always sharing whatever profit they earned. Clarence had died several years ago, but Papa kept in touch with his family in the Mississippi River Bottomland where they had settled and sometimes fetched Clarence's wife Izzy to help Mama on laundry day or when a new baby was born. Margaret often heard Papa say, "Clarence was closer to me than my own brother."

"I don't think we can wait, Papa. I gotta try to stop this bleeding or he might bleed to death before somebody can get here. Get the quilts, Frankie, before he goes into shock. Did Jenny call somebody from the Army base? They need to send a doctor."

"I don't know. She's not back yet." Frankie yelled while running to do the chores he'd been assigned.

Margaret sat down beside the man trying to assess what his injuries were. There was obviously a serious head injury. Though she had wiped the blood from his face, it was already covered again. His arm looked badly broken, maybe in more than one place. She couldn't be sure about anything else. He seemed to be unconscious now.

"Papa, help me take this helmet off. I've got to try to stop all this bleeding if I can."

They slowly pushed back the leather helmet to reveal a large gash on the side of his head a few inches above his ear. Frankie returned with the water and quilts.

Taking them up into the wagon, she sent him off again. "Go back and get me a clean white sheet, Frankie. Maybe we can use it as a bandage and compress."

While Papa and Frankie tore the sheet into strips, she cleaned the wound and tied strips across it to apply pressure and close the gaping hole. It seemed useless at first, but finally the bandages she was applying seeped only a trickle. Half the sheet, soaked with blood, lay piled on the ground beside the wagon.

"I think it's about stopped, Margaret," Papa sat back looking at the bandaged head. "What about this arm?"

She surveyed the twisted limb that lay beside the man.

"I don't know what to do about that. We need to just keep him warm and quiet until someone gets here that knows more than I do. Is Jenny back? Is someone coming from the Army base yet?"

"I'm sure it won't be long," Papa tried to assure her.

"Papa, you keep an eye on him. I'll go make some coffee and see how Abby is doing with the children, then I'll be back."

When Margaret got back to the wagon, carrying hot coffee for Papa and herself, she checked the bandage and saw that the bleeding was almost stopped. For the first time, she looked closely at his face, light skin for a black man, short, but tightly curled black hair, wide brow, smooth skin across a wide nose and thin lips. Maybe he was some other nationality. She wasn't sure, but he looked very young. She wondered how he came to be at this airbase. She knew it wasn't integrated. Probably he was just hired to help in some way.

Waiting for help and looking out over the pasture and woods, Margaret thought for the first time that there must have been others on those planes.

"I wonder what happened to the other men?" she asked Papa.

"I'm surprised anybody survived. Did you see that fiery crash?"

"Yes, I just happened to be watching when they collided. You don't think there are others out there in our woods, do you? Should we look?"

"No, we would have seen their chutes if they got that close. We'll ask when someone comes from the base. The army will send out a search team if they don't find everybody."

"I hope someone will come soon," she worried. "The sun is starting to set and it will get colder then. That will be bad for him."

Just as she finished her remark, an official car drove up the hill. Two officers stepped out, one carrying a doctor's bag. The doctor climbed into the wagon to examine the patient while Papa filled the other officer in on how the man had landed in the tree, pointing out the parachute still hanging there.

Margaret started to get out of the wagon, but the doctor stopped her. "I may need your help," he commented.

She assisted while he gave the man a shot, applied careful stitches to close the gash, and put a temporary cast on the arm.

"You're a pretty good nurse," he said to Margaret. "He might have bled to death if you hadn't stopped the bleeding. As it is, he's lost a lot of blood and is very weak. Good work!"

She smiled. "I'm not a nurse, just a mother of three. I've stopped lots of bleeding," she joked, and then said more seriously, "I couldn't just do nothing. He needed help." She got down out of the wagon as the doctor finished working on the patient.

The other officer began to explain the situation to Margaret and Papa. "I'm Colonel Clark and this is Captain Burk. As you can see, we have a serious situation here. The injured man is Gunnery Sergeant James Hayes. He was attached to our unit to learn about our air-to-ground gunnery and gun camera systems to take back to his unit in Alabama. We don't know what caused the crash. The other plane was not supposed to be in that area."

"Since he's a colored man, the mission has been kept secret to avoid trouble. It might create a major problem for the morale, training, and concentration of the rest of our trainees if a big deal were made of this, and it could even be dangerous for Sergeant Hayes. The Veteran's Hospital in Memphis takes only white soldiers. We have to find a place close by to treat him until he's able to go back to his unit or home to his family. Are there any colored families in this area where he might stay for a while?"

Margaret was appalled. How could they treat this young man who was willing to fight for his country in such a calloused manner? She couldn't bear to think about it.

"He can stay here," she stated flatly.

Papa looked at her quickly, wondering if she were thinking this through.

"There may be problems with that, ma'am," the colonel began.

"Can you get him into the house? It's getting cold out here and we need to keep him warm," she insisted.

"I don't think we can do that. This has to be kept highly secret. I don't think you understand what you're asking for. We can't be responsible for the safety of your family and Sergeant Hayes if it is discovered that he is here." The colonel was wrestling with a dilemma he had not anticipated when he had accepted this soldier onto his airbase.

"Look around you, Colonel. There are no other homes for miles, especially none where colored people live. Besides, they live in close quarters, so it would be hard to keep this secret among them. It's pretty isolated out here. We have to get him inside. We'll do whatever we can to take care of him until you find a place to move him—and we can keep a secret. My parents and brother and sisters live across the road, and my husband is in the Navy. We don't see many other people. It's the only solution I can see at the moment."

She looked back at the injured soldier and her heart bled for him. She stood up in the wagon and said decidedly, "Bring him in. We can put him in the bed in the front room."

"Well, I guess we have to do something temporarily. We'll bring him in for now," the colonel decided. "I'll have to get someone out here right away to dispose of that parachute before it draws any attention."

Margaret was already hurrying in to get the bed ready while Papa helped the men put Gunnery Sergeant Hayes on a stretcher they had brought with them and carried him inside.

Dr. Burk brought other supplies in from the car. The colonel stood to the side, observing the situation while the doctor went about caring for the injuries with Margaret's help. He added a more permanent cast to the arm, removed the torn uniform and cleaned his other less serious wounds with warm water and clean cloths Margaret provided.

"If it can be arranged, I'll stay overnight with him. The head injury needs to be watched closely for the next twenty-four hours. May I use your sofa there tonight?" Dr. Burk asked.

"Of course," Margaret was relieved that they were moving on with this soldier's care, not just leaving him when he was so badly hurt.

Addressing the doctor, the colonel began to move toward the door, "I'll get a crew out here right away to take care of that parachute. If it is noticed, it could draw curiosity seekers. I will be back here tomorrow to see how things are going. I'll work on an alternative if one is possible. Send for help if you need it and be careful." The two saluted and he left.

Papa and Frankie brought over a feather bed mattress, which Margaret put on the floor in the children's room for her and Anna Rose. As she reached into the quilt box to get extra bedding, she glanced out the window to see what was going on in the pasture. She watched as soldiers with large cutting tools and ladders made quick, quiet work of tearing the parachute from the huge tree that held it. She thought the tree seemed not to want to give up the covering, grabbing it with its branches and reluctantly letting it go.

When all traces of the parachute were gone, the men gathered all the blood-stained cloths and sheets from the ground, loaded it all into a canvas-covered truck and left as quietly as they had come.

She gave the doctor a pillow and a quilt for the sofa and offered to relieve his vigil, which she did at 3:00 a.m. Dr. Burk was grateful for a chance to stretch out on the sofa and was soon asleep.

With a cup of coffee in her hand, she sat by the bed and looked into the young, swollen face of her patient. He took a few sips of water each time she roused him, but he wasn't fully awake.

The next day, he was awake and moaning with pain. Papa sent Jenny and Abby over early to take the children to the house across the road so that the patient could have a quiet day.

Dr. Burk spent the morning showing Margaret how and when to give the pain medication and how to dress the head wound.

"We need to treat all these other minor wounds too so he doesn't develop any infection," he directed Margaret.

Early in the afternoon, Colonel Clark returned for the doctor, stating that he had decided to leave the soldier there, at least for a while. There seemed to be no better alternative at the moment. There was actually a small hospital on the airbase, but the colonel had decided that putting him there would cause trouble with the other airmen who were there.

After giving Margaret some final instructions, they left, promising to return in a few days. She was alone with two patients and the baby until Papa came by to check on her. She knew he was her lifeline, and would try to provide whatever she needed to get through yet another task that she had taken on. The enormity of it was beginning to move in on her, and fears she hadn't contemplated in the desperation of the circumstances were starting to give her a trapped feeling.

"I need Jenny and Abby to stay with me as much as they can, Papa, when they're not in school. With two sick people, I need help with the kids."

"Sure, Margaret," he answered, patting her on the shoulder. "I'll be here as much as I can too, and I'm going over to get Izzy this afternoon. She can stay for a while and help with Peggy and the kids. You need her now. You're a saint, honey. Most women would not take on so much, especially when it's something that could even be dangerous."

Through the years, Papa had made the trip to the small black community of sharecroppers who lived near the Mississippi River working on the farms in the rich delta to check on Clarence's family. Izzy, Clarence's wife, had become a part of the family, coming to stay for weeks at a time to help Mama with babies, canning, gardening, and sickness. She was small and quick, with a strong will and a heart for helping, often working for food from the garden, slabs of meat from the smokehouse, or a box of home canned vegetables to take back to her family. Papa always promised her he'd pay her in cash when the cotton crop was sold in the fall, and he never failed to do so, making the extra trip to her home to deliver the payment.

"Thanks, Papa. I need to keep busy at a time like this, but this is almost too busy. Izzy will be a great help, and you need to be taking it a little easier or your asthma will really get worse."

The next few days, Margaret hardly had time to draw a deep breath. Every few hours, night and day, one or the other of her "patients" needed attention. In between were the needs of the children. Izzy swept into the house with her apron on, easing things into a routine that made Margaret feel everything was going to be fine now. Jenny and Abby were a great help in a pinch, and Mama kept everyone supplied with hot meals. Papa was always available for whatever Margaret needed a hand with at the time. She tried to limit what she had to call on him to do. Too much strenuous activity sent him into fits of coughing.

Despite the hard work, this was bringing the family together, helping them to forget for a while their hurts from Sam's death and the dangers Carl and Robert might be in. They all felt the strain of the secrecy involved—even the children were severely warned to never even hint that they were taking care of a black soldier. The importance of this was especially impressed on Frankie, as he was so young and might be tempted to let something slip as he talked to his friends at school. He proudly took it to heart.

Margaret slept lightly on the sofa, sending Izzy to sleep with the children. Though he was receiving regular pain medication, the young soldier was in agony much of the time.

"Ohh…Ohh…Ohh…" he moaned. He cried out for his mother and squeezed Margaret's hand. She wiped profuse drops of perspiration from his face, one side of which was swollen and bruised. For days, pain and medication kept him unaware of where he was and how badly he was hurt. She tried hard to help him cope.

The few times he was able to rest peacefully, Margaret found herself staring into his young face, wondering how he came to be here in her living room. Never had she imagined such a thing, but she found that she rarely thought of his race. To her, he was a soldier doing his duty like her Carl, and she would do her best to help him recover.

She bristled at the thought of his not being allowed admission to the veteran's hospital in Memphis and grieved bitterly at the treatment he must have received at the hands of other soldiers.

She knew Carl would be extremely angry if he knew about this, but she couldn't tell him even if she wanted to. The Colonel was adamant about letting no one know he was here, and she certainly wouldn't put that worry on Carl's mind while he was in such danger himself. Besides, it would never pass censorship.

On the eighth morning, Margaret awoke suddenly, aware that she had obviously fallen into a deep sleep for several hours. Jumping to her feet, she saw that her patient seemed to be resting peacefully for the first time, even though he had missed his last pain medication. Maybe he had turned the corner—or maybe he was in a coma or something worse! Quickly, she felt his cheek and sighed with relief. It was cool and dry, the feverish clamminess was gone.

At her touch, his eyes popped open.

"I'm sorry; I didn't mean to wake you," she whispered. "How do you feel?"

"Where...am...I?" he managed to ask weakly. The swelling made it hard for him to talk.

"You bailed out of your plane when it crashed and landed in my tree," she tried to sound casual, afraid he would be frightened. "We brought you here to my house to recover. The doctor took care of your wounds and I'm taking care of you now."

"D–Does...the...Army know?"

"Yes, they wanted you to stay here awhile. It was the Army doctor from the base that treated you. He'll be back soon to check on you." She wiped his swollen face with a wet cloth and straightened his sheets. He drank thirstily from the glass of water she held up to his lips. "You look like you're feeling better."

"T...Tired," he muttered and went back to sleep.

Margaret smiled, feeling optimistic that he seemed on the way to recovery. She studied him closely. His dark, curly hair was partially visible above the bandage, his light, tan face, though badly swollen, now relaxed, without so much pain.

"I hope the doctor comes today. He probably needs a change in medication now," she said aloud as she joined Izzy in the kitchen to help prepare breakfast for the children and Peggy, who would all be awake soon.

"He better then, Miz Corwin?"

"I think so, Izzy. He doesn't seem feverish and the pain is not as bad."

The doctor did come by the time they had the dishes done, the children dressed, and Peggy settled with clean sheets, a wipe-down bath, and clean clothes. Papa sat on the porch watching Anna Rose, Janie, and Bobby play in the front yard. Junior lay on his stomach by the fireplace playing with the colorful swatches of cloth in the quilt Margaret had placed him on.

Jim was awake again and seemed to be in much less pain. Dr. Burk was pleased and explained to his patient where he was and why he was here.

"What about…the…o…others?" he asked.

"Three died in the crash," Dr. Burk told him, but you and two others survived by bailing out. They're being treated in Memphis and it looks like they'll be okay. It was a terrible crash, but we were glad there were survivors. We can't figure out what happened. Maybe when you feel better you can give us more information, but don't worry now. Just rest and get better. Mrs. Corwin here is taking great care of you."

"I…under…stand," he finally answered, looking at Margaret as if he really didn't understand why she had agreed to such an arrangement.

"He needs to start eating a little to get his strength back," Dr. Burk observed, handing Margaret an official-looking envelope. "There's money in here to pay for any supplies or food you might need to buy."

Taking the envelope, she replied, "I have chicken soup simmering on the stove now. Will that be okay?"

"Perfect! I'm going to try to see if he can sit up a little. Do you have extra pillows?"

"What about a quilt folded up behind his pillow?" Margaret asked. She had lots of quilts her Mama, Grandmama, and Aunt Abby, Mama's younger sister, had made. A quilt was always in progress at Aunt Abby's. She had no children and quilting was a favorite pastime for her.

The two of them lifted his torso gently and placed the folded quilt behind the pillow. He was sitting up just high enough for Margaret to feed him a few sips of chicken broth.

"Good," he tried to smile.

"Go easy," warned Dr. Burk. "Try again in a couple of hours if he does okay with this. You can cut the pain medication in half now, I think. Are you doing okay, Mrs. Corwin?" he asked as Margaret escorted him out to the porch.

"Yes, I'm fine. I have lots of good help," she put an arm around Izzy who was now watching the kids play in the yard. Papa had needed to go home and lie down for a while. Margaret worried that all the extra activity was a bit much for him, but he insisted on helping.

"Thank you!" He shook Margaret's hand sincerely and left, promising to be back soon.

# LOVE CREEPS IN

## 1945

Jim made slow progress then, and Margaret could see his growing suspicion and incredulity at being alive and in this isolated house in West Tennessee, and being cared for by a white woman who didn't seem to resent doing so. All of his effort now was directed toward getting better. He insisted on cutting down on the pain medication so he could think more clearly. "I'd rather have a little pain than be so sluggish all the time," he explained.

Margaret agreed and started giving him the medication only when he felt he needed it, or when he needed to sleep. She casually began to ask some of the questions she was so curious about, trying not to seem as if she were prying into his privacy. He was from Ann Arbor, Michigan, where he hadn't faced the kind of hatred he'd encountered in the South. She helped him write a letter to his parents, assuring them he was okay. Dr. Burk promised to see that it got mailed from the base post office.

She still had to feed him. One arm was in a heavy cast and the other bruised and sore. She introduced him to the children (he insisted they call him Jim) who were shy at first, but then began to enjoy listening to stories he told them about airplanes. It was obvious how much he loved flying.

Each day, she and the doctor struggled to get him sitting up higher until he could finally swing his legs over and sit on the side of the bed. That's when they discovered the swollen ankle. The pain medication and his other wounds had caused him to overlook this. Dr. Burk diagnosed it as torn or sprained ligaments. The doctor wrapped it and told him to keep it elevated and suggested that Margaret apply cold compresses twice a day for a few days.

"I must have knocked that tree out of the pasture," he joked. "Every part of my body hurts."

His laugh was infectious and soon they were all laughing.

"Ohhh!" he moaned. "It even hurts to laugh."

"You were very lucky you landed where you did. In such a crash things could have been much worse for you. I feel you will recover, but it will take some time. Be patient and do what your nurse here tells you," Dr. Burk admonished.

Margaret was amazed at how quickly the two of them fell into a routine that was comfortable and familiar. They talked easily and found no embarrassment in working together toward his recovery. That goal became their mutual obsession.

She told him about Carl and how she was worried for his safety. He asked about Peggy, whom he could hear in the other room but hadn't met. Margaret shared her concerns about her sister's illness, and her distrust of Robert. Unlike Mama, he sympathized with Margaret's assessment of Robert.

"Robert sounds pretty selfish," Jim observed.

"I think he just needs to grow up, but I can't convince Peggy. I think the biggest part of her illness is just not being able to cope with Robert's leaving and not knowing what he's doing or if he'll return alive. Despite what she says, I don't think she trusts him and that adds to her worries."

"She's lucky to have you," he spoke emotionally, "and so am I."

Taken by surprise, she felt her heart leap and her cheeks turn red. Quickly, she turned away, busying herself with gathering the tray. Immediately, he knew he had stepped over a line.

"I'm sorry, Miz Corwin, I didn't mean anything by that. Please forgive me. I'm just so grateful somebody like you would be so kind to me."

She had regained her composure and was touched by the look of shame on his face as she turned around. Smiling, she answered sincerely. "Don't be sorry, Jim. I understand how you feel. I'm happy I can help. You help me too. I'm always bending your ear with my problems. I don't really have anyone else to share with right now. Mama never seems to see my side of things, Jenny and Abby are too young, my best friend has moved to Arkansas, my husband is in the war. But I shouldn't complain. God has been good to me and my family."

"Well, the rest of my body is bent, I guess my ear might as well be too," he teased. "God has certainly been good to me too. Think of what could have happened to me in that crash or if I had landed somewhere else besides in your tree!"

They laughed and the uneasiness was gone. She had laughed a lot since Jim had entered her household. There hadn't been much for her to laugh about lately. Usually a very upbeat person, she had lost herself in sadness and busyness. She had even neglected her prayers, feeling abandoned by God. She determined at that moment to get back to that. *God, you've blessed me so. I'm so grateful.*

"I'm glad to hear you give credit to God. I forget to do that sometimes when I get caught up in my everyday busy schedule. He chuckled. "My mama drilled that into my head from the time I was a baby. That woman depends on God every minute of her life!"

He leaned back smiling, with a picture of his mother's face on his eyelids as he drifted off to sleep. Margaret tiptoed out and crossed the hall to Peggy's room, also smiling.

"What were you two laughing about?" Peggy asked as Margaret began to prop her so that she would be ready for a lunch tray.

"Oh, just something silly Jim said." She smiled at her sister, but caught the suspicion in Peggy's eyes.

"You sound like you're getting pretty familiar with him," she accused.

Peggy was unaware of Jim's race and the family had decided not to tell her. She hadn't inherited Papa's accepting nature and it would be another strain on her fragile nerves.

"Don't be silly. We can use a little laughter around here. He's a very sick soldier and God brought him here, so it's my duty to help him. Laughter helps." She was suddenly aware of her sharp tone, which brought a surprised look to Peggy's face.

Quickly, she retreated to the kitchen, trying to hide her strong reaction to Peggy's comments, and that blush that crept back into her cheeks.

She muttered softly to herself. "What's wrong with you, Margaret Corwin? Get hold of yourself! Why are you blushing? There's no sin in having a few laughs. Lord knows there haven't been many around here in a long time."

"Amen!" Margaret was startled as Izzy walked into the room and began to wash the dishes.

"Sorry, Izzy. I was just muttering to myself."

"I know," Izzy answered, never looking at Margaret, just going about her work, "but I heard you and I agree."

Margaret washed her face and hands and clattered around the kitchen, angry at Peggy's remark and even angrier at her reaction, afraid to contemplate the truth in it.

Jim had been there several weeks. He struggled daily to do more for himself, always apologizing for how much she had to do for him. He was now able to do some of his own bath with his one available hand, but she had to help him up to use the "pee pot" (as he called it) beside his bed. Papa had cut a hole in a chair and placed the "slop jar" in it as he had also done for Peggy. Jim no longer wanted to use a bedpan even though it was a struggle for him to get out of bed.

She gave him as much privacy as she could. Frankie had helped her hang a blanket from the ceiling for him to go behind and set a chair nearby for him to hold on to, but she had to help him back into bed and carry the pot out to the outdoor toilet twice a day.

"I'm sorry you have to do this, Miz Corwin," he groaned as she pulled his quilt up around him and headed out toward the back door.

She smiled. "Call me Margaret, and don't be feeling sorry for me. I'm being a good American taking care of a wounded soldier."

He groaned again. "Wounded in a stupid accident right here at home. Didn't even get a chance to go fight the enemy."

"What you were doing was important, Jim, and you may still get your chance to go fight the enemy if we get you up and going again."

"Yes, ma'am, Miz Corwin." He sighed.

"Call me Margaret," she reminded him as she left the room.

After emptying and cleaning the pots Peggy and Jim had used, she walked slowly back to the house. The February sky was blue and the sun warmed her face. She watched Mr. Wilson's horse, Teenie, graze in the pasture with her colt that Anna Rose had christened "Weenie" frolicking close by.

*I guess I'm finally adjusting to this new way of life,* she thought. *I feel so much better than I did after Junior was born. It's like a big weight has been lifted from me.*

Suddenly, Jim's face popped into her mind. She tried to shake it away and replace it with Carl's, but she realized she could hardly remember how Carl looked. It seemed so long since she had seen him or talked to him. She sat down on the porch step with a sigh, trying to make sense of it. She refused to entertain the idea that Jim Hayes had anything to do with her feeling so optimistic.

Meanwhile, inside the house, Jim's mind was whirling. He had to get her out of his head.

*She's a married Southern white woman,* he scolded himself. *Even thinking about her could get me killed around here.* He decided it was time he worked harder to get his strength back. He had to get well enough to go home. The letter Dr. Burk had brought from his mother a few days ago lay under his pillow. He touched it, remembering every word. His mother had assured him that he would be much better soon and longed for him to come home as soon as he could. He must cling to that hope.

Despite this resolve, he dozed off dreaming about how Margaret's touch made him feel. You can't control your dreams, nor should you, he decided. *God has put me here to recover and Margaret is a part of that. That's all there is to it.*

They inwardly warned themselves of the danger, but the bond between Margaret and Jim grew closer. Routines that they all looked forward to began to develop. After dinner each evening, Janie, Anna Rose, and Bobby climbed onto Jim's bed to listen to him read from their favorite book of Bible stories. His soft, expressive voice seemed to captivate them.

Margaret sat nearby listening and rocking Junior.

She looked closely at the children's attentive faces. *Carl never reads to them,* she thought to herself, then quickly felt guilty.

*It's not fair to compare Carl to Jim,* she chided herself as she sighed, enjoying the whole happy scene, the closeness of her baby son, the exciting story of Jonah, and the warmth of the fire.

After the children were settled in bed, she brought two cups of coffee, sat in her rocking chair near the fire, and they talked into the night. These were two people who had been thrust into worlds where no one around them seemed to know or care who they really were—a black soldier hiding in a white world for the sake of his fellow soldiers and a young white woman torn from her husband and his supportive family and thrust into a desperate situation where she was expected to make things all better regardless of her needs. They each felt they were in a bubble of freedom, able to open up their hearts and release all that lay inside weighing them down. Just to talk to someone, spend time with a person who listened, who understood, whom you felt had known you before you even met.

She told him stories about her childhood on the farm, funny stories about the time she and Peggy found their older brothers' homemade wine and had a tea party.

"We were so sick!" she moaned. "My brothers were furious. Their wine was almost gone, and they got into big trouble with Mama." They laughed together.

Another night there were sad stories about Sam's death and her baby brother who fell between the wall and the bed and died of suffocation while Mama was out in the garden, thinking he was still napping.

"Mama always blamed herself for not checking on him as soon as Peggy called to her that he was crying. She finished picking a few more beans, then found him behind the bed not breathing." Margaret found herself opening up to a sadness she hadn't even realized had been festering in her heart from the day these tragedies happened.

She learned about his great-grandmother who lived to be a hundred years old and had escaped from slavery with her baby girl whose father was the white slave-owner, and how frustrated Jim felt having to deny his white heritage.

His father now worked hard in the defense plant and his mother cooked at a large hotel. He showed her worn family pictures that he carried with him in his wallet. One was of his younger sister who was born with a heart defect and had died as a young child.

They never thought about the differences in their race here in the warmth of darkness, but knew it loomed as an evil shadow over every moment he was here in her house in the Deep South. He didn't fit any of the stereotypes that others in the South always characterized those of his race, and it didn't matter to her anyway. Papa was one of the few people she knew who resisted the idea that skin color made anyone inferior. He had presented an example to his family of treating all people with respect no matter what their race, but he had to be careful to whom he voiced that opinion.

"What made you want to fly?" Margaret was curious about what brought him to the point where he ended up bailing out of a plane, which took off from a Southern, nonintegrated Army airbase.

"My Uncle Stanley was a member of the National Airmen's Association established in 1939 to prove that our race could pilot planes as well as anyone else. He and a friend flew daredevil tricks at air shows all over the country. I saw the shows several times and listened to his stories. He took me up in his plane once. My mom was horrified, but dad knew how much I loved it.

"Uncle Stan used his influence to get me into Tuskegee Institute. I was in the second graduating class last year. I love flying, Margaret. It's so exciting and relaxing at the same time. It takes you away from the world of turmoil and sends you soaring toward heaven."

Finally, he had called her Margaret, and it had flowed easily from his lips as he had envisioned in his private thoughts when she wasn't around and in his heart as he felt her tender touch daily. He knew the touch was that of a sympathetic nurse, but it made his heart pound anyway.

"Well, not the kind of flying you're preparing for now!" she gasped.

He laughed at her shock. "You're right about that, I guess, but it is exciting and challenging."

"And you ended up in this airbase!"

"We needed training in the gun-camera gunnery system, but there were no facilities to do that at Tuskegee. Colonel Carter was able to find a pilot and crew here in Dyersburg that was willing to train a Negro. I had graduated at the top of my class, was an amateur photographer, and had light skin—a perfect candidate—so they assigned me to the job. I'm not sure what caused this crash. The other plane seemed to appear out of nowhere."

"I don't know about Tuskegee. Can you tell me more about it?"

"In 1939, members of the National Airmen's Association went to Washington and convinced Senator Harry Truman and Congressman Everett Dirkson to support legislation to allow us to join the Army Air Corps and to establish flight schools to train Negroes. Tuskegee Institute in Alabama was one school that applied to train black pilots. It was established in 1881 in a deal made by Lewis Adams, a former slave, with W. F. Foster who was running for Alabama State Senate as a way to secure the black vote. In March of 1940, the written test for pilots' licenses was given to those who had studied at Tuskegee and 100 percent passed the test, the only training facility of any kind that had that record. From then on, pilots trained there were some of the best ever. I'm proud to be one of them. Dr. Booker T. Washington has been principal of the institute since it started, and he is a fine man."

"It sounds like such a great place to get an education, especially for flying. Were you afraid?"

"Of course! In a plane, you're always afraid, but that's part of the excitement and what keeps you on your toes," he explained.

That hadn't been what she meant to ask. "I mean were you afraid of the white soldiers here in Dyersburg?"

He was quiet for a while, wondering how to answer that question, or if he even wanted to answer it. "Yes, a little, but it was kept a close secret from most of them and in the military during war everyone is used to secrets. I had private quarters and in my uniform with my helmet and goggles on, I wasn't too noticeable to busy men who had important work to do. I kept my distance from all but my own crew. They even served my meals in my room."

"So, at times you've been able to pass as white?" She asked curiously.

He snapped so quickly, Margaret was startled. "I *am* white! I don't need to pass."

She jumped to her feet and went quickly to his side.

"I'm so sorry, Jim. Of course, you're right. I only meant in the eyes of some white people. The truth is so different from what most people think. You know I don't feel that way."

He was immediately apologetic for his reaction.

"I didn't mean to snap at you, Miz Corwin. I wish there were more folks like you. It's just an old hurt that never goes away. My parents taught me to be proud of both sides of my heritage, but most people demand that I deny my whiteness. On the other hand, if I tried to 'pass,' I would have to deny my whole family. It's maddening."

"I know that, Jim." He noticed the tears in her eyes as she placed her hand on his. "Sometimes I'm ashamed to be a white person when I see how people like you are treated."

He had called her Miz Corwin again, falling back into the stereotype he was always expected to follow despite his resistance to it and his loathing for it.

# COMPLICATIONS

## 1945

For a while, Margaret felt that Peggy was getting better. She started eating more heartily and was much easier to help out of bed, depending more on her own strength. Maybe she would soon be able to move around the house a little more, rather than being confined to that one room, but then they would have to explain about Jim and she wouldn't do well with that news. However, that worry was soon replaced by a new development. Peggy began vomiting almost daily and eating very little.

*Maybe I'm not paying enough attention to her needs since Jim came,* Margaret thought, as she tried to understand what was going on with Peggy. *She always needed a lot of my attention when we were kids and now she's back in a similar situation.*

Margaret decided to coax her sister a little. "Peggy, you need to eat more than this," she pointed to the hardly-touched lunch.

"I can't," she moaned. "Just the smell of food makes me sick."

"Maybe I should tell Papa to get Dr. Turner out here to look at you. You can't afford to lose more weight. You were doing so well; I wonder what has happened."

"I don't think I'll be losing weight, I think I'll be gaining!" She began to sob.

"What are you talking about?" Margaret sat on the side of the bed and gathered her sister into her arms.

"I...I...think I'm pregnant!" she wailed.

Rage flew up into Margaret's brain until she felt it would explode. *Robert! That no-good scoundrel! She had warned him not to do this. Peggy is too weak to carry a baby to full term. They may both die.*

"Oh, Lord, help us!" she prayed aloud, still trying to quiet Peggy. As soon as she could get Peggy settled, she went to get Junior out of his crib and then to talk to Izzy in the kitchen.

"I need to talk to Mama about something. Can you watch the children for awhile?"

"Sure, Miz Margaret." She grabbed Junior out of Margaret's arms and swung him up in the air. He giggled excitedly.

Margaret tried to vent her anger at Robert to Mama over a cup of coffee.

"I warned him Peggy was too sick and weak for his antics!" Bitterness burst from her tight lips. "He has no regard for anyone but himself!"

Margaret could hardly bear Mama's excuses for Robert, but she felt her mother was the only source she had of venting her frustrations, so she sighed and listened.

"Now don't be so hard on Robert. Remember where he was headed—not knowing if he'd ever return. Maybe he couldn't think of anything else at the time. We'll send for Dr. Turner to look at her and see what he thinks. Maybe he can give her something to help her keep her food down."

"Mama, we're not supposed to have any outsiders in the house. Remember the Army doesn't want anyone to know we have Jim Hayes here."

"Well, we can either bring Peggy over here for him to examine her, or you could hide Jim somehow for a few minutes." She sounded irritated. She wasn't sure it was wise for her daughter to keep taking care of this man even if he was a soldier. She couldn't understand why Margaret and Sam were so determined. "Peggy's needs have to come first with us. You seem more willing to take on this dangerous situation than to be sure your sister has the care she needs. I don't like it!"

Margaret was hurt to think her mother would accuse her of such a thing. "That is not fair, Mama. I have done everything I could possibly do for Peggy, and she wouldn't even listen to me about being careful when Robert was home. Now I've been thrust in the middle of another dilemma. How can you say I don't care for her!"

"Well, I know you care for her, but something needs to be done with this soldier. His being here is dangerous to us all. Can't you check and see if the Army can move him now? He is getting better and we have another problem on our hands."

"You just don't understand! I will take care of all this as I usually have to do." Margaret had never yelled at her mother, and Maud stared at her aghast.

"You are just taking on too much," Maud scolded as she went back to kneading the dough for biscuits more vigorously than usual.

Margaret was angry, but knew she had to calm down. She began to think about what she could do so that Dr. Turner could examine Peggy without seeing Jim. It had to be done. Despite what Mama felt, she told herself she had an obligation to Jim.

" Just tell Papa to get the doctor. I will think of a way to hide Jim. Dr. Turner probably wouldn't approve of our moving Peggy and might even be suspicious of such a move."

Maud didn't want to fight with Margaret so she resigned herself to the fact that this may not be the time to continue the discussion. "Okay, we'll let you know when he's coming in plenty of time. Don't be surprised if she miscarries, Margaret. It'll be awfully hard for her to have the strength to go the full nine months."

"I know, and that's going to add to her distress."

As she headed toward the door to go home, Maud decided to try once more to convince her daughter of the foolishness of continuing to hide this soldier.

"When is the Army doctor coming back? They need to move him soon. It's so nerve-wracking having to live with this secret, and I keep getting more and more afraid that someone will find out and no telling what they might try to do about it. What if one of the children lets it slip at school? It's dangerous! We don't need the extra worry right now."

"I know it, Mama. I'm not sure when the doctor will come again, but I do hope it's soon because Jim's right foot is hurting him pretty bad. I think they need to look at it again."

Margaret didn't see the exasperated look her mother gave her as she went out the door and back across the road. *Why won't she listen to me?* Maud asked herself, shaking her head.

That evening, when all was quiet and everyone else was in bed, Margaret washed her face, combed her hair, poured two cups of coffee then headed for the rocking chair by the fireplace. Helping Jim to sit up and lean against his pillow with the quilt behind it, she handed him a cup, which he was becoming good at handling with his right hand and balancing with the thumb sticking out of the cast on his left. Once he was comfortable, she sat down in the rocker with her cup, this time emitting a huge sigh.

"That sigh sounded desperate, Miz Corwin. Is all this finally taking you down?"

She smiled at him. "Well, if you'd call me Margaret instead of 'Miz Corwin' or 'ma'am,' I'd feel a lot younger and that would help!" she teased.

"Okay M–Margaret," he answered haltingly. "I'll do anything to help out." He laughed.

"As a matter of fact," she quickly became more serious, "I am going to have to ask you to do something that may be hard for you, but we have a new development that makes it necessary." She placed her head in her hands.

His concern was immediate as he sat up straighter waiting to hear what had happened to upset her so. "What is it Miz–uh, Margaret?"

She glanced up at his strained face, surprised at the electrical feeling that surged through her body. Shaking it off, she told him about Peggy, how they would have to call in Dr. Turner and would have to hide him somehow when the doctor came. It seemed they could talk about anything without embarrassment, even subjects like Peggy's pregnancy that she usually could only discuss with her mother. They sat silently for a few minutes.

"What's behind that door?" Jim suddenly pointed toward the door to the right of the fireplace.

"It's a stairway up to an attic room. I keep it locked so the kids can't get into things I have stored there, including Carl's hunting guns. Besides, it is really hot up there when the sun is out all day."

"Could you help me up there?"

"Now?" She stared at him.

"No, not now, but sometime before the doctor comes to see your sister."

The idea began to take hold for her as she mulled it over. "I suppose with help I could, but the stairway is narrow and it may be too painful for you."

"We can't even consider that. Can it be as painful as it has already been? Can it be as painful as it may be for all of us if word gets out that I'm here? I don't want anything to happen to you or the rest of your family because of me, Margaret. I will do anything to make sure of that."

The tenderness in his voice warmed her soul, making her feel they could go through anything together.

"You're right. It's a good idea, Jim. We'll work on it tomorrow with Papa. Now we need to get some sleep."

She got up from her chair and began to remove the quilt, helping him lie down slowly. Straightening his covers, she suddenly took his hand and, looking directly into his warm, brown eyes, she shocked him with a passionate thanks.

"Jim, it means so much to me to be able to talk to you about most anything. I don't think I've ever had anyone understand and help me solve problems the way you do. Thank you."

He squeezed her hand then quickly released it, trying to gain his composure while feeling a thrill beyond measure and a dread that they were teetering on the edge of an abyss. She turned her back, busying herself with collecting the coffee cups. Her heart beat wildly and she kept asking herself why she did such a thing. It could only create more complications they didn't need right now.

"I'll see you in the morning," she mumbled softly as she returned the cups to the kitchen and busied herself there until she felt sure he had fallen asleep. As she worked, she prayed. *Dear Lord, please help us to do the right thing. Give me strength. Things just keep getting more and more out of hand. Take care of Peggy and the new life within her. I feel like I've been dropped into the middle of a whirlwind! Direct my paths.*

She sat down, laying her head on the table and cried for help from the only one that could help. Suddenly, she knew the help would come. Rising up with new resolve, she began to think of tomorrow.

*Yes, if possible, it is a good idea to move Jim upstairs,* she decided as she blew out the flame on the oil lamp and curled up beside Anna Rose on the mattress, falling into a heavy sleep. She was glad Izzy had gone home for a few days to see about her family. She didn't want to be in the same room with Jim tonight.

Papa came by early to help Margaret with her decision about hiding Jim. He found her already decided, just needing some help.

"We're going to move Jim upstairs to the attic room, Papa. It won't be easy for him, but he's willing, with our help. When is the doctor coming to see Peggy?"

"He'll be here tomorrow afternoon, so we have today to get ready."

"Okay, I need to work upstairs this morning to clean and prepare a bed, so could you take the kids over to Mama? I'll come back and get them after lunch. Tonight or in the morning, we can move Jim. I can handle the cleaning, and I don't want you up there in all that dust."

It was very dusty with lots of cobwebs, but by lunchtime she had thoroughly cleaned the floor area and the steps. Though it was still officially winter, the hot Tennessee sun on the tin roof sent streams of perspiration into her eyes and down her back. She cleaned herself up and took a tray in to Peggy.

Peggy tried to eat, but only a few bites went down before she was vomiting again. Margaret looked at her lying there looking as white as her sheets and was glad the doctor was coming tomorrow. She tried to fill her sister in on what they were doing for her, but Peggy was so lethargic, Margaret wasn't sure she heard.

Back in the kitchen, she dished out beans and cornbread and poured a big glass of iced tea for herself and Jim. Entering the living/bedroom, she almost dropped the tray. He wasn't in the bed!

"Hi," she heard from a corner of the sofa behind her. "I decided to practice moving around some before the big move," he grinned, but she could tell he was exhausted. He'd never moved that far by himself since the accident, only pivoting from the bed to the chair in his private area behind the blanket.

"Are you okay? How do you feel?" She set the tray down, ready to help him back to bed, but he shook his head.

"Terrible!" he leaned his head back against the sofa. "But I made it, so we can get me upstairs, I'm sure."

They both laughed with relief at the success of his struggle as she set the food in front of him and sat on the other end of the sofa to devour hers. She was famished and still had a lot of work ahead of her.

"How's Peggy?" he asked.

"Not good. I'm glad the doctor is coming. She looks so pale and can't keep any food down."

She collected their dishes and put them in the kitchen, then came back through his room. "Do you want me to help you get back to bed?" she asked again.

"I think I'll stay here awhile if it's okay."

"It's fine. I have to go across the road and get the kids. I'll be back soon." Going down the hill, she paused to watch a truck slowly drive by. Strange. Who had a truck like that? It was unusual to see a vehicle she didn't know on this road. Somebody down the road must be getting out-of-town company or a new truck.

By the time Margaret returned, Jim had dragged himself back to bed and was groaning with pain. She coaxed him to take some pain medication, and made him as comfortable as possible while Jenny and Abby put the children in bed for their naps. Then she, Frankie, Jenny, and Abby carried the feather mattress, bedding, a small table, and water pitcher up the narrow, winding stairway. At the end of the day, Jim wasn't able to muster enough strength to try the climb. Margaret insisted they wait until morning and watched over him anxiously through the night.

By early morning, he was feeling stronger and laughed off her concern that this might be too much for him. They insisted that Papa stay downstairs, fearing the exertion might start his coughing again.

Slowly, Jenny, Frankie, and Margaret helped Jim toward the door. There he sat on one of the bottom steps and, with their help, scooted up one at a time. It took quite a while and all were covered with perspiration when he was finally able to lie down on the mattress Margaret had prepared for him. She gave him his pain medication and made him as comfortable as possible. He needed rest.

This was all barely accomplished before Dr. Turner arrived to examine Peggy. When he was done, he spoke to Margaret on the front porch as he was leaving. Shaking his head, he told her honestly.

"She is pregnant, but I don't have high hopes for the survival of the baby. I just hope it doesn't drain her of the strength to improve herself. I'm giving her some vitamins and something for nausea. I'll be back in a week. Try to get her to eat small amounts of bland food several times a day."

As she watched his car leave, she noticed that strange truck driving by slowly again. *That's curious*, she thought to herself as she went in to prepare lunch and try to get Peggy to eat. *I wonder who that is?*

It felt strange sitting alone with her cup of coffee by the fireplace staring at the empty bed where Jim had been every night for what seemed like forever. He hadn't eaten much supper.

"I just want to rest," he had whispered when she took food up to him.

The last time she had checked on him, he was sleeping soundly. This would be the first night since his accident that he wouldn't have someone nearby to call on if he needed something during the night. She was a little apprehensive, but reminded herself he hadn't called on her during the night in several weeks. On the positive side, Peggy had eaten a little and kept it down, so maybe what Dr. Turner gave her was working.

Turning the wick of the oil lamp down very low, she climbed into her bed for the first time in months. It felt good to stretch out rather than curl up on that mattress with Anna Rose, whom she had decided could sleep in the rollaway bed with Bobby. She smoothed her hand across the sheet where Jim had lain, and wrapped herself in the quilt that had covered him, dozing off with a smile on her weary face.

She made several trips upstairs the next day, making sure he was comfortable and (she had to admit) because she missed his being close by where they could talk and laugh as she went about her work.

She had carried a kitchen chair upstairs and set it by the small window that brought in a little ventilation from the outside. The move had seemed to energize Jim and he was longing to get moving again. Dr. Burk removed the cast from Jim's arm on his next visit, which made it much easier for him to do things for himself. His ankle was also much better. Each day, he would get out of bed, move around and sit by the window looking wistfully out on the fields and woods of Papa's farm. That's where she found him one night when she took their coffee up at the end of the day.

"I've been in bed too long, Margaret. It's good to move around more, get my strength back. I like sitting here looking out at the peaceful countryside. This window's small enough that I probably can't be seen from the road. I've never really lived in the country. It looks so peaceful and quiet."

She had to laugh. "It's so dark you can't see much of anything now, can you?"

"Just the outline of the trees and your folks' house, and a million stars, but it looks so peaceful you'd never guess about all the turmoil of life around us, would you? The war, rationing, fear for our servicemen, and just all the many other things we have to deal with."

She stepped up behind his chair, placed her hands on his shoulders, and leaning down close to his cheek, she looked out at what he was describing. It was as if there was nothing and no one else in the world except this peaceful scene and the two of them next to each other caught up in it.

"I could stay here in this cozy place forever."

She wasn't sure she had uttered those words aloud until she felt his hand on hers and heard his question whispered in her ear.

"What are we doing here, Margaret?" His voice sounded desperate. "If we aren't careful I'll fall in love with you and I'm afraid there are too many great divides between us to let that happen."

He held her hand tightly and looked deep into her eyes. In the back of his mind was the warning about what could happen to a black man who approached a white woman this way, but overwhelming this was the trust they had developed with each other, making him feel he could unburden his heart to her.

She stood up and began to pace back and forth, saying nothing, crying softly. He watched her, willing to wait for what she would say, fearing what it would be, knowing that no matter what it was, it would be heartbreaking for them both. They were very young, in the middle of circumstance they could see no way out of. They seemingly had no control over what was happening.

But what stopped her pacing was not that she had thought of a way to reply to him, it was a sound they both heard. Quickly, she extinguished the lamp and peered out the window. That truck was creeping slowly past the house again. She could barely see the outline of two men in the cab and two in the backend.

"What is it, Margaret?"

"Shhhhh!"

She continued to watch and the truck soon came back by the other way, driving even slower. She was frightened.

"I'm afraid someone suspects you're here," she whispered. "I saw that same truck go by here slowly several times. I know it doesn't belong to anyone who lives around here."

A long period of silence passed before Margaret felt maybe whoever it was wouldn't be back. With the lamp extinguished, she could barely see Jim's silhouette sitting straight up in the chair.

"I think they're gone. It's probably nothing. Maybe the Army is keeping an eye on us. Let me help you back to bed." She took his arm gently to help him up.

"You didn't answer my question," he prodded.

She stood up and turned toward the stairs, making an attempt to untangle things in her mind.

"I think it's too late to say we 'might' fall in love, Jim. This is the first time I'm admitting it, even to myself. You know we just can't give in to that temptation. We'll talk tomorrow."

She ran down the steps, closing the door and leaning against it with tears streaming down her cheeks. She tried to cry out to God, but the only words that came were, "Why? Why? Why?"

She fell to her knees and prayed earnestly into the night for God's strength to do his will, then climbed into bed, trying to make sense of what was happening in her life.

# TERROR IN THE NIGHT

## APRIL 1945

Margaret's mind sailed in all directions, but she finally fell into a fitful sleep, dreaming that Carl was calling to her from a ship that sailed farther and farther away. Then she saw Jim calling from a plane that flew away from her in the other direction.

The pounding at first became a part of her dream like a drum in the background foretelling of impending doom. She finally awoke to the realization that someone was banging on the front door. Bolting to a sitting position, she listened hard. Was she still dreaming?

Bang! Bang! Bang! From the front door, then someone shouting, "Open up!"

She jumped from her bed thinking, *Oh, dear God, has something happened to someone in the family? Is it Carl or Robert or Papa?*

Unlocking the door, she swung it open and faced a dark figure grinning at her in the eerie light of the oil lamp she had grabbed from the table beside her bed. His eyes seemed to glow red in the glare of the lamp, and she had to grip it tightly to keep it from crashing to the floor. She went weak, almost fainting as if Satan himself stood before her paralyzing her with fear.

She tried too late to slam the door shut. His foot was blocking it, and he shoved it open wider, throwing her against the wall. Desperation took over, she had to do something. *Too much light!*

With all the breath she could gather, she blew out the flame on the lamp. Total darkness enveloped them all, except against the light of an almost full moon. She could make out the outline of a truck on the lawn with two other figures in the back end and one behind the wheel. That truck! It looked like that same truck! What could she do?

Grabbing her by the arm, the intruder slurred, "Hey, Miz Corwin, we hear you got a man here that ought not to be staying in a white woman's house. Where is he? Huh? We need to take care of that."

She jerked away from his grip.

*Don't panic! Don't panic!* Desperately, she tried to act calm. He had barged in, turning back the covers of her bed, looking under it and behind the sofa. She leaned up against the attic door trembling. Forcing down panic, she thought there was something familiar about him. Then a name popped into her head. *Maybe if he knows I recognize him.*

"Red Sanders," she yelled, trying to shove him toward the door. "I know you. You're from over at Nauvoo. How dare you bother me and my children and my sick sister while my husband is at war! Get our of here!"

In his drunkenness, he stumbled against the open door as she pushed him again.

He stopped and stared at her, not expecting that she would know his name or be brave enough to confront him. Pushing him with all her strength, she tried to steer him out the door.

"You're drunk! Get out of my house!" She kept getting louder, hoping her voice would carry to the attic and warn Jim to hide, knowing it could also wake the rest of the family, but that was a chance she had to take.

She heard Peggy's weak call from the bedroom. "Margaret, is somebody here?"

"See," she cried, "you've already woke her up. It's okay, Peggy. Just someone needing directions. Go back to sleep," she called, still trying to push the intruder out the door. "My sister is sick, and I have children sleeping. You're disturbing them!"

He jerked away from her, stumbling back into the living room. Her heart leapt into her throat as his eyes settled on the attic door. She ran too obviously to stand between him and the object of his interest.

"What's behind that door?"

"The attic. I keep it locked so the kids won't get up there and get hurt. Papa has the key so I can't open it. Get out of here, Red. Papa will be here any minute with his shotgun. He's just across the road." She pressed her body tightly against the door, barely able to stand, praying Jim was hiding, knowing she could only hold her ground a few more seconds.

Upstairs, Jim had also been awakened by the banging on the door. His first thought was the same as Margaret's. *There must be some bad news about someone in the family. Oh, Margaret, I hope you don't have another tragedy to face.*

Dragging himself to the window, he suddenly knew what was happening. That truck on the lawn would lead to his death unless he could think of a way to hide or escape. Turning around, he spotted the low closet under the eaves that Margaret used for storage. *Can I get my body into that tight place? Will it do any good if I do?* He moved more quickly toward the closet than he had thought himself capable of doing. As he pushed his body into the tight space, his hand touched something cold and round that he recognized as a gun barrel.

Holding her ground against the door, Margaret fixated on the intruder's hand as she watched it come toward her, grabbing her shoulder and shoving her hard toward the fireplace. Then the hand was shaking the doorknob, which always stuck (an aggravation when she had her hands full and needed to open it, but now she prayed it would stay that way). She couldn't let him open that door! She had put her hand behind her to keep from falling. It touched a familiar iron rod: the fireplace poker!

Red was leaning over to examine the lock. With all her might, she raised the iron rod over her head and brought it down hard across the intruder's back. The force of the unexpected blow sent him sprawling across the floor. Margaret watched with the poker poised above her head, ready to strike again if he got to his feet. She knew she couldn't fight him off indefinitely but maybe it would give Jim some time to get away.

Now two other men appeared at the door. They glanced at Red on the floor, and Margaret shielding herself menacingly with the poker and they laughed.

"We ain't here to hurt you! We looking for that feller we heard was hidin' here. Now where is he? Tell us that and we'll be on our way." She could tell they had all been drinking heavily.

"Get him out of here! I know who all of you are, and I'll report this to the sheriff," she tried to shout, but it came out as a weak croak. "My dad will be here any minute with his shotgun!"

Just as the word left her mouth, a loud blast burst in the air sounding as if it came from somewhere outside. Margaret was stunned and could hardly hear. The two men jumped and ducked behind the couch. Red's head jerked up. The sound seemed to sober him a bit. Trying to get to his feet, he grabbed his back and groaned with pain.

One man's head slowly appeared above the sofa and he whispered loudly, "Somebody is out there with a gun."

The fourth man called from behind the wheel of the truck. "We better get out of here if we don't want to get shot. Hurry up. I'm leaving." The truck motor started. The two men emerged from behind the sofa and grabbed Red under each arm, dragging him to the truck that had already started down the hill. Were they gone?

Margaret stood still in the silence, still holding the poker above her head. *The door—it was standing wide open—what if they come back?* She stumbled over to close and lock it, then, leaning against it, she slid to the floor and covered her face with her hands, shaking and sobbing. As soon as she could make her legs hold her up, she looked in on Peggy.

"Was that a gunshot I heard?" her sister asked groggily.

"Somebody hunting out of season, I guess." Margaret whispered as she straightened Peggy's cover. "Do you need anything?"

"No," Peggy turned over and went back to sleep.

Checking on the children, she found Anna Rose sitting up in bed.

"Mama, some loud noise woke me up," she whined.

"It's okay," she hugged her small daughter close, then tucked her back into bed. "Somebody was hunting out in the woods, I guess." She kissed her cheek and watched her eyes close. The other three had stirred a little, but never fully awoke. It was only after she closed their bedroom door that she panicked.

Running to the attic door, she flung it open and rushed up the stairs carrying the lamp. At the top, she faced Jim's bed and found herself looking down the barrel of Carl's shotgun.

"Jim! Jim! It's me, Margaret! They're gone!" she cried.

He threw the gun on the floor and she fell into his arms sobbing.

"Oh, Margaret, I could hear everything. I was looking for a place to hide when I found the shotgun. I prayed there were some shells too. There was just part of a box way back in the closet. I shot out the window over their heads hoping to scare them. If they hadn't left, I was coming down with the gun." He groaned through gritted teeth. "Did they hurt you?"

He held her at arms length, looking closely in the dim light of dawn that seeped through the small window.

"I'll be okay. You did scare them, thank goodness. I think they're gone. Oh, Jim, think what could have happened! I am so afraid. What are we going to do if they come back?" She looked into his face and he kissed away her tears.

Jim and Margaret clung together in the attic, forgetting every caution that had been a part of their ordered lives before they met, forgetting the resolve they had made to put God's will first and not allow their relationship to develop any farther. Feelings of terror that the men might return or what would have happened if they hadn't left stripped their minds of any rational thinking. There was no strength left to fight temptation; they only knew they had each other at that moment in time creating a passion that overtook their very being.

As dawn began to spread above the horizon, Jim held Margaret close. "Margaret, it's easy to see how I would have fallen for you," he touched her cheek. "But I never dreamed someone like you would care for me, or even if you did, that you would dare to admit it. Most women like you would look with disgust on a man like me and resent having to take care of him."

"Jim," she said, touching his face, "you are the most caring, loving man I have ever met, so much like my Papa. I love Carl, but he and I never had a deep, soul-connecting relationship like you and I have had. I didn't know that was even possible until I met you. Carl and I grew up together and it was just taken for granted that we would marry. I had no comparison. But I am married and I can't forget that."

She pulled away and went to the chair by the window, looking out over Papa's farm as the sun began to peek over the horizon. "My problem is not who you are, it's that I have a husband in the war and three children to consider. How could I have done this? We've sinned terribly, Jim. I'm so sorry. It's my fault. I was supposed to be your nurse. It was unethical and sinful that I used our relationship to make me feel better about all the things that were turning my life upside down."

There was a long silence while they both contemplated this reality. Jim wanted to beg her to bring her children and leave with him, but deep in his heart he knew better. He knew her now, not only as beautiful, compassionate, and loving, but also as a wife and mother, and a woman of deep faith. All that he loved about her would keep them apart. He leaned his head against the pillow and sighed with regret.

"Don't blame yourself, Margaret. You know I'm to blame. Of all people, I should have known not to let this happen. I'm so sorry. What we dream can never happen for us, can it?"

She raised her head slowly, not looking at him as she replied, barely able to speak.

"No…no it can't, Jim. When Carl had to leave, and I knew I might never see him again, I promised him and God that his children and I would be here to go on with our lives together when he returned." She turned to look at Jim now. "I have to keep that promise. I can't tear apart my whole family no matter how much it tears me up inside."

She glanced at him, as he still looked up at the ceiling.

"You know I'd be willing to bear anything we would have to face because of our race difference, but I can't put my wishes above all the others that depend on me no matter what, and I need to spend a long time with God, asking his forgiveness for giving in to temptation. I guess I know now how King David felt when Nathan rebuked him." She placed her head in her hands.

"I know that, Margaret. I wouldn't expect anything less from you. Just please don't put all the blame on yourself."

She went back to his side and laid her head on his shoulder as he tightened his arm around her.

"I'm afraid we'd grow to hate each other having to face what we know would happen. The consequences we and our families would have to endure are unthinkable. It would ruin your life, even put you in grave danger. You're so young with your whole life ahead of you. Find a wonderful girl and marry her, and you'll forget me soon. Our circumstances have thrown us together at a terrible time."

He raised himself up, and taking her chin in his hand, he whispered, "I'll never forget you, Margaret Corwin. I know you made a promise to God and to your husband that you have to keep. Will you make a promise to me too?"

She looked at him, hardly hearing his words, just memorizing his face, deep brown, sincere eyes, smooth tan skin and that determined chin.

"If Carl's drinking gets to be too much for you, or if it ever causes him to be cruel to you or the children, get in touch with me through my mother in Michigan. Here is her address." He placed the latest letter from his mother in her hand.

She resisted even thinking of such a thing. Margaret knew God expected her to be true to her marriage vows, even though she had already failed to do so, and she had to think of Jim and the impossible life he would have with her as an obstacle in his life. He was very young, just twenty-one years old, four years younger than Margaret. He had his whole life ahead of him. She would not ruin that for him.

"Will you promise?" He was insisting.

She knew it was time. Time to move on. Time to leave her heart's desire behind and live where God had placed her for his purpose. The truth was suddenly so clear.

*Get up! Go! Do what you have to do! Now!*

She felt like Judas and Joseph at the same time, betraying someone she loved on the one hand, but knowing she must run from further temptation on the other. *I should have run earlier, God. I'm so sorry.*

"I promise," she whispered, asking God to forgive her for the lie because she knew she would never do that to Jim.

She was on her feet now, talking quickly. There would be no long goodbye. She could not deal with that.

"I have to go talk to Papa and tell him about those men breaking in last night. He'll report it to the Army and they'll come soon to take you away. I'll never be the same for having the privilege of knowing you, Jim Hayes."

He wanted to say so many things, but couldn't manage to even open his mouth as he listened to her footsteps echo down the stairs. When Margaret told Papa what had happened, he quickly went to the store to call the Colonel. When he returned, she took the children across the road and asked Papa to stay with Peggy and direct the medics who came for Jim. She couldn't bear to be around when he left.

That very morning, in a flurry of secret activity, he was moved back to the base and was on a plane to his parents' home in Michigan to finish his recovery. As happy as he was to see his parents, he felt a heavy weight on his heart. Guilt and heartache made his full recovery very slow. His mother worried that this injury had traumatized him beyond what anyone knew, but kept it to herself, just trying to help him in every way she could. She knew he would never be the same.

He talked with his father about wanting to get well enough to continue his service in the Army despite what had happened.

"I'm proud of you, son, whatever you decide. I know how you love flying."

"Well, I have a long way to go before that happens." He wondered if it ever would, but knew he wanted to work toward that goal.

# FIGHTING LONELINESS

## 1945

Everyone in the family thought Margaret's tears were the result of the frightening incident in the night that hid the true meaning of her private grief.

Maud made her lie on the divan with a cold cloth to cool her face and was surprised at how inconsolable she seemed to be. It wasn't like her. Normally, she would be fighting mad about the intrusion rather than this helpless creature lying here.

"You've just had too much lately, Margaret. Maybe you can slow down a little now that you don't have all of that extra responsibility."

Maud was trying to make her feel better, but those words only magnified the pain in her heart. Maud insisted Margaret and the children stay for a while to give Margaret a chance to recover and to make sure the men who terrorized them in the night weren't going to be back again. Jenny and Papa decided to stay with Peggy as soon as the medics left. After a few days of lying in the midst of crowded confusion, Margaret willed herself to get on with life, so she picked herself up and determined to start over.

"Do you think those men will come looking for him again?" she asked Papa as he helped her take the children back across the road.

"I hope not, Margaret, but just in case, keep Carl's gun handy. I'll know to hurry over here if I hear a shot in the night again. That night I just thought it was a hunter."

*What could you do against those men, Papa?* she thought to herself, but was grateful for his protectiveness. She almost drowned in loneliness for the next few weeks, especially when the house was quiet at night and she sat down with her cup of coffee. She cried herself to sleep, praying that Jim would recover quickly and have a good life with someone who would love him and care for him.

Constant prayer became her survival tool. Only God knew her heart, and she couldn't reveal it to anyone else. She begged constantly for forgiveness. Outwardly, she went through the motions of everyday life, while struggling inside to deal with guilt, loss, and anger. She was angry at this war that kept going on, leaving her and her sister weak and struggling. She was angry for allowing herself to fall in love with Jim. She was angry with Carl for not being with her. Guilt from the sin of giving in to her passions overwhelmed her.

She spilled it all out to God every minute of every day. She prayed for things to get back to normal soon, and that Peggy would get stronger and be able to carry this baby, but she didn't pray that she would forget Jim Hayes. She knew he would always be a part of her.

Dr. Turner told Peggy that getting up and walking around the house a little would help her gain strength, so she made a real effort to come to meals at the table and sometimes joined Margaret for her coffee in the evening, which eased Margaret's loneliness. She was gaining weight and strength and having fewer coughing spells too.

Then came the greatest news they had heard in years. It was May, a nice warm day and Margaret had decided some Spring cleaning had to be done. She raised all the windows, allowing cool breezes to float through the house and, taking a bucket of soap and water, worked to remove the dust and soot of winter.

She was on her knees scrubbing vigorously when she heard shouting from outside. Leaving the bucket in the middle of the floor, she rushed to the window to see what this was all about. Jenny, Abby, and Frankie were running up the hill, waving and shouting something she couldn't understand.

"Oh, no! What's happened now?" she whispered to herself as her heart sank, dreading the thought of bad news. As the children burst through the door, she finally understood the words.

"The Germans have surrendered! The war may be over soon!" they shouted in unison.

She couldn't believe it. "Are you sure?" She grabbed Frankie by the shoulders, forcing him to stand still and wondering if this was one of his pranks. If so, it surely wasn't funny.

"It's on the radio." Jenny laughed and hugged Margaret, swinging her around. "I'm going to tell Peggy."

Peggy had already heard and was standing at the door of her room.

"You're sure?" she cried as tears streamed down her face.

"Oh, Peggy, isn't this great?" Margaret hugged her sister, laughing and crying at the same time.

Jenny was breathless with excitement as she relayed Papa's message. "Papa said that since Peggy is better now, maybe he could bring the truck over to get her and all of us could listen to the radio this afternoon. There's so much news. Is it okay, Margaret?"

Margaret looked at her sister. "Do you feel up to it, Peggy?"

"I sure do!" She looked so happy.

It was the most wonderful family afternoon they had enjoyed together in a long time. At times joy swelled to almost overwhelming heights, then at others, Mama especially, remembered Sam and grieved that he wouldn't be coming home with the other soldiers.

They all wondered and speculated about when Robert and Carl could come home, and Margaret secretly tried to picture where Jim would be and how he would be receiving this news. She hoped his mother was with him.

"Robert signed up for three years in the Navy and it's only been a year and a half. Will he have to serve the rest of his time?" Peggy asked Papa.

"I don't know, but he probably will. They can't just let all our servicemen go home at the same time, and there's still Japan. They haven't surrendered," he cautioned, which gave them all pause for reflection.

It was May and springtime and the war was coming to an end. Margaret began to force her mind to dwell on a future with Carl and the children.

A month had passed since Jim left and she had learned to look at things more objectively. She told herself their closeness was only a result of the circumstance they were thrown into and began to think of his time there as an oasis in the middle of her crisis, which they had taken too far. She still constantly begged God to forgive them, but found it hard to believe he would.

One night as she sat reading her Bible by lamplight, she found herself reading the story of David. Of course, she had read it many times before, but this time it spoke directly to her. God forgave David and he is even called a man after God's own heart. This renewed her hope that he would forgive her.

Both Carl and Robert wrote that they were still at sea and happy about the end of the war with Germany, but Japan still loomed ahead. They didn't know when things would be over for them, but longed to be home with their families.

Robert had finally received the letter Peggy wrote telling that he was going to be a father again. Peggy didn't let Margaret read her letter from him. She just said he hoped she and the baby would be okay and he might be home by the time the baby was born. Margaret knew he had no way of knowing that, but didn't mention it to Peggy.

Margaret had to quickly turn her attention to Peggy's condition. Rather than making her weaker, her pregnancy seemed to make her more hopeful, and she wanted to do more, but the doctor warned her that too much activity wouldn't be wise if she wanted to deliver her baby safely. Margaret tried to keep her busy with activities that weren't too strenuous, like folding laundry or shelling peas.

A telegram arrived from Robert saying he would be home in July for a two-week leave. Then he'd be stationed in Millington only two hours away.

Carl wrote that he was still at sea, and wasn't sure when he'd be home, but he was so happy the Germans had surrendered and longed to be back with Margaret and the children. She suspected his ship was one that was still dealing with Japan, but knew he couldn't tell her that.

Robert's visit, which Margaret had dreaded, turned out better than the last. The war had forced him to grow up some, and he tried to make up to Margaret. He could sense her anger with him since his last trip home. He stayed around most of the time and was attentive to Peggy and Bobby, leaving with a promise to find a place near the base for his family to be together soon.

The highlight of the summer was their big Fourth of July celebration with family from all over the county and lots of fireworks Papa had stocked up on at the last cattle auction. Everyone could feel that the terrible war would soon be ended for everyone.

After picnicking and listening to Uncle Wat and his sons play their guitars all day, Margaret sat on her parents' back porch when darkness set in, with Junior and Janie on her lap and Anna Rose at her feet, feeling lost, watching the bursts of color raining down from the Roman canons. Cousins, nieces, nephews, aunts, and uncles sat about the porch and lawn, drinking iced tea and oohing and aahing with each burst. She glanced at Peggy, Robert, and Bobby sitting on the steps and said a prayer for the tiny life Peggy was carrying. It would be such a hard blow to her if she lost the baby now.

When Robert left, he took Margaret's hand and sincerely thanked her for caring for his family while he was gone. She found she could almost believe him, but knowing him like she did, couldn't help feeling a little skeptical. The baby was due in October and Robert assured them he would be able to get a leave to be with Peggy when the baby came. Margaret hoped for Peggy's sake that he would be able to keep that promise.

# MOLLY

## 1945

Early on a hot August morning, Margaret was awakened by Peggy frantically calling her name.

"What is it, Peggy? What's wrong?"

"I think I'm in labor," she wailed. "I've had these pains that come and go, and I can't get comfortable!"

"Try to relax as much as you can. I'll go tell Papa to get the doctor."

She rushed across the road still in her nightgown and bare feet. Papa quickly stepped into his pants and shoes and was in the truck headed for Dr. Turner's home before she could get back to Peggy. Mama was right behind her, and soon had Peggy trying to relax and hold off any contractions. Peggy was frantic.

"Mama, it's two months early! I can't have this baby now, it's too early!"

"This doesn't mean you're having it now, Peggy. The doctor will know how to stop the contractions, or maybe it's something else. You just do your part and don't panic." Margaret rushed to warm some towels for Peggy's back to help her relax.

Margaret got the children dressed and took them across the road to give them breakfast. Keeping an eye out the window, she was relieved when she saw Papa drive up with the doctor in the passenger seat of his truck. Finishing as quickly as possible with the children, she left Jenny in charge and ran back home.

Mama was standing in the living room looking bewildered. In her arms was a tiny bundle almost lost in a soft blue blanket Peggy had pulled from her trunk just last week.

Peggy had held it to her cheek. "I saved this from when Bobby was a baby. It will be nice for the new little one."

"The baby was already coming when the doctor got here, Margaret, a little girl. I cleaned her up some, but she's so tiny, I don't think she's going to make it. Peggy is so weak and has no milk coming in for her." A tear ran down Mama's cheek.

Margaret took the bundle in her arms and dug into the blanket. She was shocked at the tiny, perfectly formed little person not much bigger than her hand. She was trying to cry, but only emitting soft squeaks. Bird-claw hands on arms no bigger than Margaret's thumb thrust out toward her.

Compassion for this tiny helpless child swelled up in Margaret's heart and spilled over as tears. The baby's eyes flickered open and she latched on to Margaret's finger. Staring straight into Margaret's eyes, she seemed to be pleading, "You're my lifeline! I want to live. Help me!"

It wasn't just the baby, it was a call from God. She felt it with all her being, and swung into action as if she knew exactly what to do.

"Well, we're not giving up on her, Mama. I know it's summer, but I'm making a fire in the fireplace. We have to keep her really warm."

When Margaret had a good fire going, she went to the kitchen and opened a can of milk. Weakening it with water, she boiled it and cooled it. Back in the living room, Mama sat near the fire, sweating profusely, but keeping the little life as warm as possible.

Taking the baby in her arms, Margaret pulled the blanket away from her face. Again the tiny one tried to cry out.

Margaret dipped the end of a clean cloth into the milk and touched it to her lips. Mama smiled delightedly as the baby immediately began to suck up the drops of milk with a loud smacking sound.

"I'm surprised she can do that as tiny as she is," Mama cried.

"Good girl!" Margaret cooed. "We're going to fatten you up."

After a few drops, the little one drifted off to sleep in her arms. Mama went back to check on Peggy, returning later with news Margaret had both hoped for and feared.

"Peggy's resting and Dr. Turner thinks she'll be okay if she gets enough rest and eats enough to regain her strength, but when I asked about the baby he just shook his head. He doesn't think she'll live, Margaret," she moaned. "He didn't even leave any instructions for caring for her."

"Well, I think he's wrong. Mama, you stay with Peggy tonight. I'm staying right here with this baby. I have to try to save her. Dr. Turner didn't really even look at her. She's breathing okay, and is really sucking up this milk. If we can keep her warm and get enough nourishment in her, who knows?"

"I'll do anything I can, Margaret, but I just don't know. She's so tiny."

Papa and Frankie pulled the mattress into Peggy's room for Mama as Margaret settled into the big rocker by the fireplace to spend the night with this new little life in her hands. Papa went for Izzy again to help with the children.

*Somehow we're connected*, Margaret thought as she felt the strong heartbeat. This tiny, surreal life reached in and grabbed her very soul and wouldn't let go. For the next three days, they fought the devil together, vowing that he wouldn't have her life.

At times, the baby opened her eyes and quietly stared, reminding Margaret of a wise sage urging her prodigy to keep up the fight. Other times she was a gasping, helpless creature, struggling for life.

Margaret left the rocking chair only very briefly for a few bites to eat, dozing only when the baby did. Like a mother bird, she dripped the weak, warm milk from the cloth into the open mouth, smiling at the eagerness with which little Molly (as Peggy had decided to name her) sucked at the life-giving liquid.

When Dr. Turner returned to check on Peggy, he was shocked. Molly was already showing signs of alertness and her little body had lost its pallor and was beginning to look like flesh rather than just skin on bones.

"You've performed a miracle here, Margaret, but what have you done to yourself? You look terrible!" he remarked.

It was only then that she realized she hadn't changed her clothes, washed her face, or combed her hair in a week. She had to admit she wasn't feeling or looking her best, but she laughed happily.

"I'm fine," she answered. "I just had to take care of this little one for Peggy's sake." *And mine too*, she thought to herself. There had been something healing that came from the struggle she and Molly had come through. God had used the miracle of this little life to help Margaret go on with hers.

"I'll have the hospital send out some bottles with small nipples made for premature babies this afternoon and a bottle of cod liver oil. You can put a few drops in her milk. That goat's milk you're giving Peggy will be good for her too. I think she's going to make it, Margaret, thanks to you," he said as he finished examining Molly and placed her back in the basket by the fireplace.

He patted Margaret's shoulder before heading out the door. "She's not out of the woods yet, but you've given her a chance. You need to take care of yourself too. You just don't look well."

When the package arrived from the hospital, Mama took over.

"I can fix a bottle for Molly, and Peggy wants to try feeding her. There's a big kettle of water heating on the stove and two extra buckets of cold water by the back door. Frankie put the tub in the kitchen, so you go soak in it for a while. You need to get some rest." She gently led her daughter toward the kitchen.

Weariness set in as Margaret sank into the galvanized tub of warm water and let her mind drift to the far corner of her mind where she kept the image of Jim's loving face which she had memorized so well to sustain her in times like these. She had not been feeling very well lately but considered it the result of her broken heart and the extra work she was thrust into.

After the bath, she curled up in the children's room and slept until evening, waking refreshed and ready to continue her vigil with Molly by the fireplace. It would be two more weeks before she felt she could go to bed and leave the baby with Peggy and Mama for the night.

Frankie and Molly

Molly was pink and beautiful and growing, with seemingly no major problems from her six-week early birth.

Robert soon got an early discharge because of his wife's health and the new baby. He decided immediately to move his family to Detroit where Margaret's older brothers had gone with their families. The jobs were there, and they were ready to move on with their lives.

Margaret was glad Robert was getting away from the influence of his rowdy pals, but she worried about Peggy and Molly. However, they would still be near family, so maybe it would be a good move for them.

It was heart-wrenching to see them walk out of her life. Another hole in her heart that was hard to fill. She still spent her evenings, after everyone else was in bed, sitting by the fire with her cup of coffee, talking to God, missing Jim and Peggy and little Molly, trying to see into the future, wondering what Carl would do when he came home for good, wondering when that would be, wondering how the war might have changed him, and wondering if he would see through her to the secret she held on to.

She promised God she would begin anew to make her marriage work and still constantly begged him for forgiveness for succumbing to temptation that caused her to violate her wedding vows and God's law. Even though she knew he had already forgiven her, she still had trouble forgiving herself.

While the family was dealing with the birth of Molly, the news came that the United States had dropped two atomic bombs on Japan, which resulted in their surrender, and the news of the signing of the treaty on the USS Missouri on September 2 came with joy and relief to the two households on Hurricane Hill Road.

# ANGEL

## SEPTEMBER 1945

Word came from Carl that he would still be overseas for at least six more months. Izzy stayed on for a while after Peggy left, sensing that Margaret would need extra help and support now that she was alone. The house creaked and echoed as if mourning the loss of human activity that had brought it back to life after years of neglect.

"I don't know what's going on, Miz Margaret, but I hear God telling me to stay with you for a little bit."

"I just haven't been feeling well lately, Izzy. I have no energy and no appetite. I guess it's just a letdown from all the people and activity that I've been used to for so long. Now that the war is over, I expected Carl to be home, but it will be at least six more months." She knew too, that the weight of guilt she carried was still there, even though she had prayed earnestly for God's forgiveness, but she couldn't share that thought with Izzy or anyone else.

Izzy, stirring the soup that simmered on the stove, uttered words that struck fear into Margaret's heart.

"I see that. If I didn't know better I'd think you was gonna have another young'un. You acting just like your Mama did every time she was with child. But I guess you just…" She turned as

Margaret jumped to her feet, the chair she had been sitting in making a loud bang as it hit the floor.

The possibility of what Izzy had said hit hard. Margaret hadn't even let her thoughts go there, but suddenly she had to. Why hadn't she thought of this before?

"I...I need some air..." She stumbled out the back door and began to run through the pasture, past the tree Jim had fallen into, through the gate, into the trees, stumbling over debris until a large tree root threw her to the ground where she lay in anguish, wanting to die, knowing her life was over. Her family, her children, her marriage; she had sacrificed all that God had given her for a love that was not hers to take. How could she have strayed so far from God's purpose? She knew that he promised we would reap what we sow. Now she would have to experience what that promise really meant.

Darkness settled around her but still she lay with her face in the dirt, begging in such a mournful tone for God to take her life that she didn't hear the footsteps that approached, until Izzy sat on the ground beside her, holding a lantern near her face.

"Miz Margaret, I been sensing something gone terribly wrong for you. Tell me about it, please. You got to tell somebody."

She couldn't move.

"Miz Margaret, I fed the babies and put them to bed. They all asleep. Come back with me. We can try to figure it out. Come on now."

She took Margaret's arm and pulled her up to sit near her. Margaret pulled her knees up and buried her face in her apron. Dirt and leaves mingled with muddy tears that streamed down her face.

Izzy coaxed her again. "Come on, let's go back to the house. Can't leave them babies alone long."

Margaret allowed herself to be pulled to her feet and guided along back to the kitchen table she had left so abruptly hours ago.

Izzy set a cup of hot coffee in front of her and washed the dirt from her face and hands as if she were a little child just in from play.

"Now take a drink and talk to me, Miz Margaret." Izzy's sincere worried face prompted Margaret to choke out the unthinkable. *I can't hide it for long anyway,* she had to admit. *I must be four months along now.*

"I…think…I…am…pregnant!" She hid her face in her hands.

It was Izzy's turn to jump up from her chair.

"Now, Miz Margaret, that can't be. Your husband ain't been home in a long time. It must be something else!"

The two women stared at each other.

"It was Jim, Izzy. We fell in love."

"No! Now, Miz Margaret, did he take advantage of you and you taking care of him so good? I hate to say I sensed somethin' going on there."

"No, Izzy, it wasn't like that at all. I loved him. I still love him. We didn't mean for this to happen. We were just scared and foolish the night those men broke into the house. We turned to each other in weakness. Neither of us meant for it to happen. We just let temptation overtake us. I love him more than I've ever loved anyone, Izzy. I let it get out of hand. I'm so sorry."

Izzy sat down slowly, shaking her head, anguish on her face. "Now, we're gonna pray about this, Miz Margaret. Just keep it between us and God for a while and let's let him show us what to do. Can you do that?"

"Yes, I guess a few days won't make a difference. I want some time with my children. When all this comes out, I may never see them again." The anguish was too much. She allowed Izzy to lead her to her bed where she collapsed into such fits of crying and moaning that Izzy was frightened the woman might lose her mind. When she finally fell into an exhausted sleep, Izzy knelt by the sofa praying for the rest of the night. As the sun rose bright across the pasture and streamed through the window, she knew she had an answer if Margaret would listen to her. She got to her feet, put on a fresh pot of coffee and made pancakes for the children.

Margaret dragged herself from her bed, took Junior in her arms, and sat nursing him by the fireplace. She held his warm body next to her, stroking his soft cheek and the ringlets of curls that fell across his forehead. He was almost a year old. Smiling, she listened to Janie and Anna Rose chatter from the kitchen between bites of pancakes smothered in sweet maple syrup.

*How long will I be able to hold them and hear their voices…I could run away with them…but where? They would have to be fed and clothed and housed. I have no money. What about Jim? I could go to him.*

She ran that thought through her mind, seeing them run to each other and embrace, hold their new baby in their arms together, and live happily ever after.

*But that's not what would happen. We would all live a life of fear, loneliness, and rejection. I won't do that to him or the children. I have to go away myself and leave them all.*

She fought to keep from breaking down again as Janie and Anna Rose came running into the room, taking their dolls from the box in the corner and beginning their favorite mommy and baby game. Junior sat up in her arms watching his sisters as they set up a tea party, Anna Rose being the bossy sister she was prone to be.

Margaret took Junior with her to the kitchen and sat at the table watching Izzy stack the dirty dishes in the dishpan. Neither woman spoke, each engaged in thoughts of the terrible truth that lay between them.

Finally, Izzy poured coffee for herself and Margaret and sat down.

"Miz Margaret, I prayed all night for you and your children and God is giving us an answer. Are you ready to hear him?"

"I'm sure God wants nothing to do with me now, Izzy. Why would he?"

"Because he loves you. You are his child. Don't be saying such a thing! Now you pay attention!" Her demanding tone and the truth in it brought Margaret's mind into focus, as she continued. "Do you know somebody in Memphis that you could tell your family you and the kids was going to visit for a while?"

Margaret thought immediately of the Wyatts.

"Well, the couple we rented from have written me several times saying how they would like a visit from us when I can get a chance to get away, but they wouldn't welcome me this way."

"They don't have to. You just have to tell your family that's where you are going. My sister in Memphis is constantly asking me to pray for their preacher and his wife who have wanted children for years but haven't had any. If you could take your children and stay three months with them and give them the baby, you could come back here and continue your life and they would have their greatest wish and no one here need to know. They wonderful people and a baby would be really blessed to be their child."

Margaret blinked back tears, trying to take this news in, but being bombarded by unthinkable reasons why it couldn't work.

"Izzy, I'd be deceiving my husband and my family. I'd be living a lie. Why would God sanction such a thing? This baby is mine and Jim's. How could I give it up?"

"God works in mysterious ways, Miz Margaret. Look at the Bible stories. What about baby Moses? He saved God's people beginning with his Mama's giving him up. What about that woman named Tamar deceiving everybody to have a child for our Savior to be born through? I tell you, God works in mysterious ways!"

"I'd be giving away my baby, Izzy. My baby and Jim's baby. I don't know if I can do that. How can God tell you that I should do that?"

"God told Abraham to sacrifice his son and he didn't ask no questions. He just raised that knife. God has reasons for things we don't know about."

Izzy reached for Junior's hand and caressed it. "These babies here are yours, Miz Margaret. God gave them to you to raise and they need you. This new baby may not be yours. He's God's. There's consequences for your sin, but God can use it to bless the Reverend and his sweet wife too, and the baby that comes would be really blessed to be with them, I tell you. God works in mysterious and wonderful ways. His ways are not always our ways. We don't have to understand, just obey like Abraham when he was gonna kill his precious son."

Margaret's mind was beginning to clear. Was this right? Could this happen? She shook her head.

"It just seems impossible," she remarked as she leaned on her hand still trying to think how this could possibly happen. She was living in a nightmare and just wanted to wake up.

"I have to write my sister and wait for an answer from her," Izzy told her. "She will have to confirm what I feel God is telling me. Will you let me do that?"

"Yes," Margaret decided. "If you think God is telling you something, who am I to stand in the way of pursuing it, but I am skeptical that God can even forgive me, much less provide a way to cover my sin."

"Well, my Bible tells me if I can help somebody like you, it will save a soul and cover a multitude of sins. Now that is in James in the Bible, and you can read it for yourself. I believe that, Miz Margaret, and you need to believe it for yourself and all your little children, especially this one that is coming."

Several weeks later, Izzy received the letter from her sister in Memphis. The Reverend and his wife were overjoyed. They wanted Margaret and her children to come and stay with them right away, to get to know them and to help Margaret with this difficult decision. Even if she decided not to give up the baby, they wanted to give her a chance to get away from the accusing eyes of family and friends and have a safe, neutral place to make a decision. Their doctor would come to the house and she would have the spiritual support of their church.

The next hurdle would be telling Mama and Papa, knowing she was deceiving them, which was one of the hardest parts for her. She waited a few more weeks then decided she couldn't wait any longer as she approached six months pregnant. There were comments about her gaining weight, and the large baggy dresses she wore couldn't hide her condition much longer. She decided to approach Mama and Papa.

"Papa, Izzy needs to go home and take care of things there. I think I'm going to go to Memphis for a while. The Wyatts have wanted me and the kids to visit them for a long time. I need to get away for a while. I'm not sure when Carl will be back. Will you take Izzy home tomorrow and then take me to the bus station the next day?"

"Yeah, honey, if you're sure that's what you want to do."

"Margaret, you don't have to stay over there in that house by yourself now. You and the kids can just move back over here," Mama added.

"I know, Mama, and I may do that when I get back, but right now I need to get away for a while."

---

Margaret stepped from the Greyhound bus and walked into the familiar bus station, a baby on each hip and Anna Rose walking behind dragging a suitcase. She stopped to look around for a black man with a red tie and a yellow vest. She soon spotted him outside the door standing by the black Buick she had been told he would be driving. As she approached, he welcomed her with a broad smile, introducing himself as Reverend Louis, and took the suitcase from Anna Rose hefting it into the trunk. He lifted Janie and placed her in the back seat and held the door for Margaret and Anna Rose to climb in.

Walking into Reverend Louis and Ella May's house was like coming home. The welcome was genuine and joyful. Ella May took as much charge of the children as Margaret would allow, entertaining them, feeding them, and watching them play. She loved putting them all three in the large galvanized tub in the kitchen and giving them as much time to play as they wanted.

Margaret loved Ella May's beautiful smile and her kind, soft voice. She had no doubt now that God had brought her to this place. Their doctor came to the house to check her and the baby, which Margaret could feel being very active in her womb. Ella May rejoiced with her at every new stage of her pregnancy and constantly told her how blessed they were to receive such a gift.

Worshipping at the church where Louis preached was spiritually uplifting and emotionally healing. Spirited singing and sermons that came straight from God's word to the heart were things she had missed while so busy being a nurse and mother. She closed her eyes and talked to God. *Thank you, Lord. This is what I needed no matter what else happens. If this plan falls all apart, I've had this time with my kids and with you.*

"I know how hard this is for you, Margaret, so I want you to be assured this baby will receive more love and tender care than you can imagine from Louis and me all the days of our lives if you allow us to adopt him."

"When I hold him in my arms, someone may have to pry him away from me, Ella May, but I know deep down in my soul that he is not mine. He is yours. The thing I don't know how to deal with is that he is Jim's too. But I can't bring myself to lay that on him now. He's still recovering and I don't want to put that guilt on him. He would be devastated. We can't deal with that now… maybe some day."

Ella May pondered the "maybe some day" in her heart and told herself she would always be prepared for the chance that

Jim would learn about his child and want to take him. *Lord, I'm going to go forward, follow your plan now, and let you take care of the future.*

Ella May saw that Margaret had drifted back to her time with Jim, and that she still loved him deep in her soul. She wondered how this frail, weary woman could ever cope after her husband returned from the war. She prayed for her daily and for the life within her that Ella May herself would soon hold in her arms and call her own. She thanked God for the miracle that brought Margaret and her precious gift to them.

Three months later, Dr. Hadman was called to the home to deliver the baby on a dark, rainy morning in December. The delivery was easy and over quickly. Margaret gazed down into the red face of a beautiful baby girl with lots of dark, curly hair, long arms flailing in the air, and a strong protesting voice. Ella May stood in the corner of the room, praising God, allowing Margaret time to let go. Margaret laughed and cried and kissed the damp curls as she whispered to her new daughter.

"I love you with all my heart, my little angel. That's why I have to give you up." She looked up at Ella May. "That's your Mama over there in the corner. She loves you as much as I do. Angel… angel…angel…" She pulled the baby close to her heart, praying that she would grow up strong and healthy and then called Ella May to take her.

"We have a name picked out, Margaret, but her middle name will be Angel, and I will tell her that her birth mother gave her that name, when she is old enough to understand." Ella May took the baby in her arms and left the room.

Izzy's sister who lived nearby had taken Anna Rose, Janie, and Junior to her house when the birth was imminent. After Margaret had rested for several hours, Billy helped her into the car and took her to where the children were. Izzy's sister tucked her into bed where she slept off and on the rest of the day. It was the only bedroom in the house, but Liza, like her sister Izzy, was loving and helpful. She made herself a bed on the living room couch while Margaret and the children were there.

She brought the children into the bedroom after dinner to spend time with their mother and made pallets on the floor for the girls to sleep in the room with Margaret. Margaret took Junior in bed with her and held him close as he drifted off to sleep in her arms.

The next day, she wrote Mama and Papa a letter telling them her visit was about over and she'd be home for Christmas. Liza, who lived alone in the little three-room house, took special care of Margaret and the children until Margaret felt strong enough to travel. Louis came to check on her everyday, bringing his lawyer one day with papers for her to sign for the adoption.

"I want to get back home as soon a possible," she told him. "I need to set my life in order and see where God wants to take me from here. I'm sure Carl will be home in a few months and we need to decide where we are going in our lives. I have no idea what plans he has for our future. I don't know if he's even thought a lot about it. He probably hasn't had time."

Louis prayed with her and reminded her that God was in charge and when she announced that she was ready, he took her and the children back to the bus station. A few days before they left, Margaret called Mrs. Wyatt and took the children on a city bus over to visit her former landlords. They spent a wonderful day reliving the times they had when they lived in the same house and catching up on what had happened since while the children played in the park. She told the Wyatts that she was visiting friends in Memphis for a few days and wanted to get back before Carl returned from the war. This was true. Never had she had such wonderful friends as Louis and Ella May and Liza had been to her.

Soon, she was back in the house that held so many memories of Jim and Peggy and Molly. She settled by the fireplace with her cup of coffee, contemplating what had just happened and trying to figure out how she could go on. She didn't know how to feel, how to think about what she had done, how to fit it into the rest of her life. She closed her eyes and on her eyelids ran a replay of the last night she was with Jim, the anguish of his leaving and her never seeing him again, the realization of a part of him growing inside her, and the heart-wrenching day that she handed that life over to another.

When she opened her eyes, she knew. She was entering another phase of being, life anew as if she had traveled through time to another dimension and was back again, but she would keep Jim and their little Angel in her heart and maybe someday encounter them again.

# TRYING TO START AGAIN

## 1946

Carl came home for a two-week leave in February. She hadn't expected to feel so glad to have him back again. To her surprise, a sense of peace and normalcy settled in, and she breathed more easily, having not even realized how tense she had been about all that had happened while he was gone. It was as if she'd been holding her breath under water for a long time, then suddenly burst to the surface. She could hardly remember the person she was when he left.

Carl took her and the children on the bus to visit his family in Arkansas. While they had exchanged letters regularly, she and Sarah hadn't been face to face in a very long time. They enjoyed long talks, sometimes serious, other times giggling like teenagers. Carl went fishing with his father and Clara Jane enjoyed spoiling the children.

"You look so thin and tired," Sarah observed. "This has taken its toll on you, hasn't it, Margaret?"

"I didn't realize how much until Carl came home," she sighed. "But the war is finally over and Peggy is much better, so things are looking up now. Carl still has another year in the Navy, but he'll be stationed close enough to come home more often. It's such a relief, Sarah."

She longed to share her deepest secret with her best friend but knew it could never happen. They had always bared their souls to each other, and it felt strange to keep quiet about the one thing she most needed to confide. She could tell Sarah sensed there was some barrier between them, but attributed it to Margaret's having carried such burdens during the war. She knew nothing of the greatest burden—the soldier who fell out of the sky into her very soul and changed everything. It had only been three months since her little Angel was born. That tiny little face constantly haunted Margaret.

Carl was so happy to be with his family again, and they were so glad to see him home from the war, alive and in good health. They were not aware of the emotional toll it had taken on him. Even Margaret was not yet aware.

Carl in uniform

Margaret had decided to stay in the Wilson house. It had been home to her for two years and it was better for Carl to have a place to come home to when he could get a chance to visit than to be crammed into Mama and Papa's house. Back home, Carl noticed that one of his guns was behind the bed.

"Why is my gun here," he asked pulling it out and looking it over.

"Peggy and I thought we heard an intruder one night so Papa suggested I keep it handy just in case."

He was checking it out thoroughly.

"It's been fired." He looked at her curiously.

"Papa showed me how to fire it. You know I've never fired a gun before." She laughed nervously. *Why hadn't she remembered to put that gun back upstairs?*

"Was there really an intruder? What would we have here that anyone would want?"

"Papa had cashed mine and Peggy's allotment checks in town that day. He guessed that someone might have watched him and figured we'd be an easy target for a burglary. If there were intruders, we probably scared them away with our yelling and screaming. We never saw anyone, so it could have just been the wind rattling the door."

"Well, it's dangerous to have it down here. The kids might get hold of it. I don't like my guns being used. I'm putting it back upstairs."

"That happened a long time ago. I forgot all about it. You're right, it's not a good idea to have the gun down here where the kids can get hold of it. It just made Peggy feel better that I had it handy." She was a little hurt that Carl seemed more concerned about his gun than her protecting herself, and her nerves were on edge wondering if he would ask more questions she couldn't answer.

Her nerves settled when he had finished cleaning the gun and replaced it upstairs with no more questions. She told herself she wasn't lying to Carl, there was an intruder but he must never know Jim Hayes was here. It would be unthinkable for him to accept that she had taken care of a black man. It would make her disgusting and unfit as a wife in his eyes.

How sad, she thought, as she watched him skillfully take the gun apart, clean it, then replace each piece. A man of Carl's abilities has no reason to feel inferior, but his mother had ingrained those feelings in him. If only he could accept God's love for him, maybe he could love himself.

Carl had absorbed the two worst character traits of his parents—Clara Jane's low self-esteem and Clyde's taste for alcohol. That combination, plus the war experience, robbed him of enjoying his family and eventually destroyed his life at a relatively early age.

Carl actually didn't seem to know what to do when he came home from the war for good. He spent a lot of time hunting and fishing with his friends. Margaret felt he deserved some time for himself and tried to say very little, but she felt he was beginning to be as irresponsible as Robert had been. He and his friends were all drinking even more than before, and she was worried. She had prayed the war experience would change him for the better, but it seemed to do just the opposite.

Margaret's older brother, Chuck, who had been Carl's best friend when they were younger, came back from Detroit to help Papa on the farm, since Papa's health was getting worse. Jenny had driven the tractor and made most of the crop last season, but she needed help.

Chuck suggested he and Carl farm a parcel of land just down the road from Papa's farm. The two of them could help Papa and farm their own parcel at the same time. He figured they could make a cotton crop and split the profits. There was an old house on the land that they leased so Carl and Margaret moved into it. Margaret didn't want to move. She had come to feel at home in the Wilson house and it was close to Mama and Papa. She felt too isolated out on that farm and the house was not in much better condition than the Wilson house had been before she and Papa repaired it.

Carl was not cut out for farming, and more and more each day, Margaret could see that being in the war had traumatized him. She tried to ask him about it, but he only wanted to avoid the subject, saying she wouldn't want to hear all that stuff.

One evening, he came home with a story that struck fear into Margaret's heart. He was hung over at breakfast, sitting at the table sipping a cup of coffee and not in a very good mood. He seemed to be in a bad mood most of the time now.

"Wayne told me a story last night about some plane crashing near your house while I was on the ship. Did that happen?"

She tried to evade the question. "There were several crashes from that training camp at the airbase. Those planes were flying over all the time."

"But somebody told him the pilot was a colored man and he was staying at your house," he accused.

She chose her words carefully. "Now how ridiculous is that?" She forced herself to laugh. "Rumors sure can go wild. There was an accident nearby and the one soldier who survived was brought to our house until they could move him, but they took him away pretty quick."

"Why didn't you tell me about that?"

"It would have been censored if I had written it in a letter and I just forgot about it. It was just part of that awful war, and I was so busy with the kids and Peggy. The colonel who came out said it was some kind of secret stuff and we shouldn't talk about it. You know how that goes. You don't want to talk about the war and I don't either. That's behind us." She feigned irritation and indifference and waited, holding her breath for the next question. It never came.

"I told him there weren't any colored soldiers in Dyersburg and they sure wouldn't bring one to a white woman's house."

Her knees felt weak as she sighed with relief, hoping that would be the last of it. Margaret was ready to move on with her life.

# JIM MOVES ON

## 1945–1953

In Michigan, Jim and his parents rejoiced at Japan's surrender. Jim's doctor gave him permission to go back to Tuskegee to take an office job helping with the paperwork needed for black soldiers who were returning home. It felt good to be able to work and especially to be helping fellow soldiers make happy transitions back to their families. He tried to picture Margaret welcoming her husband home from the war and longed to be the one she was welcoming.

Jim was living through exciting times for black servicemen. He was a part of the last unit at Tuskegee as it was discontinued and their Army Airfield was closed. President Truman made the Air Force a separate branch of the military in September of 1947 and desegregated the military. The Air Force became the first of the armed forces to officially integrate. Being a part of this helped him recover from the sadness and loneliness that had gripped him after leaving Margaret. Still his mother worried about him and attempted to convince him to look for a good wife once he was back home in Michigan.

At church, she introduced him to Juanita Harris who had lost her first husband in WWII after being married only three months. Though he had resisted his mother's matchmaking, he had to admit Juanita was capturing his heart. They both had lost their first loves which drew them close to each other. Jim told her of falling in love with his nurse when he was wounded and of their being wrenched apart never to see each again. He never told her the nurse was white. Juanita talked about learning of the death of her beloved husband and vowing that she could never love anyone else.

Juanita was lovely, interesting, and filled a hole in Jim's heart that he had held on to for too long. To his surprise, he found that he could love again. They were married and when his two daughters were born, he found himself happier than he had thought he could ever be without Margaret.

By the time the Korean War began, Jim was flying again. Hovering over devastated battlefields in a helicopter, sometimes with bullets whizzing by, picking up badly wounded soldiers and shuttling them to MASH units for medical treatment gave him a taste of war that made him almost glad that he had missed the previous one. When his time there was over and he was back home, he was ready to leave the military and go on with life with his family. He took a job with Ford Motor Company and settled into working hard and helping Juanita raise the two children.

## 1970-1975

Jim was shaving as Juanita showered, discussing her day ahead with their daughter Sharon who was sure she was pregnant for the second time. Juanita was going to babysit their grandson while Sharon went to the doctor.

"How will it feel to be Grandpa again?" she teased Jim.

"Just fine," he answered. "Being Grandpa is the best thing that has happened to me in a long time."

She laughed. "I agree, but it means we're getting old."

"Well, we'd be getting old even if we weren't grandparents. That just makes it more fun!" He laughed heartily.

No answer.

"Don't you think so?"

No answer.

"Juanita, are you okay? He stopped shaving and listened for an answer. The shower was turned off but still no answer.

Finally, she got her voice. "Jim, I feel a lump in my breast. It doesn't feel right."

A sick feeling went through his body and he shivered.

"You need to get to a doctor and check that out," he insisted. She stepped out and showed him what she felt.

"Yes, you need to get that checked right away." His heart sank.

A biopsy showed cancer. It had evidently been with her for a long time. Radical surgery followed and her recovery was slow. Sharon and Alice spent as much time with her as they could and she eventually was able to be up and about the house. They had a few more years together. Juanita was able to enjoy her three grandchildren, but by 1974, cancer had spread to her vital organs and she lived only one more year. She died in Jim's arms, having insisted on staying at home rather than going to a hospital for her last days.

## 1975-1984

He was alone again. His father had died suddenly of a heart attack while he was in Korea. He hadn't even had a chance to say goodbye. Afterwards, his mom seemed to lose her zest for life. Illnesses and hospital stays plagued her until she was finally diagnosed with a blocked colon and died during surgery.

Jim threw himself into his job at Ford and visited the grandchildren as often as he could. He missed Juanita terribly, but his time with Margaret kept coming back to him as if it was only yesterday that they were together. He looked up the address of her local newspaper and subscribed to it. Reading her hometown news seemed to comfort him, to make him feel closer to her. It was in that newspaper one day that he read Carl's obituary and began to obsess with seeing her again,

When his daughters kept questioning him about becoming sadder and sadder, he told them the story of his long ago forbidden love.

"Despite how much I loved your mother, I can't get Margaret out of my mind, especially since I learned her husband died."

"Go find her, Dad," Alice admonished. "If nothing else, it will give you closure, but who knows? Maybe she hasn't forgotten you either, but remember it is still the South and they still have their problems with interracial relationships, so be prepared."

He packed up and started on his way to Tennessee with a prayer in his heart that he was doing the right thing.

# FAMILY REACTION

## 1984

Early on, the whole Corwin family, including Margaret, had turned to Junior for the emotional support Carl had abdicated, so he soon received a call from Janie at his architectural firm in Atlanta.

"Janie, hi! What's going on?"

"Hi, Junior. Well, this may be nothing, but I wanted to run it by you."

"Okay, I have a few minutes; run it by. Is it about Mom's birthday party?"

"Well, that too, but there's something else."

"What? You sound mysterious."

"There's this man visiting Mom."

He sat up straight and was immediately interested.

"Is he bothering her? Do I need to come?"

"No, she seems to be enjoying reminiscing with him. She introduced him as an old friend from forty years ago! It's just that she's real vulnerable right now and I don't like the looks of it."

He was getting irritated at his sister's attitude. "Janie, you have no right to be saying these things. Mom has good judgment about people. Just keep an eye on it. Maybe this is a time when she needs to reminisce with an old friend. Did you see anything out of place? He isn't staying there, is he?"

"No, he came from Michigan and has rented a place in town. Mom doesn't always have good judgment about people, Junior. You know she's too soft hearted. She always takes in every stray person that comes along with a sob story."

"Well, I'll be there soon for the birthday party. Is there anything I need to do for that?"

"No, it's under control, just pick up the tab," she teased.

Janie continued to tell her story and voice her concerns until Junior became very curious and promised to call his Mom. Hanging up the phone, he leaned back in his chair thoughtfully for a few minutes then picked up the phone again.

"Mom, it's Junior."

"Junior, so good to hear from you. How are things going?"

"Fine, Mom. What about you? Are you okay?"

"I'm great, honey. Just great!" And he could tell that she was, in a way he had never known her to be just from the sound of her voice.

"Janie said you had a visit from an old friend. How did that go?"

"Ahh, Janie! I might have known she would call you." Her laugh was delightful. "He'll be here for the party and all of you can meet him. He hasn't seen you since you were a tiny baby. It's a great story the way we met. I'll tell you all about it when you come."

"Great, Mom. See you a week from Saturday. Take care of yourself!"

Margaret was still chuckling as she hung up the phone and walked back into the kitchen where Jim was dishing up soup the two of them had made for their lunch. In real time, it had been a week since that phone call from him an eternity ago.

They spent long days together talking, cooking, or watching TV, discovering with each day that what they had back forty years ago did not just happen because of the desperate times, but that they were a perfect complement to each other.

"That was Junior calling from Atlanta. Janie had called him about 'this man' who was visiting their mother. He'll be here for the big birthday celebration. I can't believe I'll be sixty-five years old!" She sat down with a sigh. His booming laugh delighted her again, as always.

"Sixty-five years young," he corrected her. "We're just beginning our lives."

She laughed too. "That's easy for you to say, you're four years younger," she kidded.

He turned serious as they sat down to eat. "Tell me all about each of your children, Margaret. I want to know all I can about them."

"Okay, I'll start with Anna Rose." Margaret loved talking about the children. "She was determined to go to college even though Carl didn't believe girls needed to go. She took loans and worked and put herself through the Christian college in Jackson. I helped her some when I could sneak a few dollars that Carl didn't know about, but she did most of it herself. She met a fine young man from Michigan who was training for the ministry. They married and moved up near his family. They have four wonderful children. Two are in college and two are still in high school. All of them are coming for my birthday."

"It'll be great to see her as a grown woman. I remember her as a four-year-old who acted as if she were twenty."

"She had to take a lot of responsibility even at that age. I had so much to do, and she and my brother Frankie were extra hands, willing to run errands back and forth for me and Mama."

"I remember that they were a big help."

"Janie married the son of our local sheriff, who eventually followed in his father's footsteps and became the sheriff himself. They have two children. They are social climbers, I'm afraid. In politics you have to keep up an image."

"She seems to be the 'take charge' one."

"No, not really. She just happens to be the only one still living close by now. She's a very sweet girl, but is pressured by living in a glass house as the sheriff's wife. I worry about John's attitude. He seems to think he's above the law at times, hunting out of season and using jail trustees for his personal servants. He's very prejudiced and Janie has to go along with the 'sheriff's wife' charade. I know that's not really her heart, but she enjoys the prestige and the perks.

"Junior is the one we all turn to because we couldn't turn to Carl most of the time. He went to Georgia Tech and has his own architectural firm in Atlanta. Jimmy is a CPA in Knoxville. Neither of them is married. Carla married young, had two girls, and then divorced. She had a very hard time at first, but went back to college and now has a good job in Memphis."

Jim had a stunned look on his face and hadn't seemed to hear the last part of what Margaret was telling him.

"You have a son named Jimmy?"

"Yes, I know what you're thinking, but it was Carl who suggested we name him after his uncle. I didn't protest. I took it into my heart as a way of confirming that I made the right decision to keep my family together, but that you would always be a part of me." Tears sprang to her eyes.

He held her tightly and tried to lighten the mood, wishing he hadn't brought up the heartache from so many years ago.

"So, will all five of them and the grandchildren be here for your birthday?"

"I think so. I usually play down birthdays, but they insisted this was a special one, and the first one after Carl's death. Janie has collaborated with them all for some kind of celebration at Reelfoot Lake. I made her promise it would just be family and she agreed."

"What about me?" he asked seriously.

"You'll be family soon" she said, laughing, "and this is a great occasion for them to learn that."

She looked at him with shock, suddenly realizing what she had said and seeing the hesitation in his demeanor. They had spent some glorious times together, but she quickly realized they had not made any permanent plans.

"Oh, I'm sorry, Jim. I'm jumping to conclusions without thinking. That just slipped out of my mouth!" She laid her hand quickly on his.

"Don't apologize, Margaret. I think it's obvious to both of us that we will never leave each other again like we had to do before, but I need to tell you about the promise I made to my daughters."

"What was the promise?" Her heart was beating faster as she tried to contemplate what this might mean.

"Before I came here, I told them our story. They loved it and encouraged me to come, but Sharon made me promise that if things worked out like I hoped, we would give both families and ourselves some time before we made marriage plans. They all need to get acquainted and come to accept each other, and they reminded me that forty years could make a big difference in two people. She said we might not even like each other now!" That laugh again.

Margaret felt better. "Well, she's a pretty smart girl, Jim. I'm certainly not the same twenty-four-year-old you knew back then."

"And I'm not the same twenty-one-year-old. We do need time to get used to each other again and decide how much we have to face or are willing to face in opposition from our families. I promised her we would wait six months at least."

"You're right, of course. I can't wait to meet those daughters of yours. They sound like wonderful people."

"They are, and they'll love you."

"I hope so," Margaret worried. "I gave you up for family once, but I don't think I could do it again."

The March day could have easily been in May. Warm sunshine streamed through the windows and red buds were already beginning to show their colors as Jim drove along the highway toward the restaurant where Janie had reserved a large table in a private room for the family birthday party for Margaret. Junior had insisted that they all go on ahead and allow Margaret to come in after they were seated.

"Jim will drive me there," she had confided to Junior. "I want you all to get to know him, and this will be a good occasion for that."

Jim had stayed away the last couple of days as her children had come in from their various homes and were staying with her. She had talked at length with Junior about Jim—how they had met, why they hadn't seen each other in over forty years, and why he came back. Junior was touched, but agreed with Jim's daughters that everyone needed time to get used to the idea of seeing them together.

As they walked in, Junior began clapping and the others followed—some of them (including Janie and her family) unenthusiastically, as their attention was riveted on Jim.

Before sitting down, Margaret introduced him to her family. "You are just the best kids any mother could ever have," she began. "All this was not necessary, but it is very much appreciated. I love all of you so much, and your help and support since Daddy's death has been what has kept me going."

Turning to Jim, she continued, "I want to introduce you to Jim Hayes. We met over forty years ago while your dad was in the Navy during World War II. Jim was badly hurt in a plane crash near our home, and I had the privilege of being his 'nurse' for a while. We're renewing our friendship and I want you all to get to know him."

Jim waved slightly, saying, "It's great to meet all of you. Your mom is a special person who saved my life years ago."

Junior began the applause again and they sat down.

After the meal, there were gag "over the hill" gifts and laughter. Junior took Jim around to each of the others who welcomed him enthusiastically. Only Janie and her family were cool to him.

Carla and Jimmy had to go back home the next day because of their work schedules, but each told Margaret they were impressed with Jim and glad she could renew the friendship that meant so much to her all those years ago.

Anna Rose's family and Junior stayed the week. Jim came for dinner each evening. They talked, played games, and relaxed together. Janie stopped by a couple of times in the afternoon to visit with Anna Rose and Junior, but was conspicuously absent for the evening family times. Normally, she was the perfect hostess at her lovely home for family get-togethers, but while Anna Rose and the children spent several afternoons at her home enjoying the swimming pool, she issued no invitation to the whole family this time.

As they watched Janie pull out of the driveway after a brief, businesslike visit, Jim shook his head sadly. "How are we ever going to win her over, Margaret?

Margaret was furious at her daughter's behavior. "She's allowing herself to be influenced by the aristocratic, Southern family she married into. I've taught her to act better than that. She has a lot of Carl in her, I'm afraid."

"She's your daughter; maybe she'll come around. Remember, we're giving them time, Miz Corwin, ma'am." His eyes twinkled mischievously as he took her hand. They laughed as they remembered how hard it had been for her to get him out of the habit of calling her that.

Margaret fell deep into thought about her family, Jim's family, and the life she and Jim wanted together. It had to work out this time. They both knew they wouldn't part from each other again as they had to do so many years ago.

# CATCHING UP

## 1984

Sitting in their favorite place on Margaret's back porch, Jim and Margaret had been silent for quite a while, looking out over the pasture toward the woods as the sun set behind the trees in a great orange ball that was almost breathtaking. But the silence wasn't awkward. It was comfortable and exhilarating at the same time.

As darkness settled in on them, Jim turned to Margaret. "I have a request that may be hard for you, but I feel it's important to us."

"What is it? Anything you ask," she leaned back against the chair, closing her eyes, feeling truly blessed to be able to grant a request from this love of her life that she had thought she'd never see again.

"You've referred to Carl's alcoholism, and I get the feeling there's a lot of heartache that went on for you because of that. Would you be willing to just start from the beginning and tell me all about what you went through? It's amazing to me that you stayed with him all those years. There's no excuse for abuse, Margaret."

She opened her eyes and stared at his profile in the dark. "Why do you want to hear all of that? It'll only make you angry and I want to forget it. It's in the past now. Besides, I can't dismiss my part in the turmoil of our marriage. The secret I had to keep drove me to guilt feelings that came out in terrible actions sometimes."

"I know. My part in that breaks my heart, Margaret. That's another reason I need to hear what you went through. Back in the forties, our attraction to each other happened because we could just open up and pour out our hearts to each other. It freed us, it cleansed away that stuff that was weighing us down. I sense that we need that again." He reached over and took her hand. "It will make me angry and hurt and sad, but if I know, I can understand better and it may help us move on from it. I feel such a need to catch up on that gap in our lives."

She became very quiet, unconsciously squeezing his hand tightly as she thought about reliving those years. She didn't want to go there! What she had hidden she could not even admit to him, at least not yet. She would protect him as long as she could from a guilt that she knew he would take on if she confessed her darkest secret. Yet, they had never kept things from each other. She began making excuses.

"I feel so guilty complaining about Carl. So many women are abused physically, but he never hit me. I often think I should count my blessings instead of whining."

"Of course it's just like you to say that, but mental and emotional abuse can cause just as much damage, Margaret. That's one reason you need to go back over it with me. We need to get rid of that guilt you feel. It wasn't your fault that he couldn't cope."

"Jim, we can't ignore that I was unfaithful to him at a time when he was in terrible circumstances that he had no control over, and I hid that from him. He never knew. I couldn't forgive myself for that. I guess I thought I deserved whatever he gave me." She was spilling out anguish she'd never voiced to anyone before.

"Margaret, you said it yourself. He never knew so that doesn't enter into his behavior. God has forgiven us. I know that, and you know that Carl never could have forgiven you if you had confessed. Nothing good could have come from that. If I had been a white man, maybe he could have, but never a black man."

Her mind was screaming, *I need to confess to you too, Jim. I need to ask your forgiveness too, but I can't...I can't...not yet...maybe never.*

She leaned back, took a deep breath and fought for control. "Where would you want me to start?" she whispered.

"What happened when Carl came home from the war?"

"Okay." She finally decided she could start there, skipping over the biggest problems she faced before Carl came home. "But it won't be pretty." She relaxed her hand and he patted it gently.

"We're used to things not being very pretty, but I think if we take this journey into the past together, things will become much better for us the rest of our lives."

She closed her eyes and forced her mind back to those days she'd rather have forgotten, surprised at how vividly they came back

## 1946

Margaret hated moving to the old farmhouse on the land Carl and Chuck were trying to farm. She was alone with the children most of the time. At least while Carl was gone to war, she had her family right across the road; now there was no one for miles around. Very soon she was pregnant again. The loneliness became unbearable at times.

Carl wasn't much of a farmer, he'd rather hunt and fish, but he tried hard. He and Chuck did their best to raise a cotton crop, but the weather didn't cooperate. It rained and rained and most of the cotton rotted in the fields. When that happened, Chuck decided to move back up north where his two older brothers were and find a job there. Margaret's folks provided what they could spare from their farm to feed her family. Otherwise they might have starved.

Time for the baby to be born came closer and closer. Carl was never at home, or he came in drunk. The war had changed him so. She had worried about his drinking before the war, but after he came home it was much worse. On top of his war experience came his failure as a farmer with a family to support. He had never been good at taking responsibility. His father had always stepped in with a way out for him before, but now Clyde lived several hours away, and Carl was on his own. Rather than depend on God, as Margaret constantly tried to coax him to do, he relied on his whiskey, trying to forget about his failures with his hunting and fishing.

Papa never drank so Margaret had no experience in how to react to such behavior. She didn't do it very well, nagging and complaining because she was scared. He told her he was looking for a job in town and she wondered if this was true.

One August morning, she woke up early with a nagging pain in her side. Carl was already waiting for Wayne's wife to drop him off to go fishing with Carl.

"Carl, I don't think you should leave," she pleaded. "I feel like I may be ready to have the baby. Don't leave us today. I have no way to get help if I need it."

"Aww, it's not that time yet. Quit whining. You're always whining about something. There's Wayne. I'll be home early."

A car horn sounded and he was out the door, leaving her sitting at the table with her head in her hands. She didn't dare move around much, asking God to either provide a way for her to get a message to Mama or hold off this baby's birth until Carl got home.

Anna Rose was only five, but under Margaret's direction, she got Junior and Janie up and dressed and gave them a cold biscuit and some milk. Anna Rose entertained her little brother and sister as her mother sat trying to think what she should do. She would just have to hold out until Carl returned, or maybe Papa would come by as he often did. She prayed he'd come that day."

It was midmorning when she heard his rattletrap truck chugging down the road. "I have to make sure he stops," she said to Anna Rose. "Watch your brother and sister and I'll go out and flag him down." Slowly, she walked out to the road and waved as Papa came around the curve.

"Where are you headed, Papa?"

"Mama is canning beans. I'm just headed to the store for some lids for her canning jars. You need something?"

"Well, I'm not feeling the best and Carl's gone. This baby's acting like it might come soon. Go ahead and get Mama's lids, but could you bring her back over to stay with me when she's done—at least till Carl gets home?"

"I'll get her right now! The beans can wait."

He whirled the truck around in the driveway yelling that he'd be right back. He soon brought Maud, who took one look at her daughter and sent Sam into town for the doctor.

By the time Carl got home late that night, Dr. Turner had delivered his second son. Mama had gone home and had taken the other children with her. She left Abby to attend to Margaret and the baby. Carl took a quick look at the baby then left again to take Wayne home.

Janie, Anna Rose, Junior and Jimmy on the old farm

1984

Reliving that stressful time left Margaret distraught and exhausted. She squeezed her eyes tight to shut out the memories. Jim took her in his arms, remembering another time when he had kissed her tears away forty years ago.

Jim was anxious to learn how Margaret coped with the four children and Carl's constant absence, but didn't want to push her into the anguish of reliving it all, "Don't feel you owe it to me to finish," he said. "We're doing just fine."

She smiled and he could see she had already gone back to those days; almost as if he wasn't there, she opened a window to the life she had with Carl and the children.

## 1947

Things got better for a while after Jimmy was born. Carl got a steady job at the Cotton Oil Mill and, with a regular income, he was able to buy a house in town—a tiny four-room house in a newly developed community called Milltown. There was no plumbing and no running water, but Margaret had close neighbors, and the children had friends to play with. Anna Rose started school in the fall at the neighborhood school within walking distance. There was an outdoor toilet, and they walked down to the corner where they could fill buckets with city water at a faucet sticking out of the ground. It wasn't the best, but it was better than being stuck out in the country with no one around.

Margaret would often send Anna Rose and Janie to the corner with a gallon bucket. It took two of them together to bring it back full of water, but sometimes it was almost empty again by the time they got back home sloshing so much out of the bucket trying to carry the heavy load.

"Mother, Janie kept dropping her side of the bucket and the water would slosh out," Anna complained.

"It's too heavy," Janie whined.

So Margaret would have to put Jimmy and Junior in the stroller and go get the water herself, taking the girls along to push the stroller back. On laundry day, this might have to be done many times. She would reuse the laundry rinse water to bathe the children and herself. Carl didn't have to worry about that. He showered at work each evening in a nice warm shower!

Margaret soon found out from the neighbors that all Carl had to do was go by the courthouse and sign a document and the city would run the water line down to their yard. She kept reminding him to do that, but he kept saying he forgot. He went to the pool hall in town after work rather than going by the courthouse, so the office was closed by the time he started home.

"You ought to be glad you've got running water," he would chide. "At least you don't have to draw it from a well. You're always complaining. I have to work, you know."

"If I had a well it would at least be in my yard. Running water could be in my yard if you would just go by and sign that paper."

"I'll do it when I have time. Stop nagging!" He dismissed the subject and she didn't want to escalate the argument in front of the children. She was never sure how far she could push him.

Finally, she started meeting him at the door with two buckets every day when he came home, no matter how late it was, saying, "We need water from the corner. Would you go get some, please?"

He would give her that angry look, but knew that his dinner couldn't be prepared without some water so he would reluctantly go for water.

Soon he "remembered" and they had a faucet in their front yard! Such a primitive improvement was a great blessing at the time.

# LOOKING BACK

## 1984

Later in the week Margaret continued to catch Jim up on the life she had with Carl and her children after they moved to Milltown. He listened with interest, learning more and more about the years that had separated them.

"Living in that neighborhood built specifically for workers at the local cotton mill was such a blessing to me," Margaret continued, "even though the house was small and crowded—just four rooms built on a concrete cone foundation. The living room opened into the kitchen straight ahead with a bedroom on the left. A door in that bedroom led to a very tiny back bedroom. Carl and I took the back room, which barely held our bed, and all four kids slept in the front room. We had electricity with a bulb hanging from the ceiling in each room but just a potbellied coal stove for heat.

"In the kitchen was a kerosene cook stove, a standalone cabinet with a flour bin, an ice box, and a table with a water bucket, dipper, and wash pan. The ice man delivered ice in a horse-drawn wagon several times a week for the ice box, and I could get kerosene for the cook stove for ten cents a quart at the little neighborhood store two blocks away.

"Carla was born when Jimmy was two years old, so we added a baby crib to the kids' bedroom that already had two beds. I had a hard time with the birth, so the doctor strongly urged us not to have more children or my health could suffer. Carl didn't want more children anyway, so Carla was our last."

Margaret was actually enjoying sharing this part of her story. It had been many years since she had thought about that time in her life.

"Am I boring you?" she suddenly realized how long she had been talking about herself.

"No, you're fascinating me," Jim replied sincerely. "I have to admit I never had to live without those basic things like you did. Being near a big northern city had its advantages, especially for my race. What was the neighborhood like?"

She chuckled as she thought back about the people who lived around her. It was indeed a different time. The houses were close together and everyone became like family.

"The neighbors were a colorful lot," she continued. "Mr. and Mrs. Kent lived next door, an older couple, having one of the few yards with a fence around it. They raised pigs in the back lot, even though it was in the city limits and smelled up the whole neighborhood." She laughed. "There were not yet any zoning laws in the area. We bordered on woods and pasture.

"Mr. and Mrs. Kent had a phone and we didn't. They would allow me to use it for really important calls, like if I needed to call a doctor for the children. They were very proud of their one granddaughter who would sometimes come for a visit. The children wanted to play together but the granddaughter wasn't allowed to go outside the fence. They found a way to sit on each side of the fence and still play together.

"Across the road was Mr. West who lived with his daughter Lana. She was a nurse and had been married several times, but wasn't married at that time. She was very glamorous and had many suitors. Mr. West was a handyman and would voluntarily do things around the house for me. In a fence beside their house, they kept a solid white Spitz dog they named Truman after the president."

"Lana West, Carla and a neighbor boy".

"Mr. Johns lived alone on the other side of us, but his house faced the crossroad a block away. His backyard fence backed up to our side yard and he grew a large vegetable garden there. He kept to himself and seemed very mysterious, but we often saw him working in his garden. Sometimes, he would hand me a head of cabbage or some onions over the fence when he saw me in the yard.

"On the corner where we had to go to the faucet to get water lived 'Crazy' Mrs. Hendricks, as the children called her. Her daughter, Joan, still in her late teens, lived with her and had a baby girl. Mrs. Hendricks had mental or emotional problems and probably should have been in an asylum. Joan was not at home very much, and left her baby daughter with Mrs. Hendricks, which seemed dangerous, but no one wanted to interfere. Mrs. Hendricks cleaned and scrubbed constantly. Some days if she was angry with Joan, she ranted and raved all day long about how terrible things were and how awful her daughter was. You could hear her all over the neighborhood. The children were afraid of her and stayed close to home on those days. She was the only one there to take care of the baby most of the time, and who knows what kind of care the child got! In those days, you minded your own business. Joan somehow provided their necessities. I did pray for them many times hoping that the baby was cared for. She seemed to do fine.

"Mr. Bradford owned all the land in that plot, and he and his sons built the Milltown homes. He and his wife lived behind us and his relatives lived in several of the other houses they had built.

"The land had been cotton fields when he bought it, so there were no trees. Mr. West planted a row of Locust trees for me for some shade in the front yard. There was hardly any grass, so dust was constantly in the air and tracked into the house. When it had been hot for a period of time in the summer, we sprinkled the lawn with a garden hose to keep down the dust. The road was mainly a dust bowl too. A city sprinkler truck would come by and sprinkle water on it. The kids liked to stand beside the road to get sprinkled with the water from the truck.

"There were lots of kids and the whole neighborhood was their playground. Ball games were organized during the day and hide-and-seek at night. It was a good place for the children to grow up.

"The war seemed to have increased Carl's antisocial behavior. He withdrew emotionally further and further from the children and me. He came home late most nights having been drinking at the pool hall in town, but he never missed work and eked out a living for us. We had a roof over our heads and food on the table. I was grateful for that. If he'd left us, I don't know what I would have done. I had no other way of taking care of us."

"Do you remember promising me that you would get in touch with me in such a case?" Jim asked with some irritation.

"Of course! But I would never have kept that promise. I couldn't do that to you. What if you were married and had your own family? I couldn't, Jim." She reached for his hand. "Anyway, it never happened."

"So he was there, but not really there for you and the kids," Jim observed. "How did you manage to have any kind of life?"

She chuckled. "You know me, Jim. I got involved with my neighbors, the children's school, and the church. When Carl wasn't around, the children ran and played freely and joyfully. When he was home, they tiptoed around him fearing his disapproval. He ate, read his newspaper, and slept, rarely talking to any of us. The children didn't know what it was like to have a relationship with a caring dad."

"He did care about them. I know he did—why else would he have stayed and worked so hard to make a living? But he didn't know how to show it. It was so hard to get him to talk about it. I tried to draw him out. I tried to get him to go with me to their activities. He just wouldn't do it. He went to Junior's graduation, but none of the others. Anna Rose wanted him to give her away at her wedding, but he went fishing instead. I don't think he could handle it emotionally. I don't know what happened to him, Jim."

"How did the kids grow up to be such wonderful people?" Jim wondered aloud.

"Oh, it left emotional scars on all of them. Anna Rose exhibited her grandmother's tendencies to withdraw and feel inferior until she went away to college and saw that she could have a life outside her shell. She was fortunate to marry a loving man and get into a profession she loved. I think Janie's inferior feelings led her to marry someone from a prominent family that could give her things that made her feel important. I don't think hers is a very loving marriage. And the boys have shied away from intimate relationships, which I think is due to their father's bad example. Carla is divorced.

"I can't blame it all on Carl. I was far from the perfect parent. A lot of times, I was just trying to hang on and find a way to keep us all going, and I reacted in inappropriate ways many times to what I know now was his need for understanding. Neither of us knew how to cope with life as it came to us. A marriage needs two people pulling in the same direction. We were such opposites."

"I waited a long time, Margaret. before I asked Juanita to marry me. But as I look back on it now, I see that's just what I did—waited. I could have tried to contact you. I just left it up to you. That wasn't fair."

"We can't say that, Jim. If God had wanted that to happen, he would have impressed it on you. You did what he led you to do."

"I would have loved to take you away from all that, but I'm amazed at how that same strength that drove you to take care of me and your sister and all the children during that awful war still shines out of your soul. Somehow you didn't let that die."

He hugged her tightly and she sighed contentedly, basking in the honest praise of someone who loved her. It was a new experience.

"You could have taken me out of that hurt, Jim, but that would have created other hurts for us, the children, and both our families. That's why we parted in the first place. Life hurts, but it's also good. God's brought us back together. Let's forget the past and go on from here."

He got to his feet and stretched. "It's getting late. I'd better go."

He headed to his car and down the road, leaving Margaret longing for the time when he wouldn't have to leave at all.

# COPING

## 1947–1960

The Tiny House in Milltown

Anna Rose, Junior, and Janie

The Corwins lived in the little house in Milltown for twelve years. After eight years, Carl finally had two rooms built on the back so that the girls and boys had separate bedrooms. While it was an improvement, he never had them finished inside, so the bare drywall became an inviting canvas for the younger children's crayons and pencils.

A bathroom was installed in that tiny bedroom that had been Margaret and Carl's. There was no hot water heater, so they still had to heat water on the stove, but there was a tub and toilet in the bathroom and a sink in the kitchen.

Carl bought a refrigerator when the old man who delivered ice became too ill to do so anymore. Margaret had no say in the decision. The delivery truck just showed up one day and asked where she wanted the refrigerator put. When natural gas was piped into the neighborhood, Carl was forced to replace coal and oil with a gas heater and cook stove.

Margaret struggled to provide for the needs of the children since every spare penny Carl made went toward his hunting and fishing equipment—and his whiskey, of course. While Carl felt they should be satisfied with bare necessities, she was determined to help the children rise above what he expected.

Margaret had to beg and plead and endure Carl's ridicule to get him to give her the least bit of money for the children's needs. When time came for Anna Rose to start school, she needed clothes and supplies. Carl said she could just wear what she had, handing Margaret only enough money to pay the grocery bill. Mr. Barnwell allowed her to charge her groceries during the week and pay the bill on Saturday when Carl got paid. Margaret looked at the money and made a decision she felt she had to make.

When Carl left for work, she took the children and the stroller, boarded the city bus, and went into town. Anna Rose was fitted with shoes, new underwear and socks, and two dresses. When Margaret returned home, she went to Mr. Barnwell and told him what she had done. She picked out school supplies for her daughter from his shelves.

"Here is the money I have left, Mr. Barnwell. Anna had to have school clothes, so you can see Carl for the rest of the money." The storeowner knew Carl and chuckled at Margaret's ingenuity. He carried the remainder of the bill over to the next week.

That evening, Anna proudly displayed her new clothes and supplies to her dad. Carl looked at them and then at Margaret. "Where did the money come from for these?"

"You can see Mr. Barnwell for the rest of the grocery bill that didn't get paid." Margaret picked up Anna's display from the couch and headed into the bedroom to put them away.

"Well, we may have to cut down on eating next week if you are going to insist on blowing our grocery money," he called after her.

She peeked around the door and stared into his face. "No! You may have to cut down on the pool hall and the fishing equipment and the whiskey next week!"

He broke the stare, grabbed up his newspaper, and was silent the rest of the evening.

Margaret grew a large garden in the spring and summer and faithfully cooked the fish and game Carl brought home to supplement their meals. She scrimped to save as much as she could of the grocery allowance for clothes, lunches, and supplies for the children.

She'd always worked hard and knew no other way to live, so she determined not to feel sorry for herself, feeling blessed that Carl had a job. She took pride in her ability to make something out of what at first seemed to be nothing.

Another battle came when she insisted that she needed to get a driver's license. She knew how to drive and had driven all the vehicles on the farm at a time when a license wasn't required, but now the children were becoming more and more involved in school activities and she needed to transport them.

"You don't need a license. We've only got one car and I need it to go to work. We can't afford gas for you and the kids to run around."

"I don't want to run around. The kids need transportation and I can't keep depending on others for that. I need to take my turn."

"You couldn't pass the driver's test anyway," he shot back, trying to shame her into backing down. Though he kept trying, this tactic never worked with Margaret. It only made her more determined. Where the children were concerned, she would find a way.

"Okay! If you won't take me, I'll walk over there and borrow a car from someone to take my test in, but I will get a license."

He sneered at her and refused to discuss it further.

The next day she put in a call to Mama.

"Will you ask Papa if he'll take me to get my driver's license? Carl won't take me. He thinks I don't need to get one, but I have to take the kids to their school activities. I need to have a license."

She could hear Papa in the background when Mama told him what she wanted.

"I don't want to go against Carl if he don't want her to get one," he hedged.

"Well, she's going to walk over there and borrow a car if you don't help her," Maud growled, exasperated at all of them.

"Okay, tell her I'll be over tomorrow morning, but my car's not in the best shape. They may not even let her take the test in it."

The passenger side of Papa's old car was wired shut, so the examiner had to crawl in the driver's door, but he was a friend of Papa's and saw right away that Margaret knew how to drive, so when Carl came in that evening she showed him her license and said she would need the car Friday afternoon for a PTA meeting at school. He had nothing to say, but reluctantly took her with him back to work after lunch on Friday so that she could have the car for her meeting.

"Now you better not be late picking me up after work," he warned. "I don't want to be sitting around here waiting after I've worked all day"

"I'll be here," she promised and she was careful not to be late, though she often had to wait for him to take his shower or he would take her home, then go back to take his shower, and then go the to pool hall.

The door was opened for her to do what she felt she had to do for the kids. Some days she could keep the car and go out to the farm to pick cotton while the kids were in school, giving her another source of extra income.

Papa's health continually got worse. He was diagnosed with emphysema. His doctor told him frankly that if he continued to farm, his life would end quickly and painfully. The dust and pollen from the farm was slowly killing him. He began to make plans to sell his beloved land and start a business in town. He bought a house in a mostly residential neighborhood and built a concrete block building behind it to house Lane's Washerette.

He installed rows of wringer washers with two rinse tubs each. This was the perfect business for the times, since automatic washers were not yet in the price range of the average family and it was expensive to install the wiring for them. As with most new inventions, many women were also skeptical that these automatic machines could even get their clothes clean. They felt scrubbing on a washboard was the only way.

Rural areas had water from wells that was hard or had sulfur in it, so women from the country came to wash their clothes in soft city water. Also, women who lived in the city often didn't want the mess of setting up a washing machine and rinse tubs in their houses so they could get the job done more easily and quickly at Lane's. Papa added an automatic washer and dryer exclusively for Mama to use to do laundry for some customers who could afford to hire their laundry done for them.

The middle class neighborhood, which bordered on a wealthier one, was a couple of blocks from the golf course, public swimming pool, and park, and had a florist and small grocery store nearby. It was a good move; they were closer to Margaret and the family and enjoyed the closeness of neighbors and friends that the location provided.

Papa added a refreshment area where patrons could buy a candy bar and a cold drink from the ice chest while doing their laundry. These treats also attracted neighborhood kids and grandkids.

However, after a few years, Margaret found she had to help out frequently as Papa became weaker, having stayed too long on the farm to save his health, and when Mama underwent an emergency appendectomy, it became apparent the business was becoming too much for them. Papa's doctor advised him to take it easier, so they began to look for a smaller house to retire to. Ever the businessman, Papa came up with an idea to keep the business in the family.

"Margaret, Miss Maud and me have found a house we'd like to buy on a quieter street so we can retire. I wondered if you might talk to Carl about you and him buying our house and business before we put it on the market. It's a bigger house for the kids and you could use the extra money from the business."

"Do you think I could handle it, Papa?"

"Of course you can. You've had to take over when Miss Maud and me were sick, so you know how to run it, and I'll be close by if you have questions."

Margaret was excited about the prospect, but Carl was skeptical. "We couldn't get anybody to buy this house in the mess it's in and I don't know if we can afford your mother and dad's place."

"Mama has a customer that is interested in our house, Carl. Two widowed sisters need a small place and they want to fix it up a little. The business will pay for itself. Please consider it," she begged.

He finally gave in. "Well, if you can pull it off, I'll go along, but I'm doubtful."

Papa's business sense and her tenacity prevailed. The sale of their house and Carl's good credit rating made it easier than they anticipated and they were soon owners of the larger house and the business.

It was a drastic move for Carl, but Papa and Margaret took care of all the details, Carl signed the papers, and they found themselves in a nice neighborhood with a good business to help them financially.

"How are we going to get all this stuff over to the other house? I don't have a truck." Moving day was approaching and Carl was still worrying about all the details that seemed to overwhelm him.

"Wayne has a truck that you two go fishing in all the time. He'll let you use it. Isn't there someone at work that would help us load and unload it?"

"I guess ol' George will help if I ask him," he muttered, referring to the black janitor who worked at the mill. George was a friendly, outgoing man who pastored a church as well as worked at the mill. He would come over and talk to Margaret and the children if he saw them in the car waiting for Carl after work. Margaret hated the way Carl referred to him, but felt helpless to change her husband's prejudiced mind.

Moving day was exciting and fun for Margaret and the kids, although Carl looked with disdain on their giggling and joking.

George Parsons was a jolly, helpful Christian man. He and Margaret carried on a lively conversation about their children as they worked. Out of the corner of her eye, she saw Carl's scornful looks of disapproval.

By late afternoon, all was moved and Margaret overheard Carl on the porch offering George a pint of whiskey as payment for his help.

"No, sir, I can't accept that, Mr. Carl. I don't want a policeman catching me with that in my car. I'd be in trouble for sure. Anyway, I don't drink. You don't owe me anything. I'm just glad to help you and your nice family."

They shook hands and George carried in the last box. Margaret took ten dollars from her purse and tried to slip it to George, but he just smiled and said, "I don't want no pay; I'm glad to help, Miz Margaret."

Watching him leave, she thought, *Carl looks down on him because of his color, but he sure has more sense than Carl about how to live his life.*

This business was perfect for Margaret—the everyday socializing with other women raised her spirit and the extra income provided things for the children that Carl didn't think they needed and insisted he couldn't afford. They were mostly teenagers now and it cost more and more to provide for their needs.

What should have eased tensions for Margaret and Carl ended up causing more problems. She tried to make sure there were hot meals for him when he came home for lunch and dinner, but sometimes got tied up and ended up being a little late. Even though the business was attached to the house, juggling tasks both in the house and the business was a little stressful.

In the evening, if the meal wasn't on the table, Carl went for the whiskey bottle in the refrigerator, or sometimes he used her working as an excuse to stop at the pool hall after work for drinks with friends. She knew the alcohol was what was making him more angry and jealous, but felt powerless to get him to cut down.

This arrangement was great for her and the children. She was always there when they came in from school and had money available when extras were needed, such as Anna Rose's plea near the end of her junior year.

"Mother, they're fitting us for class rings tomorrow and I need to pay half the money. Can I order one, please?"

"Sure you can." She went to the cash box and counted out the amount that was indicated on the paper Anna Rose had showed her. "Put this in your purse for tomorrow—and don't lose it!" Anna had bounded out the door with a fleeting "thanks" before her mother was finished, but Margaret smiled at being able to make her so happy.

# LAUNDRY BUSINESS

## 1960–61

Carl wanted nothing to do with running the laundry business. He didn't like dealing with people and became jealous of Margaret's doing so. She was friendly and accommodating to all the customers, and built a regular clientele on top of what Mama and Papa had done. However, Carl would stick his head in occasionally, always finding something to criticize.

"If you wouldn't talk so much to the customers, they'd get done sooner and wouldn't tie up the machines," he offered one night after a particularly busy day that had made her late getting dinner on the table. "We'd make more money if you'd just tend to business and not be so nosy."

"Nobody ever has to wait for a machine," she tried to reason. "We get a lot of our business because of our friendly service." She was tired and in no mood to take his criticism.

Once in a while, he took a look at the ledger she kept where Papa had showed her how to do the business records.

"Where does all this money go?" he demanded. "I sure don't see any of it. We have to pay income tax on this, you know. You better be saving some."

"Some has to go back in the business, electricity and water bills, you know. The machines have to be kept in good working order. The rest goes for things the kids need and for groceries. You can see I don't spend it on myself. I'll start a savings account for the income tax. I had forgotten about that."

She hated to think what it would be spent for if he got hold of it. She tried constantly to appease him, to keep him even-tempered, to avoid a blow-up. All of this took its toll on her nerves. Not knowing how to change things, she found herself unable to relax, feeling in a constant state of turmoil.

Curling up at night, trying to relax her mind, she'd take herself back to 1945 where she could see Jim's face smiling at her, feel his kind touch, hear his laugh, and immerse herself in unconditional love. At times, she even imagined their little angel baby girl running and playing with her other children. She tried to imagine Angel at every stage of her life, growing up in a happy home. *Does she ever wonder about the mother who gave her up? Does she ever wonder who her father is?*

She knew it was an impossible dream, but gave herself over to such thoughts when she couldn't fall asleep, or was in desperate need of calming her spirit. She told herself God was in it, talking to him like a friend as she often did.

*I know I'll never see Jim or our daughter again, but it's the only experience I've had with a man who accepted me and respected me, other than you and Papa,* she'd tell the Lord.

She was trying to bargain with God, but at times she wondered if her bargain was with the devil. Would God allow her to use her love for another man to keep her sane? She didn't know the answer to that, she only knew her prayer was always for Carl and her children—all of her children—and holding on to that time in her life kept her from unraveling.

No one else knew. She felt sure no one would ever know. The secret took on a life of its own, driving Margaret to react more and more in seemingly bizarre ways that left others wondering why.

She cringed, as usual, when Carl walked into the Washerette one Saturday. She had been preparing to close at noon, but a soft drink delivery truck had pulled up. She had to take the delivery since supplies were getting low and they wouldn't be back for two weeks. Two young men jumped out and began to load her usual order onto a dolly.

"Oh, Carl, dinner is on the stove in the kitchen. I'll be there in a minute to dish it up as soon as I take care of the boys here." Immediately, she knew she had used the wrong words, but she hoped he would take the hint and go back in the house. "The boys" were used to taking their time and having a laugh with Margaret, so they were in no hurry.

"She takes good care of us, Mr. Corwin. You ought to keep an eye on her," Joe teased as he filled the icebox with a variety of cold sodas.

She knew Carl couldn't take a joke like that, but she laughed, too loud, too nervously.

"You boys think you're something, don't you? How much do I owe you? You'd better get back to work. You can't make any money standing around here. I'm ready to close for the day." She tried to hurry them along without being too obvious.

"You trying to get rid of us?" They faked disappointment, then began to load the drink cases with the empty bottles back on their truck and waved as they pulled away. "See you in two weeks."

She could see Carl was fuming and braced herself for the verbal abuse she knew would be coming. Placing her hands on the top of the icebox, she prayed, *Help me stay calm. Carl's going to make something bad out of this, I know.*

He had gone back into the house and she followed, putting beans, potatoes, and fresh sliced tomatoes from the garden on the table, chattering too much. Placing a plate in front of him, she turned to pour a glass of iced tea, so her back was toward him when the accusation came.

"How do you "take care" of the boys?" he sneered.

"Oh, they're just a couple of kids that like to tease people. I guess it makes their work more fun." She tried to casually dismiss them.

"Well, all that flirting could lead to anything. You better watch yourself!"

Her resolve to stay calm left in a whirl of anger and disbelief. She turned slowly toward him.

"What are you accusing me of?" she almost whispered through clinched teeth. "How dare you! Those kids are half my age!" She rushed over beside his chair and was standing over him with her hands on her hips, not knowing what to say or do.

Taking such posture as a threat, and knowing he had allowed his criticism to go too far, he reacted out of desperation, immediately jumping to his feet, his fist drawn back. She felt as if she had already been hit.

"Go ahead! Hit me, Carl! But you'd better make it a good one, because if you hit me once you'll never have the chance to do it again!" She stuck out her chin, with determination on her face. He stared at her, then dropped his hand, picked up his hat, and left.

She wasn't sure what she had meant by that threat. She didn't know what she'd do if he hit her, but she felt sure that she could never stay with him if he did. She could withstand a lot, excusing him because of how he had been raised, and feeling that the liquor made him do things he wouldn't have done otherwise, but he'd never come that close to violence before, although there had been other times when she felt if she had not left him alone he would have hit her.

Shame and anger consumed her as she sat at the table with her head resting on her folded arms.

"If you only knew," she cried. "If I was going to choose someone else, I'd have done it years ago." She talked to him as if he was still there. "Why do I put up with this? Why do I take the humiliation?"

She knew the answer. The humiliation Carl heaped on her could be hidden. The humiliation of breaking up her family and becoming a "divorcee" was too public. With her upbringing, she couldn't handle it. Mama and Papa said, "If you marry, you marry for life. Don't come whining to us just because things get tough." Her oldest brother's wife had divorced him and the things said about her in the family were horrible. Margaret had always been the "good girl" of the family, the dependable one, the one that could take the heat and keep going. It wasn't in her to give up on her marriage.

Besides, what about the children? She couldn't take care of them by herself. She had nowhere to go, and the truth was, she felt responsible for Carl, like God had placed him in her care. He needed her and she needed to be needed. It was his own feelings of insecurity that made him so jealous. His sister was her best friend; his family was her family. No, she'd have to find a way to endure. Leaving was not an option for her.

Hearing a car in the driveway, she dried her eyes and wearily took care of more customers, although she had planned to close early. Her mind probed for a way to teach Carl a lesson. She had to do something, this was more than she could take.

Anna Rose was in college and Janie had quit high school and eloped with John, so there were just the boys and Carla at home. By the time the last customer pulled out of the drive, she had made up her mind. Locking the door for the final time, she painted a large sign and nailed it across the door. "CLOSED FOR GOOD."

Phone call after phone call came in for days. Customers were outraged that she would just close with no warning. What were they going to do about their laundry? She could only refer them to another laundromat on the other side of town. The children were upset and confused and Carl just used this as another opportunity to berate her further. All this left her exhausted and wondering why she had done such a thing.

"What good did that do?" Carl huffed. "You just cut your nose off to spite your face. We won't have the money to spoil the kids like you're used to doing now." He was disgusted.

The satisfaction Margaret thought she would feel only turned to loneliness and sadness and the loss of income was unbearable. She decided she had to go job hunting.

"You can't get a job. You don't have any work experience." Carl tried to keep rubbing in what a foolish mistake she had made, and she had to admit that he was right. But had she continued the business, what would he accuse her of next? It had become too much for her to handle. She had to do something else.

She found that her experience running the business was a blessing and she soon was hired at Danby's Rubber Company. It was hard factory work, but it paid well and was out of the reach of Carl's scrutiny. She could help Anna Rose at college and provide extras for the other kids and not have to worry about the meticulous bookkeeping of running a business.

Her drastic reaction to Carl's accusation was definitely a turning point in their relationship. Their intimacy was gone, and she spoke mostly in a cool, indifferent tone to him, but she also noticed his criticism of her wasn't as sharp. They began to live separate lives, with his drinking, fishing, and hunting and her becoming more involved with church, family, and the kids.

She advertised and sold the washing machines and tubs, saving the money to help Junior and Jimmy get started in college. Although Carl was willing to help the boys, his philosophy being boys needed to go to college to be able to get good jobs, but girls would marry and stay at home with kids, so the money would be wasted on them. Anna Rose was able to go only because she took government loans and worked part time.

Junior and Jimmy immediately adopted the large vacated quarters that had been the laundry for a bedroom/hangout with their friends. They dubbed it "The Armpit" and a parade of her sons' friends made it their second home, their clubhouse.

Her biggest regret was Mama and Papa's disappointment. They had put a lot of work into building the business and making it respected in the community and had wanted it to stay in the family. They couldn't understand her throwing it away. Of course, she never told them about Carl's accusations.

She tried to explain to them that she had to spend too much time with it, couldn't do as good a job as Papa had done keeping up the accounts, and needed more money to help Anna Rose, but the suddenness of it made them shake their heads at their daughter's impetuousness. As much as she came to regret it, she couldn't go back. It was done and she had to live with it.

Papa and Margaret.

# REGRETS

## 1966

The next crisis came when Carl learned that the mill where he had worked for almost twenty years was closing. He'd thought this would be where he'd spend his life, and looking for a job at this point in his life was too hard for him to even know where to begin.

Margaret felt sure he could find something else with all those years of experience, but he just sank into despair. Secretly taking things into her own hands, she called his boss who promised to recommend Carl if he heard of any jobs available elsewhere.

"Carl has been a great worker for us for a lot of years. I won't hang him out there without anything if I can possibly help it, Margaret."

"Thank you, Mr. Richards."

Two weeks before the mill closed, Mr. Richards told Carl he had accepted a job at Tartan Mills just twenty miles away, and he had asked to take Carl with him. They needed a good millwright. Carl worried that he wouldn't know how to do the new job, but it turned out to be very similar to the one he had done for all those years at the mill in Dyersburg.

His severance pay was enough to make a down payment on a house out in the country, which would be closer to Carl's new job but still close enough for Margaret to keep hers. They moved as soon as their house sold. Carl was more relaxed out in the country away from a lot of people. The American Legion became his new place to go after work for his drinks.

The drinking accelerated then. Margaret became afraid he would be arrested for drunk driving. Several times when he came home late, he almost missed the driveway. She watched from the window and held her breath until he made it, parking the car halfway on the grass and tottering up the back steps. Would he make it? "No!" she screamed as she ran to rescue him where he had fallen down six steps onto the grass. "Carl, are you hurt?" She helped him up and saw the gash above his left eyebrow, streaming blood down his face. She was finally able to help him up into the kitchen and doctor the wound. When it was covered with a bandage, she tried to talk to him.

"Carl, you can't keep drinking and driving. You are going to get hurt or hurt someone else. If you get caught, you might have to go to jail. That would be terrible. You might even lose your job!"

"I only had a few," he muttered. "I just lost my footing in the dark. Quit your nagging!" He pushed past her and headed to the front bedroom where he had started sleeping separately from Margaret.

Only a few days later, as he tried to make it into the driveway, he missed the turn and one wheel slipped into the shallow ditch on the right side. Margaret pulled him out of the driver's seat, then got under the wheel herself. Rocking back and forth a few times, she was able to get out of the ditch and drive on in the driveway. Carl had gone on into the house and climbed into bed. As she stopped the car, a police car drove in behind her.

"Are you having car trouble, Mrs. Corwin," he asked as she stepped out.

"No, Parker, I just missed the driveway a little there in the dark. I got it out okay. Thanks."

She was shaking when she went in, thinking how close Carl had come to being arrested for drunk driving. When she looked in on him, he was sound asleep with his clothes on. She removed his shoes and covered him up with a blanket, feeling so helpless and ashamed that they had to live this way.

Carla was the only one of the children still at home and she had to change schools in her sophomore year. She wasn't happy about the move and began spending more and more time in town with her friends. Margaret was worried about her and tried to talk to Carl about it.

"I'm worried about Carla. She doesn't like it out here where we're so isolated. She doesn't even come home half the time. I hope she doesn't get into trouble."

"She ought to be glad she's got a roof over her head. You worry too much. She's old enough to take care of herself."

Just four months before her high school graduation, Carla stunned Margaret by telling her that she and her current boyfriend, Gene, were getting married as soon as school was out for the summer. Everyone in the family was puzzled. The decision seemed so out of character for Carla.

Anna Rose and Junior tried to convince her to wait.

"You're so smart and have great grades. You ought to go to college, at least for a while. Why don't you just try it for a semester? You'll be so glad you did," Anna Rose pleaded.

"You can stay with me in Atlanta and go to school there if you want to," Junior offered. "I'll help you all I can."

Finally, the truth came out.

"I'm pregnant!" she yelled. "And that's that. I'm getting married! And don't tell Mother and Daddy. That's my job. I'll tell them when I'm ready."

A few months after her graduation, Carla and Gene eloped, and that's when Carla told Margaret about her dilemma. Margaret felt terrible, disappointed, and responsible, but now all her energy went toward helping Carla through her pregnancy and the birth of the baby, then another baby just a year later and a marriage that became stormier as the years went by. Carla's girls were seven and eight years old when her divorce became final.

The three of them moved in with Margaret and Carl and depression overtook Carla. It was all she could do to drag herself up each morning and get the girls off to school. After they left, she sat in a rocker, staring into space. While she was glad Carla didn't stay in a marriage that had turned out to be more abusive than her own, Margaret was desperate to try to find a way to bring her daughter out of this terrible state of mind.

"Let's go over to Dyersburg State College and talk to somebody about your taking some classes," Margaret kept suggesting. Carla had been a good student and enjoyed studying in high school.

"I don't have any money for college," she objected.

"We'll ask about financial aid. Your brothers and Anna Rose didn't have any money either, but they managed to go. I know you can too."

Finally, she relented and Margaret made an appointment. Carla insisted on going by herself, and came back with a new direction for her life.

The next four years, she and Margaret juggled taking care of the girls, working, and getting Carla through school, but when she graduated, she was offered a good job in Memphis.

After Carla's move to Memphis, Margaret and Carl found themselves across from each other at the dinner table, married for over forty years, but almost strangers. She had been too busy with Carla's family to even notice the change in his health recently. He didn't stay out late drinking much anymore, but kept his whiskey in the refrigerator at home. He dragged himself in from work each day, and had to take pain medication to sleep. His face was pale, he had lost weight, and he seemed to cough constantly.

Suddenly, her life with Carl began to flash through her mind like an old newsreel, coming to a halt with the end of the film flapping around the reel. She looked again at Carl and noticed that he looked so tired, and was wheezing with each breath. The cigarettes he had smoked since he was a child had taken their toll on his health. She suddenly realized he was seriously ill.

"You look pale, Carl. Are you okay?"

"I'm fine," he mumbled without looking up.

She gazed at him as she thought about all their years together. *What happened to our life? We started out loving and sharing and planning together, but after the war, we became combatants. I know Carl drinks and smokes too much, but I could be a better wife. I betrayed him, and the guilt and secrecy of it has made me act crazy. I need to be a better wife…and I will…starting now! I've ignored Carl's needs.* Resolve to change things took hold of her then.

"Carl, why don't you go sit in your recliner and watch the news. I'll bring you a cup of coffee. I know you're tired."

He looked at her with surprise, but saying nothing, he shuffled down the hall to the living room. Things changed for them then. She spent her time trying to make him comfortable, cook what he liked to eat, and convince him to see a doctor.

He was grateful, having a foreboding of the seriousness of his illness, but not wanting to face what it might be. Fifty years of excessive smoking and drinking and daily working in cotton fibers had taken its toll on his lungs. Any physical exertion made it difficult for him to breathe, and a chronic cough racked his body, but he insisted on going to work everyday and couldn't give up the cigarettes and whiskey he was so addicted to. He refused to see a doctor until one early morning when Margaret found him sitting on the side of the bed coughing up blood into his handkerchief.

He was admitted to the hospital where oxygen and pain medication eased his symptoms, but Dr. Conyers didn't give Margaret much hope.

"I'm sure it's lung cancer, but we need to send him to Memphis for further testing. They have a great oncology department. They'll do a biopsy and x-rays to see how extensive it is. We'll make the arrangements in about a week. We first need to get him a little stronger to withstand the trip."

The biopsy showed cancer, which had spread to vital organs. Margaret called all the kids and by the time all of them arrived, he was gone. She anguished that her resolve to make Carl's life better was too late. Why hadn't she seen that sooner?

Margaret's minister had visited Carl in the hospital everyday and tried to console her with a report of his visits.

"I didn't push religion on him, Margaret. I just read the Bible to him and prayed with him. We talked honestly about his condition and he regretted the way a lot of things had gone in his life. He made peace with God in those last few days. He knew how serious his illness was, but didn't want you to know. He just couldn't talk about it."

She knew that was so much like him, and hung on with gratefulness to the hope that he did find that peace in his last hours. *I guess God had to find another way to reach Carl since I failed to do it.*

Junior stayed with her for a few weeks and helped her face the many surprises that kept coming out that Carl hadn't taken care of. He had borrowed money on his life insurance policy leaving barely enough to even pay for the funeral. At the same time, she found savings bonds he had purchased hidden all over the house. Junior helped her find out how to get them in her name in order to be able to use them.

There was a large bill he had run up at the American Legion for food and drinks and he had charged a TV at the local furniture store. Secrets he kept from her kept cropping up, making her wonder what she might find out next. This prolonged the sadness, making it hard to know how to go on with her life.

Then after Junior left, the loneliness permeated her soul. She began to feel her life was over. What could she do now with the kids all grown and gone and now Carl too? It was in the midst of this sadness that Jim Hayes called.

# FIGHTING OLD BATTLES

## 1984

Margaret sat up quickly in bed, still not quite awake. Was that the phone she had heard? What time was it? She put on her glasses and reached for the clock. It was 6:00 a.m. There it was again. It was the phone. She jumped to the floor and rushed to the hallway. Who would be calling this early? She grabbed the receiver.

"Hello!"

"Margaret, this is Jim."

"Jim, is something wrong?" Her heart was pounding. What could have happened?

"It's okay, Margaret, don't get upset, but I need you to come down to the jail and get me, please. I think it's all a mistake, but one of your son-in-law's deputies arrested me last night after I left your house. He said I was 'driving erratically' which is not true. I'm sure he was watching me leave your house."

Anger and embarrassment overwhelmed Margaret. She could tell Jim was angry too. She couldn't remember ever hearing this tone in his voice.

"Oh, Jim, I'm so sorry. I'll be right there. Why didn't you call me last night?"

"There was no need to disturb your sleep. I need you to take me to where my car is impounded. We can discuss it when you get here."

Tears stung her eyes as she drove toward town, but she quickly suppressed them. This was John's fault and she would not give him the satisfaction of seeing her hurt, but he would be confronted by her anger.

Entering the front door, she charged toward the front desk.

"I'm here to see John," she barked at Nina, the deputy on duty.

"He's…"

She could see Nina was going to come up with an excuse to make her wait.

"Never mind. I know where his office is." She bypassed Nina, startling John at his desk as she burst through the door.

He immediately began to try to calm her.

"Now, Margaret, don't be so upset. This was an honest mistake. It's okay now." He leaned back in his chair, but his hands trembled a little as he tried to light his cigar.

She placed her hands on his desk and got near his face speaking slowly and deliberately.

"It is *not* okay and it *wasn't* a mistake! You've had someone watching my house, haven't you? This would not have happened to a white man."

"Okay! A deputy goes by there a few times a week since Carl died. You're a woman alone in an isolated area. I was just trying to make sure you're safe."

"No, you didn't do such a thing until Jim came into my life again. It's not that. You're trying to scare him away, aren't you? Admit it!"

This comment hit home, and his sudden anger at her peeled away his protective facade, making him impulsively say what he had determined not to admit. He jumped up from his chair.

"For God's sake, Margaret, you're seeing a black man! You've done some crazy things, but this is the worst. Why are you doing this to our family's reputation?"

There it was, the family's reputation. She forced herself to speak calmly.

"Now you listen to me, John. Just because you're white doesn't mean you are even worthy to shine Jim Hayes's boots. I've lived in that neighborhood for twenty years and I do not need your protection. If anything even remotely like this ever happens again, I promise you, Jim and I will get a lawyer and bring you up on charges of discrimination even if you are my son-in-law. That's against the law now, you know. Are we clear on this?"

She could tell she had hit a cord of truth and watched him scramble to change her mood.

"I'm sorry to have upset you, Margaret. It was a mistake, that's all. Nobody's trying to target Jim. The deputy was just doing his duty." He laughed nervously and tried to lay his hand on her arm. She jerked away.

"I know what it was, John. Just remember my words. Where's Jim? I'm taking him home and there better not be any record of this arrest. It might be proof of something you don't want investigated."

There was a knock at the door as a deputy escorted Jim into the office. Margaret quickly went to his side as John handed him an envelope that contained his belongings and tried to shake his hand.

"I'm sorry about this mistake, Jim."

Jim ignored his hand. "It was no mistake, John. I hope it doesn't happen again. I told Margaret I'm not here to cause trouble in her family, but this was beyond our expectations. I'm willing to forget it for her sake, but you need to inform your deputies it must not happen again."

Margaret could see that John was almost unable to control his anger at the humiliation of having a black man talk to him with such confidence.

Jim took Margaret's arm and escorted her back to her car where she laid her head on the steering wheel and sobbed uncontrollably. He tried to comfort her.

"It'll be okay, Margaret. I remember you saying many years ago that if we wanted to be together, we'd face a lot of obstacles. Back then it would have been worse than this, but it's still not going to be easy. We're just learning what we're up against, especially in this area."

"But to think someone in my family would treat you like that, Jim. I just can't stand it."

"You don't have to, Margaret. We're going to make a life together." He took her gently in his arms. "There may be more things like this to put up with, but we at least have the law on our side now, if we are willing to fight the battle. To me, it is worth it."

Margaret's nerves were still unsettled as they sat on the back porch with their iced tea, a cool breeze washing over them. She tried to relax. It was the beginning of summer and Jim had been back in her life for almost three months, but it seemed he'd always been there. She'd kept his memory so vividly in her heart and mind as the years slipped by.

While the children were small, she'd watched them play, bringing him to stand by her side, smiling at their joyful, carefree games. After they had all left home, she had bouts of insomnia that only left when she took her mind to a serene island where the two of them sat close together with the sun touching their faces, then she'd fall into a restful sleep.

All those years of dreaming and now he was here—not a dream, really here. The years of struggle with Carl seemed like the dream now, like it had happened to someone else in a movie or a book.

She had to admit she had been so elated to have Jim back in her life that she hadn't considered that their racial differences would still be hated by bigots who would make it their business to punish them. While the civil rights movement had put the law right, changing hearts and minds of many in the South still had a long way to go. They had to face this and cling to God's promises to keep it from tearing them apart.

"We used to drink coffee together in the evening. Now we've graduated to iced tea," Jim said, breaking the silence.

Smiling, she remembered their evenings by the fireplace years ago. It was so much simpler when everything was a secret.

She knew in the silence that followed that he wanted to say something that he didn't know how to approach. She waited.

"Margaret, I think it's time we looked at our circumstances and made some plans, don't you?"

"Yes, I do."

"First, I have to ask you, has this incident with John given you any second thoughts about marrying me?"

"Of course not!"

"I was sure that would be your answer, but I had to ask."

"It's just made me feel so ashamed that you had to put up with such treatment," she growled.

"There will be more to come and maybe worse. For this to work, we have to take the attitude of pitying these people, and not let it create anger and resentment in us. I was proud of you today. You handled John well and didn't let him get away with his vicious plan. Let's just go on with our lives now."

She saw clearly what he meant. It made so much sense. "I promise I won't let it ruin my attitude. We have better things to do with our time."

"Now, I have to ask you another question which I don't want you to answer right away. Give it some thought, Okay? We'll discuss it tomorrow."

"Okay."

"How committed are you to living here in the South, in this town?"

She did have to think about that. She'd never lived anywhere else, but she'd seriously entertained the thought of moving to Memphis with Carla after Carl died. Janie was the only one of the children still here. She needed to know more about what he was thinking.

"Well, I can see this might not be the best place for us to make a life. Before you came, I was thinking about selling the house and moving to Memphis with Carla. What did you have in mind?"

"Well...my daughters want us to come and live in Michigan. Each time I talk to them, they're anxious to meet you. They'd like us to live near them. We'd be better accepted there, but I'm not going to insist on moving you to a strange place where you'd be miserable just for that reason. That's why I want you to give it some thought."

It was a new concept, but she felt immediately it was the perfect answer. She started to speak, but he placed his finger on her lips.

"I don't want an answer now. I told you, I want you to think about it."

After he left, she walked the floor into the early morning hours mulling everything over, asking God for answers, praying she would make the right decision. She knew Janie wouldn't like it. What would the other kids say? Well, it wasn't their life, it was hers! What would her friends say? She'd lived here all her life! The church? A plan began to form in her mind to put out a fleece and see what God's answer would be. Above all she wanted to be in his will.

The next morning, she called Jim early.

"I've thought long and hard about what you said, and it's just hit me that I'm just as bad as others who condemn us!"

He laughed. Surely she was joking.

"I mean it, Jim. You've been here several months and I haven't ever taken you to church with me. I told myself you were enjoying the church in town, but deep down I think I just didn't want to deal with what people in my church might say. There are some things I need to get settled before we make our final plans. Will you go to church with me tomorrow?"

"Well, sure. How do you think it'll go over?"

"We are going to find out! Come on over and I'll have lunch ready."

Margaret's thoughts went back a few years ago when a visiting missionary from Africa came to preach a series of sermons for them. No white church members invited him to their home to stay or even for a meal. He stayed at the home of the local black preacher and came into the church building only for the service in which he was involved. Margaret remembered being appalled and ashamed, but told herself she couldn't invite him to her home because of how Carl would react. He didn't want any preacher in his home, much less a black one. Now she could see she was just making excuses too. That had been years ago, but she had to see if things had changed.

"Of all the people who should accept any person without prejudice, it should be God's people," she told herself.

They walked into the church building early and met with either stunned silence or a half-friendly nod. Margaret went to her regular seat near the center of the sanctuary, speaking to her friends as she usually did. Jim followed, sticking out his hand to shake the hands of those she introduced him to. The pew they sat in, usually crowded, stayed almost empty. The ladies who often sat with her found other places. A couple of latecomers scrunched themselves on the end of the pew.

It felt so right to have Jim worshipping with her. His deep baritone voice blended with her soprano, giving new meaning to the hymns they both loved, but they still felt all eyes bearing down on them through the whole service.

Jim was the first to comment on the way home.

"That went pretty well, don't you think?"

She gave him an exasperated look. "That's because you don't know how they usually act toward me. I might as well have been a stranger to my 'friends.' I'm not going back there. They're not who I thought they were, or maybe they are who I suspected they were."

"Well, you did give them a shock. Maybe they felt they just didn't want to intrude when you had a gentleman with you," he teased.

"Maybe you're right, but this isn't really about them. It's part of my making a decision for us."

He could see that she was trying to sort all this out in her mind, so he dropped the subject and left her to her thoughts.

That evening, as she watched one of her favorite late television shows, she was startled by a noise outside. Going quickly to the door, she called out. "Who's there?"

Suddenly, there was something bombarding the screen on her front porch. Frightened, she slammed the door shut, locking it with trembling hands. Shouts of insults she hadn't heard in a long time came from her driveway. The pelting of her screen porch continued. "What do they want?" she whispered. Fear gripped her and her imagination leapt to seeing herself beaten and dragged behind a car, or taken to a tree and hanged, now knowing the terror that Jim and others of his race had often felt. On her knees, she crept into the hallway and dialed the police. She could hardly gasp out the words.

"S–S–Someone is throwing things at my house. Please come out r–r–r–right away!"

A squad car came immediately. One officer came inside while the other sped after the car that was just peeling out of her driveway, scattering stones in its haste. The officer took down her account of what happened, but she hadn't much to go on except a messy porch and a glimpse of a car she couldn't identify.

John came, bringing Janie with him. *How does he know everything that is going on?* She didn't have time to reflect on that.

"Rotten tomatoes," he observed. "It was probably just kid's pranks, but I'm leaving Janie here for the rest of the night, and a deputy will be patrolling nearby—if that's okay," he added quickly, not wanting to face her anger again.

"It's fine," she agreed, leaning into the shoulder that Janie offered. She had been so frightened.

When everyone had left, Janie brought her a glass of water and a sedative the doctor had ordered for her after Carl died. She hadn't taken one in a long time and hesitated to do so now.

"You need some rest, Mom," Janie insisted. She had to agree and swallowed the pill.

"This is about you and Jim, isn't it? You can't live this way. It isn't safe! Don't you see that?" Janie was distraught and treating her like a child.

She took a long time to answer.

"Yes, I do," she muttered softly, "but I can't discuss it tonight."

Alone in the bathroom getting ready for bed, she stared at her pale face in the mirror. Things had to change beginning tomorrow. She and Jim only wanted to live their lives together quietly. They had a right to that. They had other serious matters to deal with. She knew that she had to find a way soon to tell him about their daughter. That could make all the difference in their relationship, but she just didn't know how or when to approach it.

The next day they observed the mess. The screen would have to be replaced in some places. Who would do such a thing? And why? She secretly suspected taking Jim to church with her had triggered it. This was confirmed when the police called saying they had caught the culprits—juveniles whose last names she recognized from church.

Janie left late the next morning after being assured that Margaret was fine. John sent his work crew out to clean up the porch.

Now she knew she had received an answer to Jim's question. She called him immediately, giving him a brief version of what had happened.

"Oh, no, Margaret! Are you sure you're okay?"

"I was really scared, but I'm fine now. Janie stayed the rest of the night with me. I did a lot of thinking, and I've made some decisions. Can you come over?"

"Of course! I'll be right over!"

He made the short trip with mixed emotions. Had she decided she couldn't handle the stress? Was she going to ask him to leave? Of course, he couldn't blame her. She was just coming off the death of her husband, and now this! He had pushed himself on her too soon. He so wanted them to live a quiet, happy life together. Fighting the civil rights movement over again wasn't in his plan. He decided to make it easier on her. *Is God telling us this won't work?*

He could tell she was still a little shaken as he took her in his arms for a long time and felt her clinging to him. Then she moved away and sat on the couch motioning for him to sit next to her. He wanted to begin before she did.

"Margaret, I've made a decision too. I'm going to leave and go back to Michigan right away. We'll keep in touch and maybe things will work out later. I know I shouldn't have just shown up. I should have corresponded awhile and had you visit me first when you felt up to it. Let's just try to start again slower."

She stared at him in disbelief. "I hope you don't really mean that. I hope you're just saying that because you're upset. I've decided that moving to Michigan would be perfect, Jim. I really mean it. We'd be nearer to Anna Rose and her family, as well as your daughters. I'd love it!" She sounded excited.

Relief and joy almost brought tears to his eyes. "You're sure about this?"

"I asked God for an answer and as far as I'm concerned, last night was it."

He caught her excitement. "You know we promised the kids we'd wait six months for everyone to get acquainted. I've been here three. We could spend the next three in Michigan while we plan our wedding. You would know by then how you would fare in 'Yankee-land,'" he teased.

She felt completely at ease. This would work. She was ready to shed the weight of life with an alcoholic and take on a new beginning with a Christian man who loved her deeply and whom she loved with all her heart. One hurdle remained. What would he say about the baby she had given up? She knew she had to tell him before they went to Michigan, but she so feared it would turn him against her. How would he take the news that she had given away his child?

After Jim left, Margaret began to take herself back to what happened to her life with Carl. "Did I make it worse?" she wondered. Then it was as if God took her to a movie, a replay of the last few years of her marriage.

*I went to church and I prayed, but I didn't listen to you, God. I did things my way. I see now that if I had allowed you to direct my path, things might have been different. I went my own way and left Carl to his. I should have thought more about him and less about myself and maybe I could have been a better witness to him. It seems I always have to ask your forgiveness for my rash mistakes. Forgive me again, Lord. Help me know when to tell Jim that he has a daughter he never knew about.*

# DISASTER

## 1984

The news that Margaret was moving to Michigan, maybe for good, met with differing reactions from her children. Carla was the most encouraging.

"Go for it, Mom. You're still young and you put up with Daddy all those years. You deserve to do whatever makes you happy. I've never been to Michigan. I'm looking forward to visiting you."

Jimmy and Junior were a little more cautious.

"Mom, we like Jim a lot and can see he's been really good for you, but don't trade one set of problems for another. Make sure you can be at home there before you make your final decision."

"Do what you want to do, but be sure you're taking care of yourself," Junior added.

Anna Rose was very happy at the prospect of having her mother move closer to her and her family. The twice-a-year trips she and her family had made for years would not be necessary and they could visit with Margaret a lot more often. They invited Margaret to stay with them until she and Jim finalized their plans.

Janie was the problem. She was making her case in Margaret's dining room over coffee one early morning.

"Mother, I've come to accept that you and Jim are going to be together, but I just can't believe you would take off to Michigan with someone you barely know. If one of us kids did that, you'd be so against it!"

Janie was pacing back and forth. Margaret put her head in her hands. She had awakened in the night with indigestion and still felt achy and weak, so patience with her daughter was wearing thin.

"If you'll remember, you did what you wanted, eloping with John, not finishing your education. How can you lecture me?"

"This is not about me! It's only been a year since Daddy died. You're still not over that. How can you make such a decision so soon?"

"I need to go on with my life, Janie. Jim loves me and I love him. We need…need to go…wh…wh…"

Her head was aching. She had to stop this and get some rest. Standing up, she felt her head spin. "Oooooh…Janie…I…need…to–"

"Mom, you have no idea where you're going or what kind of people you'll be with. What kind of neighborhood will you be in? You may be the only white person there! Will you feel safe?"

Turning toward her mother for an answer, she could see something was wrong.

Sharp pains blasted through Margaret's chest, down her arm. She tried once more to speak. "Janie…" Dizziness…fireworks in her head…nothing!

"Mom! Mom! What's wrong?" Janie's arms were wrapped around her as they both went to the floor.

---

John was startled as Nina rushed through his office door without knocking.

"Your wife on line one, she's upset."

He grabbed the receiver and pushed the button. "Janie, what's wrong?!"

"John, it's Mother. We were talking and she just collapsed! I'm going in the ambulance with her now to the hospital. Go get Jim Hayes and meet us there. Hurry! Oh, John, I'm scared. I think she's had a heart attack."

"Calm down, now. We'll meet you there!" John hung up and quickly told Nina he had to rush to the hospital.

Stopping his car in front of Jim's apartment, he rushed upstairs and knocked loudly on the door, but didn't know what to say when Jim opened it.

"What are you arresting me for today, John?" Jim finally broke the silence.

John ignored the bitter remark. "You need to go with me. Janie called and said Margaret collapsed while they were talking. We're meeting them at the hospital. Come on."

"Oh, dear God. What happened?" he asked as he quickly turned off the stove and began buttoning his shirt.

"That's all I know. Janie called an ambulance and they're on their way to the hospital. Hurry!"

The two men rushed down the steps and into the patrol car. John turned on his rotating light to get through traffic.

In the emergency room, Janie was nearly hysterical. "She's had a heart attack."

"Calm down, now. How bad is it? Did they say how she is?"

"That's all they will say. I can't get any information from anyone." She wailed.

Jim was at the nurse's station trying to get someone to tell him what was going on, but was only told the doctor would see them as soon as he could. They were trying to stabilize her and assess the damage.

He came back to the waiting room and collapsed on the couch, his head in his hands. Janie went to him.

"It's my fault, Jim. We were arguing about her going to Michigan with you. I'm so sorry. I should have kept my mouth shut. It's none of my business."

He looked up into her pleading eyes and then took her in his arms. It was natural. He was suddenly filled with sorrow for her and saw things from her point of view. She'd just lost her father and he—a stranger to her—was about to take her mother away. Now, this terrible news!

"It's not your fault, Janie. It just happened. It probably would have happened anyway. She'll be okay. She has to be!" He couldn't fathom losing her now as he silently petitioned God. *Take care of her, Lord. Let her be okay! Help us all through this.*

John went to the desk and tried to exert his authority as sheriff, but came back with little news.

"They're doing a lot of testing to decide what to do. The doctors will let us know how she is as soon as they can. I think we should call Junior."

Junior said he'd be on the next plane to Memphis and he and Carla would drive over from there. Jimmy and Anna Rose decided to wait for further news on her condition before traveling.

The three of them walked the floor for two hours, and then rushed to the doctor when he appeared at the door.

"She's had a heart attack, but we aren't sure how much damage there is to the heart muscle. She's stable now, but we need to do some tests in the morning to determine what to do next. We suspect a blocked artery or a damaged valve. She may need surgery. We'll know more tomorrow. She's being transferred to intensive care.

"Can we see her?" Janie wanted to know.

"One at a time, for just a minute. Come with me."

Jim and Janie followed him. John decided to wait, not knowing if seeing him would upset her.

"Mom, I'm so sorry," Janie whispered, taking her mother's hand. "I don't know if you hear me, but I love you."

Tubes and machines were everywhere, and Margaret looked lifeless.

"Jim's here. He'll be right in. I love you, Mom." She kissed her mother's hand and left with a heavy heart, but she had made up her mind she wasn't going to stand between Jim and her mother anymore.

After seeing Margaret, Jim came back saying he would be staying the night, so John and Janie should go home and get some rest and plan to relieve him tomorrow.

"Please call if there's any change," took the place of the protest Janie wanted to voice.

"Of course I will! Try to rest."

He headed back to the room in the intensive care unit where they had told him Margaret would be transferred.

Jim spent the night at Margaret's side, dozing off and on in the recliner by her bed, always with one hand resting lightly on hers so that if she moved the slightest, it would wake him. Nurses were in and out and assured him she was resting comfortably.

Early the next morning, he was sent to the waiting room so they could take care of her morning routine. The rest of the family began gathering there with questions for him about how she was. Junior and Carla had arrived at Janie's late in the night.

They listened intently to the doctor when he walked into the waiting room.

"The x-rays show a damaged heart valve. She'll need surgery to repair it. She's awake and I've talked to her about this. We've decided to send her to Memphis where there's a Dr. Johnson who specializes in this kind of surgery. She'll be in good hands and should make a full recovery."

They were all frightened, but happy to hear the words "full recovery."

# A DIFFERENT PATH

## 1984

While everyone else followed in cars, Margaret was taken to Memphis in an ambulance. An anxious dread hovered over them. Jim said very little, using the time to pray and think. They soon found out that more tests would be done the next day to determine when to schedule surgery.

Everyone except Jim said goodbye to Margaret and went to Carla's for the night. He preferred to stay in the large waiting room where pillows and blankets were provided and he could check on Margaret every two hours. *Besides*, he thought to himself, *I don't know how Carla's neighbors in the condo would react seeing me there, and I can't face that now.*

At midnight when he tiptoed in, he thought she was asleep, but suddenly her eyes flickered open and she looked at him with a look of desperation. He took her hand and tried to reassure her.

"You're going to be fine, Margaret. Just relax. I'm right here close. The kids went home with Carla for the night. Can I get you something? Do I need to call a nurse?"

"No, Jim…Jim, I have to tell you something. Listen…listen."

"Don't worry, Margaret. You'll be fine. God wouldn't bring us this far to take you away now. Don't talk, it may weaken you."

"No, Jim." Her voice was weak and barely a whisper. "Show me the pictures of your daughters again. Please!"

He pulled out his wallet and put the pictures in her hand, thinking this may calm her. She looked at them for a long time.

"What's wrong, honey? Don't even be thinking that you won't see them. We'll be with them soon. I talked to them yesterday. They are so anxious to meet you. Just don't be so worried."

"Jim, listen to me. I have to tell you something. I never told you...I never told anybody. Jim...you have another daughter. She was born in December after you left. I gave her up for adoption. I'm so sorry I never told you, but if I don't make it through this, I wanted you to know. I had to tell you. I'm so sorry."

She was sobbing uncontrollably now and holding onto his hand with such a tight grip, he could hardly move to comfort her, but he didn't know if he could move anyway. He couldn't believe what she was telling him. Maybe it was the medication. He just held on to her not knowing what to say, trying to take in the words that hung between them. His heart felt as if it had fallen into his stomach and he thought he might be sick. Was she saying what he thought he heard?

"Margaret, please, you have to just think about getting well now. I want to know all about this, but not now. Now we have to concentrate on what you're going through."

The nurse walked into the room and took control quickly. "Mrs. Corwin, you need something to calm you. Take this and rest. We want you to be at your best for this surgery tomorrow. Mr. Hayes, perhaps you should leave now."

"She's upset!" he insisted. "Will she be okay? Margaret, calm down now. You will be fine. We'll talk when you are better."

"Jim...are you angry? Don't be angry. I did what I thought was right."

He patted her hand softly as the pill began to take effect. "I'm not angry. I'm anxious to hear all about what you told me. Just concentrate on getting through this surgery and we'll talk when it is over." He walked out of the room and headed for the hospital chapel. Falling on his knees, he cried and prayed the rest of the night, trying to imagine what Margaret must have gone through to keep such a secret, and lamenting that he was not there when she needed him most.

At times, he told himself she was just under the influence of medication. People say strange things at those times. Maybe it wasn't even true, but the agony in her face when she said it would flash before him and he knew she was not imagining.

On the day of the surgery, the waiting room was filled with Margaret's concerned children and Jim. Jimmy and Anna Rose had arrived at Carla's the night before.

He was anguishing in silence until his two daughters surprised him by walking in at midmorning. They held him tight and he cried, as he hadn't done since Juanita's death.

"We had to come and see how you and Margaret were," Sharon explained to her father. "We couldn't let you go through this alone."

"He's not alone. We're all here." Carla extended her hand to both Sharon and Alice. "I'm Margaret's youngest daughter, Carla."

Jim introduced them to everyone else and the waiting continued. Though the surgery started at 7:30 a.m., it was after two before the doctor came in to report to them.

"She came through the surgery very well. There were no complications. The valve has been repaired, so she should recover slowly but steadily if no infection or other complications develop. We will be closely monitoring and intervening so that won't happen. It may be a while, but the nurse will let you know when you can see her. She'll be monitored in the recovery room for a few more hours."

They hugged each other happily with teary eyes. John came in bringing sandwiches for late lunch as they waited for word from the nurse. Jim excused himself saying he had to take care of something by himself. By the time he came back, they were allowed to see Margaret briefly.

It was the next day before Margaret opened her eyes and looked around. She tried to take in the myriad of tubes and monitors around her. Then her eyes fell on Jim, sleeping in the recliner beside her. She tried to smile even though every muscle in her body seemed to be sore. *He's still here. What is he thinking? Did I really tell him about the baby or did I just dream it?*

Rising up quickly, he asked almost in a whisper, "Hey, how do you feel?"

"Like I bailed out of a burning plane and landed in a huge oak tree," she groaned.

His booming laugh was heard across the hall at the nurses' station, prompting a nurse to come and see what was going on.

"She's awake, and obviously telling jokes to make you laugh so hard," she grinned. "Let me in on it."

"It's a private joke," he chuckled.

As Margaret's condition progressed each day, they began to discuss what she had told Jim before she went into surgery. He approached it first when he felt she might be ready.

"Do you remember what you told me before you went to surgery?"

"Yes. How could I forget? But I wasn't even sure I had told you."

"Now do you feel like telling me more about my other daughter?"

"I'll try. I want you to know everything. I've kept this secret so long, I can't keep it anymore. After you left I felt terrible, of course, but I never even thought about being pregnant. Then Robert came home and took Peggy and the kids to Detroit, and I just kept thinking I felt so bad because of everyone's leaving, then Izzy, you remember Izzy who helped us so much, made an offhand remark about my acting like I was pregnant—and I knew. Suddenly I knew! I don't know why I hadn't thought of it before. I thought my life was over. I was sure I would lose my family, my children, and everything. I prayed that I would die. I felt I had nothing else to live for. I had lost you and now I would lose my children." She leaned her head back on the pillow unable to go on.

"Oh, Margaret, if I had only known! Why didn't you get in touch with me?"

"Of course I wasn't thinking straight, but what could you have done, Jim? I couldn't think of a thing that would make a difference if I told you.

"Thank God for Izzy! She prayed for me all night and convinced me God had given her an answer. She knew a preacher and his wife in Memphis where her sister lived that could not have any children and wanted them desperately, so she made arrangements for me and the kids to go there before anyone here could tell I was pregnant. I had the baby at their home, and they adopted our little girl. I signed all the papers their lawyer put before me and left her with them. They were so kind and loved her so. I have longed to see her again some day, but never knew how to contact her and wasn't sure if I should try."

"If I could have taken her, my mom would have loved to help me raise her."

"That never occurred to me, Jim. I couldn't see how to work out telling you without everyone else knowing."

"I feel so terrible that you had to go through that by yourself."

"I wasn't alone, Jim. The Reverend and his wife were wonderful to me and my children. Their church was such a spiritual and emotional help, and Izzy's sister took great care of the children and me as I recuperated. Izzy prayed for me constantly and convinced me God was answering her prayers by providing a good life for our baby and providing a baby for a couple that so wanted one."

"Maybe we can look for her together," he sighed, "but do we want our children and the world to know about this? What kind of Christian witness will we be if they know what we did? You were married. Your husband was fighting in the war! What will they think of us?"

"We don't have to tell anyone yet, Jim. I just had to tell you. I have been praying for God to show me the right time to tell you, and he just suddenly laid it on my heart that you had to know before I went into surgery. If something had happened to me, you would have never known. Our families will eventually understand that we were so alone and frightened. We gave in to temptation in our vulnerable condition. That can happen to anyone.

"I know I messed up, but I just didn't know what to do and I took the only door I saw open. It seemed like what God wanted me to do, but maybe it was just an easy way out for me. Izzy assured me that the baby wasn't mine, it was meant for the Reverend and his beautiful wife. I know I left our baby in good hands and feel sure she's had a good life."

"No, no...I am not saying that you messed up. You did do what God led you to do. Maybe I was the one who wasn't following his lead. I should have contacted you and checked on how you were doing. I left it all up to you. Why didn't I think of the possibility of your being pregnant? It's in the past now, but when you are stronger, we can decide what we might need to do to find her. Do you want to do that?"

"Yes, I've thought of doing that for years, but didn't know how, and couldn't deal with Carl's knowing who she was as long as he was alive."

"It will be our quest after you are well." He smiled and changed the subject.

"One thing that hit me as you were in surgery was how insensitive I have been. I should have taken care of this before now." He pulled a small box from his pocket and placed a beautiful diamond ring on her finger. "This was something I needed to do to help you know how serious I am about us no matter what happens, or has happened."

"I knew, Jim. You didn't have to do this, but it is wonderful."

Margaret's favorite nurse walked in just in time to be the first one to see the new sparkle on her finger. She smiled at her patient's happiness.

"It's beautiful," she hesitated, then went on. "I'm curious about how you two met."

They looked at each other and laughed, then gave her a brief version of their story. She was fascinated.

"My husband works for the Commercial Appeal newspaper here in Memphis. I think your story needs to be told. Could I get your permission to bring him in to interview you and do a feature story in the newspaper?"

What a surprise! They'd never dreamed of such a thing!

"We'll discuss it and let you know," Margaret answered.

They quickly decided it might be beneficial and encouraging to other interracial couples to hear their story, so they got permission from the doctor to make sure it wouldn't be too much for Margaret, and spent short sessions with Milton Underwood, the reporter.

Meanwhile, they planned their small wedding to take place in the hospital chapel. Milton had a photographer on hand for the happy occasion.

They experienced a few days in the spotlight when the article came out and the TV stations picked it up. A TV crew that came into the hospital interviewed them and they began receiving letters from other interracial couples. They answered them all, suggesting there should be some kind of support group started in the city. One young couple very interested in starting such a group came by the hospital and Jim gave them the names of all the couples that had contacted them as a basis for beginning.

"This may turn into a ministry for us, Jim. These couples are so desperate for support."

"Yes, it will be good to be a help to others in our situation."

But they were happiest when the doctor said Margaret could go home. Jim tucked her into his car, determined to take care of her as she had taken care of him so many years ago. They had so many things to do together.

---

This article that appeared in the Commercial Appeal in Memphis made Margaret and Jim celebrities for a while.

## REUNITED AFTER FORTY YEARS

Memphis, TN – The chapel at Baptist Hospital is rarely the scene of a happy occasion. It's often filled with grieving family members praying for the health of a very ill loved one or sobbing quietly over the death of someone close to them.

Yesterday was quite different. The chapel was filled with beautiful flowers and family and friends of James Hayes and Margaret Corwin as they became husband and wife soon after Margaret's emergency heart surgery.

The fact that the ceremony was held in a hospital chapel was just the beginning of the unusual circumstances leading up to this marriage.

Jim and Margaret met in 1944 as WWII was raging in Europe and Japan. Jim was stationed in Alabama as a member of the Tuskegee Airmen when he was sent to Dyersburg Army Air Base to learn a new technique to take back to his unit. His plane collided with another one in a fiery crash and he bailed out, landing in a large oak tree in Margaret Corwin's pasture. Margaret lived there with her three children, her sister, and her sister's small child while both their husbands were in the Navy.

Jim was seriously injured, but at that time the Veteran's Hospital wouldn't take black soldiers. Margaret took him into her home and took care of him.

"I was appalled that a person fighting for our country would be rejected at the veteran's hospitals because of their race. I was brought up to honor all people regardless of their race," she told this reporter from her hospital room.

*238*

Jim was in her care for several months and the two forged a bond that lasted through both their lives. They never saw each other again until recently when Jim read that Margaret had lost her husband to cancer. He had also lost his wife to the same disease, so he traveled from his home in Michigan hoping to reunite with Margaret. He happily found that she had never forgotten him either.

They will now start their life together, eventually moving to Michigan to be closer to Jim's two daughters and one of Margaret's daughters. They were making plans to be married when Margaret was stricken with a heart attack.

"I have the opportunity to take care of Margaret now as she was so willing to do for me forty years ago," Jim says.

# GETTING BETTER

## 1984

Jim's daughters stayed long enough to see Margaret when she was able to meet them. They told her how much they were looking forward to her move to Michigan when she had recuperated.

"Thank you so much for coming. I know it meant a lot to your dad. He needed some family around him and he has missed you so much."

"We've missed him too, but we know this is where he belongs right now," Alice replied.

Jim took Margaret to her own home and tucked her into her own bed to recuperate. She was weak from the surgery and had to be very careful not to overwork her heart until the new valve was healed.

His loving care soon had her on her feet and walking around her yard on his arm, enjoying their new life together. Not only was her heart healing, but a place on her leg where they took cartilage to repair the valve had to be closely watched. Plans to move to Michigan were postponed until they could be sure she was able to make the trip.

Meanwhile, they worked on a plan to look for their daughter. Margaret tried hard to piece together where she was and whom she had met that they might contact. When they drove to Memphis for Margaret's monthly checkup, they went by the neighborhood where she had stayed with Louis and Ella May and Liza. It was gone, torn down and replaced with a strip mall.

"I'm sure this is the area," Margaret sighed, "but everything is gone. There were rows and rows of tiny homes, a whole black neighborhood. They are all gone. The church is gone too. Louis and Ella May would be in their eighties if they are still alive. Where do we go from here?"

"Don't worry about it. We'll think of our next step soon. Remember you have to take care of your health first."

She smiled and settled into the seat for the two-hour drive back to Dyersburg, but her mind strained to remember something else that would give them a clue to follow.

Suddenly, she sat up straight. "I wonder if we could find any of Izzy's family? I can't remember her last name right now, but if I think hard, I probably will think of it sooner or later."

Jim patted her hand. "It'll probably come to you when you aren't even trying to think about it. Just rest now."

She leaned back. "I'm always thinking about it."

The doctor had said that Margaret was doing remarkably well and could begin to do more around the house as she felt like it, and a walk each day would strengthen her heart and her breathing now that her leg was healing. She was delighted to be able to help Jim out and looked forward to their daily walks up the road and back.

"Would you like to go to church with me Sunday?" he asked as they prepared their lunch one afternoon. "I think you'll like the service and you know Reverend Brown is a wonderful man of God. You'll like his wife Mirna too."

Solomon Brown was a little younger than Jim and a true man of God. He had worked his way through seminary, and came back to Dyersburg, his hometown, to marry Mirna, his childhood sweetheart. They had raised three children—two sons who moved to Detroit to work and a daughter who still lived near them with her husband and little boy.

Solomon had come to visit Margaret and Jim several times when she was in the hospital in Memphis, but hadn't been to their home. Knowing Margaret's son-in-law John for many years, he didn't want to cause more problems for his family or for Jim and Margaret, but he kept them on his prayer list.

"Yes, I think it's about time I got back into church. That would be great, Jim. We need to have Solomon and Mirna over for lunch or dinner sometime now that I'm able to help with the cooking. We need to return the favor for all those delicious dishes Mirna sends home with you each Sunday."

"That's true!" Jim laughed.

Margaret had never received a more warm welcome in a church. Handshakes, smiles, and hugs abounded as she came in the door and walked down the aisle on Jim's arm to his usual seat near the front. The singing was joyous and sent up as a sincere praise to God. Prayers brought a sense of God's presence that filled the sanctuary. Solomon's sermon seemed to be sent directly from God to her.

"My text for today is found in Romans 8:28," he began. "You can open your Bibles to that passage which has so often spoke to me and I hope will speak to you today."

Jim turned to it in his much-worn King James, holding it where they both could read along as Solomon read. "And we know that all things work together for good to them that love God, to them who are called according to his purpose."

"Now we all have things happen in our lives that we think could not possibly be God's will. They are seemingly bad, evil events that cause us to ask why God is allowing this to happen to us. We've been good. We don't deserve it. That's how we think. Now admit it. We all do." There was laughter and lots of "amens".

"Now, I've heard this scripture used time and time again and quoted like this, 'We know that things work together for good to those who love God.' But so many times we leave out the main word. The main word is that little word *all*. God is telling us here that *all* things work *together* for good to those of us who love him. You know sometimes God and Satan want the same thing but for different reasons. For example, the Crucifixion of Christ. Satan wanted to get rid of the Son of God, Satan wanted the people to think that he was just a man blaspheming God, but God wanted to save the world through this horrific event, and God wins. God wins every time. Satan had tried and tried time and again, but he can't defeat our God."

Amen, and Praise the Lord, echoed through the sanctuary.

"All of us have gone through hard times in our lives. We need to ask ourselves, 'Where is this leading? What good does God want to come from this?' If you love God and are called according to his purpose, he will work *all* the things that happen to you *together* for good. Now it may not even be 'good' for us personally, and we may not even be privileged to know what good came out of it. Christ's death wasn't 'good' for him personally. He left his home in glory for that suffering, but it worked for good to all those who trust in him."

At the door after the service ended, both Jim and Margaret shook Solomon's hand and thanked him sincerely for those words that they so needed to hear. On the way home, Margaret commented on the sermon.

"We need to let go of our guilt, Jim. God had a purpose for our daughter being born, even under those bad circumstances and when we find her we will know what that purpose was. God has forgiven us. We need to forgive ourselves."

"You're right, Margaret. I think God gave that text to Solomon for us this week. It will be easier for us to go on from here." They both felt a renewed love for Christ and each other.

"I'm feeling good, Jim. Let's go out to eat and then drive out by the Mississippi bottom where Izzy's family used to live. We could at least find out if there's anyone still living around there."

"Okay, we'll eat at Boyd's where we first got together again, but let's decide about the ride out to the river after we eat and see how you feel."

Margaret actually felt better after she ate, so Jim followed her directions and headed out to where the little shacks, on stilts because of flooding, used to stand. There were a few remnants of stilts and fallen down houses, but no one lived in the area anymore.

"We seem to hit a wall wherever we go," she sighed.

"Right now, we can't do a lot until you are better, Margaret. There are a lot of other things we can do when you are well. When we really get into this in earnest we will have to let others know what we are doing. We aren't ready for that yet. Just hang on, honey."

He patted her hand and she laid her head back on the seat, beginning to feel tired and frustrated. Would they ever find their daughter? She could be anywhere by now.

# YOUNG MARION

## MEMPHIS, 1946

"Look! Look, Louis!" Ella May dragged him into the living room where one-year-old Marion stood banging her toy on the coffee table. "Just stand right there and watch." She knelt down a few feet away from the baby. "Come on, Marion. Come to Mama." The baby laughed and took a few teetering steps toward Ella May, plopping down on her bottom, then crawling the rest of the way.

Ella May grabbed her up in her arms, hugging her tight. "She can walk, Daddy. She can walk!" The two parents laughed with delight.

Louis patted his little girl's soft hair and planted a kiss on her forehead. "Good job, Marion. You're gettin' to be a big girl."

They never ceased to thank God for this beautiful baby and could hardly believe she was theirs even after a year of caring for her. Each milestone in her development was a miracle for them. In their early forties, they had waited and prayed for so long for a child.

Ella May ignored the stares she often got when she was out with the baby. With Marion's fine hair, light brown with relaxed curls, and her light olive skin, she was definitely a white child, despite her black father.

They walked into the kitchen and Ella May placed Marion in her high chair as Billy washed up at the sink and sat down to dinner.

"Did you go shopping today?"

"Yes. We walked down to the store for a few groceries. Another lady stopped me and asked if Marion was my baby or if I was babysitting her."

"What did you say?"

"I just said 'she's mine' of course and went on by. Wasn't any of her business!" The two of them had a good laugh over that reply. It happened often. They wondered how it would eventually affect Marion's life as she grew older, but they wouldn't let themselves worry about it.

## 1952

As she approached school age, Marion became more outgoing and longed to be more social, but she Wasn't very successful at making friends. Not only was she outspoken and bossy, but she looked so different from most of the other children that she was teased a lot, always getting her feelings hurt. Her parents grieved over that, but tried to make up for it by being more attentive to her at home. Louis often told her it was because she was so special.

Ella May was surprised one day after school when eight-year-old Marion came running through the front door pulling a small boy along with her.

"Mama, Mama, meet my new friend, William. He just moved in that house down the street. We played tag and he let me win."

Ella May dried her hands on a dishtowel and looked at the two kids. Marion was flushed and excited. William, a head taller than Marion with dark skin and hair, was quiet and calm, looking into Ella May's eyes through thick glasses. She had to laugh at the contrast.

"Hi, William." She thrust out her hand and felt his strong handshake. "Tell your mama I will be over tomorrow with a blackberry pie for you all to welcome you to the neighborhood. Do you like blackberry pie?"

"Yes'm."

"What time will your daddy be home from work? My husband would probably like to visit with him."

"He don't live with us. He run off."

"Oh, I'm sorry, William. I'll come by tomorrow to see your mama. Is she at home during the day?"

"No, ma'm. She work at the school cooking lunch."

"Well, I'll try to catch her when she's not working. You two want some cookies?"

She watched the two children eat their snack and play games at the same time. William seemed enthralled with Marion. Ella May was so happy to see them having fun together.

Trudy Barnes, William's mother, was a small, hard-working woman who was determined to make a better life for her children. Her husband had walked out on his family after their daughter Jona was born. Trudy had not seen the man since William and his sister were very small. Trudy had gone to work for a white lady, leaving the children with her mother most of the time. Her little girl had been born with a heart defect and was frail, needing a lot of care. So when Trudy heard about the job at the school from a friend who lived in Memphis, she applied for it. She knew it would give her more time with her kids.

## 1964

William's mother rode with Louis and Ella May to Marion and William's high school graduation. She had become a good friend of the family, and Louis had taken the place of William's father on many occasions. Ella May gladly helped out with William and Jona after school until Trudy came home from work. Ella

May became alarmed one day when Marion came into the house leading Jona. "She's sick, Mama. She needs to lay down."

The little girl collapsed in Ella May's arms as she picked her up and ran for the phone. An ambulance came quickly but it was too late for Jona. Her heart had just given out.

Louis and Ella May tried to be a comfort to Trudy, praying with her and helping her with arrangements. The church was filled with mourners as Louis delivered the funeral sermon.

"All of us know what a bright bit of sunshine this little girl brought to all who knew her. God put her here for a little while to brighten our days, and especially to fill Trudy's heart with love. Now she is at home with him," he concluded.

Ella May had shared with Trudy how God had provided for them to adopt Marion. For a while, Izzy kept them up on how Margaret and her other children were doing, but after Izzy died, the secret died with her. She never told anyone else about the forbidden romance between Jim and Margaret.

The three of them clapped with pride as their two children got the top two academic awards for their four years of high school. William, having been behind when he first started in grade school, under Louis's coaching, had come to be at the top of the class almost every year, with Marion sometimes beating him by a few points. However, it was William who came out on top at graduation. No one was prouder than Marion about that. Their close friendship had budded into a deep love for each other and they had made plans to spend their lives together.

They were both registered and ready to attend LeMoyne-Owen College with scholarships, excited to be able to dig into the subjects they were passionate about. The fight for civil rights was gaining momentum and the two of them were ready to take up the cause, hoping to become lawyers.

## MARCH 1968

Marion stood across the street and gazed up at the beautiful façade of Clayborn Temple, its golden stone surface gleaming toward the sky in the bright sunlight. Men of all ages streamed from the doorway and down the steps to the sidewalk, each carrying a sign that proclaimed their desperate message: I AM. A MAN. They were braced for the march to Memphis City Hall in support of the sanitation workers' strike. She and her fellow students at LeMoyne–Owen College had spent many hours inside the beautiful church making those signs and attaching them to sticks that could be held high with the urgent proclamation. Her father had cautioned her not to come here. "It could be dangerous, Marion. You've done your part to help by making signs. Now wait for me at home with your Mama."

But she couldn't stay away. Dr. Martin Luther King was there. If she could only get a glimpse of him, it would be a blessing, a confirmation that the prayers she had sent up daily for him and all of those involved in the strike had not been in vain. William stood beside her. He had been protecting her since they were in third grade when the other children made fun of her. She was different—almost white, more white than black, many accused, but no person of color had ever defended civil rights for blacks more than Marion. The two of them stood close together in the crowd craning their necks for a glimpse of their idol waiting for him to address the crowd.

There he was, just stepping out the door! Marion and William looked at each other with an excited smile. She could hear the great preacher's commanding voice but couldn't understand the words of assurance he was speaking. Then he locked arms with the other ministers, her father doing the same in the row behind Dr. King, and they watched the huge parade head toward city hall. Several blocks down, she could see the barrage of policemen with nightsticks, tear gas, and guns at the ready. With a prayer on her heart for her dad, Dr. King, and all the marchers, Marion gripped William's hand. They were skipping their college classes today. This was too important to miss.

William wasn't comfortable going against Marion's father, but he knew he had to stay with her, to never leave her without protection. He had a sinking feeling this could get ugly, and he feared for Reverend Louis, Dr. King, and all the men who were daring to take on this injustice. It had been less than two weeks since Louis had participated when the local ministers led a group of high school students that ended in two of them being arrested. William hoped Dr. King's presence would be a calming influence. As the end of the line neared them, Marion grabbed William's hand and pulled him into the crowd of marchers.

"Marion, your dad will not like this," he chided, but picked up on the excitement and grabbed a sign that lay on the ground, holding it high as they marched along.

"This is a peaceful, nonviolent march," Marion answered and laughed with excitement. It was going fine until they began to hear shouting and glass breaking somewhere ahead of them. "What's going on?"

Marion stood on tiptoe to try to see, but William didn't have to stand on tiptoe. The peaceful march was now a near riot. Nightsticks were being wielded, gunfire popped, and the smell of mace permeated the air even as far back as they were. He had to get Marion out of there. Grabbing her arm, he pulled her toward a parking lot behind a large apartment building. They hid behind a tall hedge, shaking from the chaos they were hearing.

"Stay here," William told her. "I'm going to look down the street to see if it is safe for us to run home."

She crouched on the ground, watching him slip out of sight around the building. As she watched, two policemen ran past her with guns drawn, chasing a young black man. She screamed in horror as she watched the boy open an apartment door, shots rang out, and he lay lifeless on the steps. Before she knew what she was doing, she ran toward him screaming, "No! No!"

One of the policemen grabbed her and warned, "You had better go home as fast as you can, young lady. You should not be here."

She ran toward the street yelling for William, but he was nowhere to be seen. Panicking, she ran to the nearby church where her father had been pastor for twenty years. Sinking into a pew, she began to pray. "Dear Lord, help us. Keep my father and William safe. Keep Dr. King safe." She couldn't get out of her mind the sight of the young man she had watched being shot. She lay her head on the back of the pew ahead of her, sobbing and praying until she felt a gentle hand on her shoulder and looked up into the tearful face of her mother.

Ella May sat down beside her daughter and listened to her account of the horrible things she saw. She hated to bring this up to Marion, but she was sure that policeman thought she was white or he wouldn't have let her go. "It's bad, Marion, but I fear it's going to get worse. We have to brace ourselves for whatever comes. We are on the edge of changing things for our people and it won't come easy, but it must come. God has given us a leader in Dr. King to free us from oppression, like he gave Moses for the Israelites." She hugged her daughter close.

"What do you think is happening to Daddy and William? They could be jailed or hurt, or even killed, Mama."

"I know, honey. Your dad and I have talked about this and thought about it long and hard. We agreed that he had to do what he could and we would pray that nothing bad happened to him, but we know it is more likely than not. Let's go home and wait for news, okay?"

The two women sat in their living room, listening to the radio, trying to take in the news about the march that had gone so wrong. Hundreds had been arrested and many injured. At midnight, a knock on the door sent a feeling of dread through both of them. Ella May opened the door to find Trudy standing there.

"William hasn't come home. I thought he might be here. I've been listening to all that is going on. I'm afraid."

Ella May hugged her friend. "Come in, Trudy. Join Marion and me. We are as worried as you are. We can worry and pray together."

She poured coffee while Marion told the story of how she and William had lost each other in the crowd and of her witnessing the shooting of a young man. The three women talked, walked the floor, and prayed the rest of the night.

Early in the morning, they heard the front door open and Louis walked in. Marion ran to the door as she heard her father finally enter. Embracing him, she began to thank God that he was home. He gave them what news he had been able to find out. Things had gone terribly bad, with many injured and arrested and a sixteen-year-old boy dead. Louis had been visiting and praying with as many of the injured as he could.

"Dad, Dad, I'm so glad you're safe. What happened? How did this go so wrong? It was a peaceful march. Dad, I saw them kill that boy. I was there hiding in a bush. They just shot him when he was running away. Did you see William anywhere? He was with me but we got separated"

"No, I didn't see him. You two were not supposed to be there, Marion."

"I know, Dad. I'm sorry. I just wanted to see Dr. King. Now I've lost William. How can we find him?"

"Please, Louis, tell me where to look to find my son!" Trudy cried.

Louis hugged his daughter and his wife; then shaking his head, he collapsed on the couch.

"I'll find him," he assured Trudy and his daughter. "If he's not here by morning, I'll go down to the jail and look for him.

"I think it all went wrong when some of the young boys just couldn't hold their rage. They might have been sent by some of the more militant black groups that go counter to Dr. King's efforts. They started breaking windows and looting. That wasn't what he wanted, so we're going to try again tomorrow even though Dr. King can't be with us. It's got to be peaceful like Dr. King says."

Ella May brought her husband a cup of coffee and a sandwich, loosening his tie and pulling off his shoes, rubbing his tired feet.

Marion walked the floor silently praying for William's safety. As dawn began to break, they heard another knock at the door. Marion hurried to open it and there stood William with blood streaming down his face. Trudy jumped up from the couch where she had been sitting with her head in her hands. Everyone rushed to bring him into the house and attend the wound on his forehead.

"As I stepped out into the crowd, I felt something hit me and I guess I blacked out. When I came to, lying on the sidewalk, I crawled into some bushes and I must have blacked out again. When I woke up the street seemed empty so I just stumbled on over to my house. Mama wasn't there so I figured she would be here. I don't know what hit me."

"I came here looking for you, son," Trudy told him. "I didn't know what else to do when you didn't come home."

They were all so glad to be safe and together, knowing this wouldn't be the last of their struggle and that it would probably get worse before it got better for them.

The march of three hundred sanitation workers and ministers the next day was peaceful and silent, escorted by armored personnel carriers, military trucks, and national guardsmen. News that Dr. King had postponed his trip to Africa to return to Memphis in support of the sanitation workers further encouraged the men who were laying their lives on the line for their rights and dignity.

Only a week later, Dr. King lay dying on the balcony of the Lorraine Hotel in Memphis, shot by an assassin.

Marion stayed glued to the TV. There was rioting in more than 130 cities in America as a protest of the senseless death of this nonviolent leader. Marion had cried until no tears were left. Now she was angry. Dr. King would not want violence to mark his death, but within a week the Open Housing Act he had fought for was passed by Congress. His life was not in vain. Dr. King's work would go on and their cause would prevail. Marion resolved at that moment that she would dedicate the rest of her life to doing her part to see that his dream would come true.

"Dad, William and I have decided to study law. I want to be a lawyer and help our people in this struggle for civil rights."

Her parents looked at each other. "That won't be easy, Marion," her father spoke slowly, trying to sound reasonable. "There aren't many women lawyers."

"I know, Dad, but I also want to run for some kind of government office. That's where I can help the most."

"What does William say about that?" Ella May asked her daughter. It was expected that they would marry soon, since they would be finished with college in May.

"He thinks it is a great idea, Mom. He will support me all the way. We've been working a lot at school on trying to help carry on Dr. King's work."

Louis and Ella May had to smile at her words. They knew their daughter well enough to know that when she set her mind to something she was determined to accomplish it, but worry also lined their faces. They were glad she would have William to support her.

# MARION AND WILLIAM

## 1969–1970

Marion stared at her image in the mirror as her best friend Susan adjusted her veil and her mom looked on from a seat behind her. Suddenly it hit her—the dark, smooth face of Ella May, black, curly hair that she had spent hours trying to tame were so different from Marion's. Her mother looked so lovely in the beautiful pale blue hat that matched the sheath dress and long jacket she had chosen for the wedding.

Looking back at her own light olive face, long, almost reddish-brown hair, laying in soft relaxed curls on her shoulders, and her small facial features, she wondered for the first time, *Who am I? Where did I come from?* She knew she was adopted but had never thought it mattered. There could be no better parents than Louis and Ella May. *Why is this bothering me now? Well, it's not bothering me, I am just curious. Getting married makes a person reflective.*

"Are you ready?" Susan squeezed her elbow, bringing her back to the matter at hand—her wedding, her marriage to her best friend, William, who had supported and encouraged and loved her for as long as she could remember.

"Yes!" she smiled at Susan and turned to plant a kiss on her mother's cool cheek. Ella May stood and hugged her beloved daughter, wiping the tears quickly to try and save her makeup. They moved out into the foyer of the church.

In the foyer, Louis stood with admiring eyes fixed on this cloud of loveliness as she walked toward him and took his arm for their trip down the aisle. His mind went back to 1945, the day he picked up a forlorn young white woman and her three children who carried the most precious gift he and Ella May had ever been given. He closed his eyes and said a silent prayer to God for that young woman, wishing she could see her gift now.

At the altar, he placed Marion's soft hand into that of young William Barnes, knowing that she would be as cherished with William as she had been with him and Ella May. William had become a son to them at a very young age. These were truly their two children. After walking Marion down the aisle, he turned and became the minister who joined Marion to her fiancé in marriage.

Both William and Marion had been accepted to the University of Michigan Law School. Louis had looked for a church he could pastor near the school so they could all move to Michigan together. He had been accepted to pastor a church in Ann Arbor, so all four of them would be moving there as soon as the young couple returned from their honeymoon. Louis and Ella May had visited the church there a couple of times and the lovely parsonage was big enough for all four of them to live comfortably while Marion and William were in school. It was another blessing from God that they were all so thankful for.

---

William looked at the lovely bride he had so longed to have for his wife. She was not only beautiful, but also smart and compassionate, and so anxious to help eradicate prejudices against their race. Passion for civil rights permeated her very being and he was determined to help her move toward her goal of getting into a position to be of utmost help in that endeavor.

His own father had left his mother with two small children and he watched her work hard for white families to keep food on the table for the three of them. They had lost his sister, and his mother still worked hard to keep the family going to make sure he didn't have to do what she had to do for a living. Marion's father had been a father to him too, for as long as he could remember. Coaching him on the church baseball team and helping him with problems as he went through his teen years, keeping him on track with his education and spiritual growth. It had made all the difference in his life, and now he was a real part of the family he so loved, and they would soon be in Michigan together on the next step toward their goals,

He would miss Mama, but hopefully he could bring her to Michigan in a few years. If things went well with law school, he and Marion could afford to take care of her too.

The newlyweds were sitting in lounge chairs around the pool of the hotel in New Orleans where they were honeymooning. He wondered what she was thinking. The book she had been reading lay idly in her lap; her eyes were closed but he could tell she wasn't asleep.

He touched her arm. She smiled up at him. "You seem to be deep in thought," he remarked.

She didn't answer immediately, then asked a strange question. "William, do you ever wonder who I am?"

He laughed. "I think I know you pretty well. We didn't just meet, you know. We have a long history together."

"I don't mean that. You know I'm adopted. I have a whole other family out there somewhere. I just wonder about them."

"Well, that's natural. Maybe someday we can find them. Have you asked your Mom and Dad about them? Maybe they could shed some light on all that. They may just be waiting for your interest, your questions."

"I haven't asked. That's true. I guess I thought it might hurt them. But I also know that my birth mother is white. She might want nothing to do with me, you know. "

"Maybe your parents would know that, Marion. They are very understanding people and would want you to ask rather than worry about it."

"You're right. I think I'll do that when an appropriate time arises."

While the two young people were on their honeymoon, Louis and Ella May moved to Michigan and set up their new home to welcome the newlyweds. William and Marion went back to Memphis, gathered their personal belongings, said goodbye to friends and William's family, and then headed to Michigan. They had both thrived in college life in Memphis and were looking forward to law school, knowing the challenge would be greater than they had ever experienced but excited to take it on.

Michigan was a different world for the four Tennessee natives. More freedom was available to them to travel where they wanted to go, eat where they wanted to eat, and attend activities they wanted to take in. Having lived under Jim Crow laws of the South made it so joyful for them to live with more freedom. They quickly made friends in the middle-class neighborhood. The church welcomed them with exuberance and love.

It soon became obvious that William and Marion needed to be closer to the law school. The long hours they put in and with such different schedules, they needed to be within walking distance of their home.

"Dad, we can get a student apartment for a really good price and we'll be right on campus. It's pretty basic, but I think that would be best for all of us, don't you?"

"Well, it probably would work better for you and William, but we sure would miss you. Will we ever see you?" he teased. "Let's go run that by your Mama."

Ella May hid her disappointment and just came up with one condition. "Every Sunday we all have dinner right here around this table," she tapped her fingers on her dining table.

Marion gave her a quick kiss on the cheek. "That's a deal. One of the worst things will be missing your good cooking." She waved goodbye, and was off to her next class. William had left early for his first one. Louis had gotten up to drive him so Marion could get in another hour of sleep since she had worked into the night on a mock case that she would participate in today.

Ella May and Louis hadn't realized how lonely it would be when the kids moved out, but told themselves it was something they needed to get used to.

"We knew they were not going to be with us forever," Louis commented. "It will be good for them to start on their own."

The first Sunday dinner was exciting for them all. Marion and William had a very busy week at school, but it was much easier for them to live so close and come and go easily when they needed to. It was giving them more time together too.

After dinner, they were relaxing in the living room when Marion decided to approach the subject she had been wondering about for a long time.

"Mom, Dad, I've been wondering about my adoption. Would you be willing to give me some information about that? I guess getting married and all the things I'm learning in law school have made me more curious."

Louis took a deep breath, and Ella May remained quiet. "Well, as we told you, your birth mother was a white woman who had an affair with a black man. She came to live with us until you were born, and gave you up to us for adoption. What other things do you want to know? We'll tell you what we can." Louis offered.

"How did you find out about her or did she find out about you first?"

"The sister of one of our church members was working for her family, and she knew how we had prayed for a baby for so many years, so she told this lady about us and we made the arrangements."

"You got to know her for three months. What was she like?"

"We came to love her and her three little ones very much, Marion. She was a wonderful person, and told us she was very much in love with your birth father, but, of course, especially at that time, she was afraid it would endanger his life if anyone knew about them. He was a soldier and had to leave the area. He never knew about you."

"He never knew about me? I wonder if he ever found out. You said she had three other children. Did she have a husband? Was she divorced? Was he still alive?"

"He was on a ship in the Navy. I don't know what happened to her marriage when or if he returned from the war. I don't know if he ever knew about you either. She was a Christian and very penitent about allowing herself to be unfaithful to her husband. I don't know if she ever could forgive herself. I tried to tell her that God forgave people in the Bible who committed much worse sins, like Paul who persecuted Christians and David who committed murder to cover his adultery, but I'm not sure she could accept that for herself."

"Did you know her name or where she lived?"

"We knew her name. It is on the adoption papers, but we didn't know where she was living or how she came to know your birth father. I picked her up at the bus station and took her back there when she went back home. We didn't think it was wise to try to contact her after she left and she never tried to contact us."

"Did she give me up because I was black?"

The bitterness in her voice saddened Ella May. Louis thought for a while before answering.

"It made no difference to her that you had a black father. I know that. She was caught between keeping you and losing all her other children and the rest of her family too, or giving you to a family like us who would love and cherish you and raise you in a good home. She had no way of making a life for you by herself. I think she wanted to do what was best for all her children, including you."

Ella May finally added what she was thinking. "She anguished at handing you to me after you were born. She spent a long time just talking to you and calling you her angel. When she laid you in my arms, I told her we would give you 'Angel' as your middle name and that someday I would tell you that."

Marion got up from her chair and went to her mother, crawling into her lap like a little child. Ella May cradled her as she had done when she was a baby. "Thank you, Mama. I just wonder sometimes who I am."

Louis went to her and stroked her hair. "You are our precious daughter. No one could love you more."

"I know, Daddy. That is not even in question. I just think about where I came from sometimes."

He squeezed her hand. "That is only natural, and I'm glad you asked about it instead of just wondering."

After the young couple left, Louis put his arm around his wife. "Are you okay? Did I say the right things?"

"Of course you did. I kept waiting but she never said she wanted to find her birth parents. I wouldn't know how to help her and I'm so afraid of how she might be accepted if she did find them. A rejection could be very hard on her."

"We'll just pray for wisdom as to how to handle it if she mentions that."

# LIFE CHANGES

## 1973–1975

"There were five law firms at school interviewing the graduates yesterday," Marion told her mom and dad as they ate their usual Sunday dinner. "I think William has decided on one that he would like to take a job with, haven't you, William?"

"Well, I'm looking closely at Goodman and Mantz. The partners are Christians and they try to do some pro bono work for people who need a lawyer but can't afford one. That's what I would like to do, you know."

"That's great, William. We will pray about your decision. What about you, Marion? Anything interesting?" Louis asked.

"Not really. I guess I just haven't found the right niche for me. Goodman and Mantz would take us both, but we've discussed it, and we would like to go with different firms. As you said, we're praying that we'll find the right thing so I know we will."

She did find the right thing. The city of Ann Arbor was looking for someone to work in the attorney's office. She felt it would be a good way to get her feet wet in politics. It wasn't the kind of money one makes with a law firm, but a step toward what she really dreamt of doing, and she soon found that she loved it.

"It is so interesting, Mom. Even when I'm looking for information on cases that set precedence, I find myself in the middle of local politics. I'm going to work on Paul Rogers's campaign. He's such a good man working for equality in all areas and wants me to help bring out the black vote for his state senate run."

Marion was a tireless campaigner, going door-to-door and organizing other aspects of the campaign, talking passionately to people—her genuine personality drew people to the candidate. She even got her father in on helping out. He had retired from the ministry, and he and Ella May moved into a little apartment after they helped William and Marion buy their first house, hoping they would fill it with grandchildren soon. But Marion seemed bent on another path at this point.

William and Marion joined a Community Bible study in their new neighborhood that met in the home of Jim and Juanita Hayes. They were impressed with the couple's two beautiful daughters that attended the university while still living at home. Sharon, their oldest, was very interested in Marion's work and they talked often about the need for more minorities in the government. The Hayes's had an obvious love for the Lord, and had invited anyone in the neighborhood to study and pray with them. Several churches were represented in the group, all united in praying for their families, their children, their churches and their nation. Not only was it a place to gain spiritual strength, but became a forum for bringing people into the campaign.

Marion was busy, but not too busy to notice that her father was not looking well. After dinner one Sunday, she approached her mother about her concern as they cleaned up the kitchen together.

"Mama, is Daddy feeling okay? He doesn't look well lately."

"I've noticed that too. He's lost his appetite and is losing weight. I'm trying to get him to see a doctor, but you know him. He keeps putting it off."

"Well, maybe I'll nag him about it a little bit." She laughed.

"Come on," Ella May decided. "Let's gang up on him."

The two women were able to convince Billy he needed to find out what was wrong with his health, and the appointment was made for two weeks from Monday. With her job and the campaign, and trying to spend time with William at home, Marion almost forgot about her dad's appointment until her mother called early one morning before she and William left for work.

"Mom, is something wrong? It's so early!"

"Your dad went for his doctor's appointment yesterday, you know."

"Oh, yes, I had forgotten that was yesterday. What did he find out?'

"Well, he has to go in for exploratory surgery Thursday. Marion, he may have cancer." She could hear her mother's voice tremble.

The shock on her face made William come to her side asking, "What's wrong?" She couldn't answer.

"We don't know for sure yet, but the doctor wasn't very positive. Oh, Marion, please pray for him."

"Of course I will. William and I will be over tonight to pray with the two of you, and I'll call our prayer group. Oh, Mom, I'm so scared."

"Me too, honey. We'll see you tonight."

The diagnosis was the worst—colon cancer. A tumor was removed with the hope that it hadn't spread to other organs in his body. Slowly, he recovered from the surgery and seemed to be getting stronger. He was able to get back to helping Marion with her work on the campaign, folding and mailing.

It was at Christmas, when William's mother came to visit, that his decline once again seemed so obvious.

"Is your father okay, Marion? He is a shell of his former self. I hadn't seen him in so long it was a shock to see how he'd changed," Trudy confided in her daughter-in-law.

"He was doing better, but I think he's going down again. The chemotherapy took its toll on him. He got over that and bounced back, but lately he has been losing weight again. He promised to see the doctor after the holidays.

Marion could see the sadness in her mother's eyes as she watched Louis open his gifts barely able to untie the ribbons. His strength was slipping away. At home later, she cried on William's shoulder. "I'm afraid he won't get better this time," she cried. "Oh, William, what will we do without him?"

"I don't know, honey. He's as much a father to me as he is to you. Don't jump to conclusions until he's seen the doctor. Let's wait and see."

The news was devastating. The cancer had spread to his liver and kidneys. Ella May took him home and could only try to make him comfortable and watch as he turned into a thin-skinned skeleton. He tried to eat a little, but never enough to gain any strength. May 1975, just a few days before his 75th birthday, they stood around his bed and watched as he breathed his last.

At the funeral, Jim and Juanita Hayes paid their respects, handing Marion a book of Psalms with a sympathetic inscription. "God knows and feels our every heartache. You are in our prayers. Jim and Juanita Hayes"

Ella May and Marion were totally lost. They had always relied on Louis. They never had even thought about being without him. William tried to step in as best he could. He had learned a lot from Louis. But the loss would be forever with them all.

William and Marion insisted that Ella May move in with them. They could not bear to have her living alone. She had never lived alone, and Marion needed her nearby. Soon after Louis's death, she had discovered she was pregnant. She and William had been married over five years. They were excited that finally they would have a family, but lamented that Louis wouldn't see his grandchild. Marion hoped and prayed that everything would be fine with her pregnancy, but she didn't slow down her workload.

Ella May took over the housework and cooking so that when Marion was at home she could relax. At three months, she had to be hospitalized and then on bed rest at home for several weeks. William and Ella May fretted and worried about her and the baby, but she soon stabilized and was up and about again. Their next surprise came when the doctor announced that he heard two heartbeats—twins. Everyone insisted that she do her work in the office now and not run around the city campaigning. Paul Rogers won his senate seat and attributed a big part of his success to Marion's hard work.

"This young woman needs to run for office," he announced. "She has everything it takes to represent the people. If you ever see her name on the ballot, vote for her. She'll do you right." He brought Marion up on the stage and everyone clapped wildly.

Problems arose again as time neared for the babies to be born. Marion spent the last month in the hospital, trying to hold on to full term, but the two tiny boys were born three weeks early. Tiny Louis and William spent two weeks in an incubator, but turned out to be healthy as soon as their lungs caught up to their original birth date. Marion, Ella May, and William had their hands full at home, but considered it a joy, so happy to have the two little ones to love and cherish and help them get over the loss of their grandfather.

"I think he's looking down proudly at them," Ella May whispered as she and Marion laid the two babies in their cradles. Mother and daughter smiled at each other over that thought.

# RUNNING FOR OFFICE

## 1990

William and Louis Barnes were twins but hardly even looked like brothers. Willy, as the family decided to call him, had his mother's light skin and hair and if he had seen a picture of his great grandfather Samuel Lane, he would have known what he would look like when he grew older. Of course he knew nothing of the great grandfather from whom he got his looks and his wonderful sense of humor. Louis was a replica of his father—a head taller than his brother, dark eyes and hair, thin and studious.

The boys were their mother and father's delight. Louis's favorite thing to do was to help out in his father's law office. Filing, running errands, doing research—anything that was needed by his father or any of the other law partners was what he loved to do. He had already made it known that he would follow in his father's footsteps.

Willy was a football player. Stocky and strong, but very fast, he was already a star running back as a sophomore on the high school team. Friday nights found the whole family in the stadium cheering him on. Even Ella May, at eighty-five, didn't miss very many games in which her grandson played.

Friendly and outgoing, Willy loved helping Marion in her campaign for the state senate. Paul Rogers was retiring and strongly supported Marion to take his seat. The campaign, while not yet in full swing, was gearing up for a tough political fight. The governor was supporting her opponent and it was well known that he didn't want to deal with a black woman in the senate.

Marion had moved from working in the local attorney's office to working with the state attorney general. She became a favorite of many in the state, supporting anti-discrimination in voting and wages.

"I am not running for office as a woman or an African American. I am running to be a senator who will work for equality and fairness for all the people of Michigan," she often emphasized in her speeches. She knew that the fight for civil rights had come a long way, but also felt it still had a long way to go. She could never forget her promise to do what she could to see Dr. King's dream come to a complete fulfillment.

"You will win, Mom. I know you will," Willy kept telling her. "Everybody likes you."

"Well, not everybody." She laughed. She had tried to protect the boys as much as possible from the many encounters she had had in her forty-five years with those who still judged her and her family on the color of their skin. She knew this campaign would bring more of that out and that she couldn't shield them much longer.

She had seen the shock on faces of some potential donors when she introduced her husband and sons, obviously they had been thinking to that point that she was white—maybe now thinking she had married a black man.

Marion's hero was Barbara Jordan. She constantly studied her life and her way of approaching her politics, wanting to emulate this great woman's success. Marion could relate to a woman like her, a black woman from the southern state of Texas, and hoped to learn how to put herself in a position of leadership to make the kind of changes Barbara Jordan did. However, she knew Senator Jordan had won her seat campaigning in predominately African-

American precincts. Marion was trying to replace a popular senator from a predominately white middle class area.

Ella May was frightened for her daughter. She knew that several threatening letters had been sent to Marion's office. Having spent most of her life in the South, she knew that many people made good on their threats. Though Marion shrugged them off as kooks, Ella May prayed constantly that her daughter would be safe. She talked to William about her concerns.

"William, I'm concerned about Marion's safety. Please make sure she is careful not to run around alone. Those threats she is receiving could be serious."

"I'm concerned too, Mama. I try to be with her or have one of the boys with her as much as possible. But you know how she is. She thinks of something she needs to do and just takes off to do it without thinking she may need to take someone with her. I've cautioned her to be careful, but I can't police her. I feel she needs a bodyguard but she won't have it."

"Well, this may only be the beginning of what she has ahead of her."

---

Marion looked up from the papers in front of her that she had been studying for several hours. Something here was not right. Surely there was a mistake. Case after case that she had looked at seemed to point to this office and maybe even the attorney general himself targeting investigations of people of color and women. She had accidentally found the list in the files of one particular investigator who was very close to the attorney general.

Lost in her thoughts, she was startled by a knock at her open door.

"Working late, Marion? I'm leaving and that leaves you the only one in the building. You gonna lock up?"

It was him—the lawyer whose file sat right in front of her. She quickly covered it with another file.

"Sure, Dan. I'll lock up."

He stared at her for a few seconds then turned and left. Had he seen the file she had taken from his drawer? She had to bring this to someone's attention, but who? The attorney general himself could possibly be in on it.

*I think I'll talk to William about this,* she decided.

Grabbing the list, she headed down the hall to the copy machine. Placing the list on the glass, she quickly copied it and returned the file to Dan's drawer. Glancing at the clock, she was alarmed at how late she had stayed. "I hope William and the boys went ahead with dinner. I know they're getting tired of my being late all the time," she mumbled to herself. Throwing things into her briefcase, she put the list on top of everything else and headed down the hall toward the elevator.

Inside the elevator, she pushed "M" for the main floor and leaned back against the wall, suddenly realizing she had developed a splitting headache. The jolt when the elevator jerked to a stop threw her to the floor. Everything went dark.

" Oh, no! What now?" She pulled herself up and felt for the buttons pushing all that she could find. "What am I going to do? There's no one in the building!"

One of the buttons she had pushed began to blink. She felt better. Maybe it would alert someone. She sat down and tried to relax. There was nothing she could do until someone came. She knew William would very soon be hunting for her.

William dialed Marion's office number for the fourth time and listened to it ring, ring, ring—no answer. It was 10:00 p.m. and Marion should have been home hours ago. She never went elsewhere without letting him know. He went to the boys' bedroom door and knocked.

"Yeah, Dad, come in."

"I'm going out to look for your mom. She should have been home before now. You need to listen for the phone or any message from her while I'm gone, okay?"

"Sure, Dad. Should one of us go with you?"

"No, you need to be here if she comes or if we get a message from her. I'm going to call the police to let me in her office building."

The police met William in front of the building and opened the front door. It was immediately apparent that the elevator was not working and that it was stuck somewhere.

"She must be stuck in the elevator," the policeman observed. He yelled, "Is anyone in there?" and banged on the door. They heard a returned banging and a muffled voice. William knew it was Marion. The officer called for an electrician that could find out how to get it started again.

William went to the payphone in the hall and called the boys. "Willy, we may have found where Mom is. The elevator is stuck here at the office. She's probably in there. We are waiting for someone to fix it. I just didn't want you to keep worrying."

"Are you sure she's in there?"

"Well, not a hundred percent, I guess, but I heard a voice and I think it was her. We'll know soon."

It was midnight before the elevator started moving slowly to the bottom floor and William pulled his wife, gasping for air and sweating from the heat, from the small space where she had been confined for four hours.

"It looks as if this cable has been tampered with, officer," the electrician called the policeman to look at what he had been checking. "It is a botched job. If whoever did this had been successful, she might have plunged to her death."

William looked at his wife and hugged her close.

"We will investigate," the officer promised.

The next day, when an investigator came to question Marion, she showed him the list of targeted investigations with Dan's signature on them and a note at the bottom specifying the course he would take against these people.

"He left just before I did," she added. "He knew I was in the building alone and would take the elevator."

Soon, Dan's fingerprints were found on the broken cable and he was arrested. An investigation of the attorney general followed to determine if he was involved. Dan implicated everyone who was in on this in order to take some of the heat off himself, but he was the only one who had tried to kill a person. There was no proof anyone told him to do that.

Marion's campaign received a new energy and donors came seeking her. She received so much publicity she barely had time to go about her daily routine. It looked as if her run for the senate was turning into a sure thing.

# SEARCHING

## 1985

In Memphis for another checkup for Margaret, she and Jim searched through the phone book, looking for Dr. Hadman. Margaret remembered that he was the doctor who came to the home and delivered her baby. He was a young man then, so he might still be around. There were two Dr. Hadmans. They took down the addresses and drove to the first office.

At the desk, Margaret asked for information. "I'm looking for an African American Dr. Hadman who had a practice in 1945. Could this doctor be the one I'm looking for?"

"No, ma'm. This doctor is young and white."

"Thank you for the information."

They drove to the next office. This looked more like it might be the person they were looking for. Several black patients were in the waiting room.

"You might be looking for Dr. Hadman's father," the nurse told Margaret. "He isn't practicing anymore."

"Could we make an appointment to talk to Dr. Hadman," Jim asked.

"He's not taking any new patients, but he can refer you to someone."

"We don't want to be his patient. We just would like to talk to him about a matter."

She looked over the appointment book. "It would have to be next week, I'm afraid. He's all booked up this week."

"Okay. When can we see him next week?"

"I have Wednesday at 10:00"

"That's good." Jim looked at Margaret for reassurance. She nodded her approval.

"Who can I put down for the appointment?"

"Margaret Corwin." They had decided they would use the name Margaret had when she was Dr. Hadman's patient before. Maybe he would mention it to his father and jog his memory before they talked to him.

When they walked into the doctor's office on Wednesday, Margaret was nervous. Could this be the lead they were looking for?

He shook their hands. "Have a seat. Sally said this was something about my father."

"We're hoping your father might have some information we are looking for. In 1945, he delivered a baby girl at the home of Rev. Louis and Ella May Cross. The baby was mine and I gave her up for adoption. Jim is her birth father. We would like to find her. We wondered if your father would remember that birth and maybe could tell us how to find the adoptive parents."

"I see. Well, I can call him and ask if he would talk to you."

The doctor picked up his phone and talked with his father. When he hung up, he told them what they hoped to hear. "My dad isn't sure he can help you, but he will be glad to see you. Here is the address. It's not far from here."

The old doctor welcomed them and listened to Margaret's story. She could see that the memory was coming back to him.

"Yes, I do remember Rev. Louis and Ella May, and I remember delivering that baby in their home. There weren't many times when I delivered a white woman's baby in a black home at that time. I think the Crosses moved to Michigan in the late sixties. I'm not sure where in Michigan. They came by my office and picked up their medical records to take with them when they moved."

"You have no record of where they went?"

"No, I'm sorry. I wish I could help you."

They gave him their phone number and asked him to call them if he thought of anything that would lead to finding the Cross family. It was time to see a lawyer.

When they got back home, Margaret made an appointment with Thurmond Morris, the only lawyer she knew. Janie had hired him to help settle things when Carl died. They told him that they wanted to locate a black minister and his wife, Louis and Ella May Cross, who had lived in Memphis until the late sixties and had moved to Michigan. Margaret remembered the name of the street and the name of the church, but told him the home and church were no longer there. He promised them he would see what he could find out.

Two days later, Janie came by as she usually did with a fruit salad for dinner and to check on how her mother was getting along, but they soon found out she had another matter on her mind.

"Mom, I happened to run into Thurmond yesterday and he said you had consulted him on a matter," she tried to act casual.

Margaret was immediately upset. "I thought lawyers were supposed to keep their clients' matters confidential," she snapped.

"I'm sorry, Mom. We're family. He didn't think we had secrets from each other."

"It's a matter between Jim and me at the moment. We will eventually share it with our kids, but now is not the right time. Maybe I chose the wrong lawyer."

"It's okay, Mom. If I see Thurmond again, I'll tell him he shouldn't be disclosing his clients' business."

"Well, you shouldn't have to tell him that. I will call him. What did he tell you?"

"Just that you were looking for a black family that lived in Memphis in 1945."

"That's all. You're sure?"

"Yes, Mom. I'm sure. I'll just forget it until you're ready to tell me."

Margaret knew her daughter too well to believe she would forget it, and she was right about that. The next day, there was a call from Junior.

"Don't tell me." She laughed. "Janie called you."

"You're right. You know her, don't you? Well, I can't say I'm not curious, but I wanted you to know that I told her it was none of our business unless you wanted it to be."

"Thank you, son. It is your business and we will let you in on it eventually, but we are just not ready yet. It's not that we want to keep something from you. We just have to right now."

"That's fine, Mom. How are you feeling?"

"Things are going really well. The doctor says I will be as good as new very soon. Jim and I are thinking more seriously now about our plans to move to Michigan."

"So that is still in the works?"

"Yes, we feel it will be the best place for us, but we're not going to rush it. I have to be strong enough to take it on."

"Okay, Mom. I feel really good about the turn your life has taken now that you are healthier. Let me know if I can help with anything. Will finding those people throw a kink in any of your plans?"

"At this point, I honestly don't know, Junior. But it is something we have to pursue. I hate being so secretive, but that's the way it has to be right now."

"I understand, but my advice is that Thurmond is not the best person to confide in. If I were you, I'd find another lawyer."

"I know that now. I've already decided to do that. Keep in touch."

"Bye, Mom. I love you."

She hung up and poured two glasses of iced tea, and then went to the yard where Jim was mowing the grass. He stopped the mower and they sat on the front porch while she relayed to him her conversation with Junior.

"I've been thinking," Jim began as he listened to her dilemma. "If this couple have moved to Michigan, it might be easier to find them there. Let's talk to the doctor and our kids and finalize our plans to move there. From there, we can find a lawyer that can help us. We might even find them in the phone book!"

They had a good laugh about that.

# TOGETHER AGAIN

## 1985

Margaret put her house in Janie and John's name and they put it up for sale with a realtor. She and Jim booked flights from Memphis to Ann Arbor, Michigan, where Sharon and her husband picked them up. They would stay with them until they decided where they would live. Jim and Juanita's house had stood empty for nearly a year, but Jim wasn't sure he should go back there. Memories of Juanita's illness and death were everywhere, and he didn't really want to bring Margaret into that. He left Margaret to rest at Sharon's and went over to look at the house. Alice and Sharon went with him.

He was shocked when he walked in. The two girls had spent hours remodeling and removing their mother's belongings.

"We each took mementoes that we wanted to keep, Dad, and all the rest is stored so that you can go through it at your leisure and keep what you want or get rid of what you don't want. All the medical supplies were returned," Sharon told him.

"It is ready now if you want to bring Margaret to live here, or if you want to sell, it's ready for that too," Alice added.

"It looks like a different house." He was awed at the transformation. "The furniture isn't even the same."

"Well, some is re-covered and repainted, but some is different. Not necessarily new, but very nice." Alice laughed. "I think Margaret would like it here."

"Well, we'll just see," he sighed. "I think you might be right."

Back at Sharon's, everyone gathered for a special dinner. She had invited Anna Rose's family to join them. Since they had to come from Dearborn, they were invited to stay overnight. The next day, Anna Rose went with Margaret and Jim to look at his house.

"This is a beautiful place, Mom," Anna Rose remarked.

"Yes, it is," she sighed. It felt warm and inviting and like home. She looked at Jim, wondering what he was thinking. He grinned at her.

"You think you could live here?" he asked.

"The question is, can you live here with memories of Juanita."

"Of course, I'll always have memories of Juanita, but nothing here is hers now, and that is the past. We are starting over. I don't think it will be a problem at all for me."

"Then we're at home," Margaret decided.

The two of them settled in as if they had always been together. Jim was able to resume his place in the church he had always been a part of with Margaret at his side. They decided to resume their quest to find the daughter they both longed to see.

Jim came in with an armload of phone books after his prayer breakfast one morning and they began to look at all the last names of Cross and circle any that were Louis. They started with Detroit, feeling that was the place that Southern people most often migrated to.

There were more than fifty, but they took turns for days calling each one, asking if the one on the other end of the line was a minister from Tennessee or if someone in the family had been a minister in Tennessee. They didn't find a single lead, so they spread out from there with the Detroit suburbs.

After several weeks, Margaret was exhausted and discouraged.

"We have to do something else," she determined. "This is too overwhelming and getting us nowhere."

"You're right, honey. We'll look for a lawyer." But they weren't sure where to start looking for one and the years slipped away.

## 1990

Jim turned on the TV to watch the news while Margaret prepared a snack in the kitchen.

"Margaret! Margaret! Come and look at this."

On the screen was a young woman running for state senate. She was being interviewed concerning a scandal she had exposed in the attorney general's office. There had even been an attempt on her life.

Margaret looked close. "Is she black?"

"At least partly," Jim remarked. "Look, that is her husband and two sons with her."

They watched with growing interest as the beautiful woman articulated her position on different political views and her desire to work toward equality for all those she would represent. A law degree from Michigan School of Law and years in the attorney general's office as well as organizing and working on campaigns for other politicians made her uniquely qualified for the job she was running to win.

"I can certainly vote for her," Margaret decided.

"Yes, she seems to know what she's doing," Jim agreed. "What was her name?"

"Marion Barnes, I think is what she said," Margaret thought she remembered correctly.

They sat for a while enjoying their popcorn and listening to the rest of the news. Suddenly, Jim blurted out, "I think I know her. She and her husband were in a Bible study Juanita and I had in our home back in the seventies. They were young law students at the time, but she doesn't look much different. I know I would vote for her. Unless they've changed, they are very dedicated Christians."

"That's great to know. How nice to really know someone you are voting for."

"I have an idea!" Jim jumped up and grabbed the Ann Arbor phone book. Turning to the Yellow Pages, he looked under 'Attorneys'.

"I think I remember the name of the firm her husband worked for. Maybe he's still there. I know he would help us. This is it, Goodman, Mantz & Barnes. He's a partner now. I'll call him tomorrow." He wrote the number down.

"This is an answer to prayer, Margaret. I just know it."

---

"Jim Hayes! It is so good to see you again. It's been a long time. I don't think I've seen you since you lost your wife. How are you?"

William had gotten up from his seat and walked around his desk to shake Jim's hand.

"I'm doing great, William. I want you to meet my new wife, Margaret."

"So happy to meet you Margaret." He took her hand in both of his.

As they settled into seats, he got down to business. "What can I do for you?"

Margaret began. "We are looking for someone and would like some help. Do you have time for a long story?"

"I sure do. Where do you want to start?"

Margaret started with where she was living and why when Jim bailed out of the plane and landed in her tree. She continued with how close they became and told about the men who broke in and would have done great harm to Jim. She told how they allowed that incident to put them into a state of mind where they gave in to their passions. At this point, she broke down.

"We all have sin in our lives, Margaret," William spoke with compassion, offering her a box of tissue. "Can you continue?"

"Yes, yes, I have to."

William had been intrigued thus far, but his interest turned to not believing what he was hearing when she continued.

"I became pregnant, but kept it a secret from all my family, even my husband who was still on a ship somewhere in the Pacific Ocean."

"The black woman who worked for me told me about a couple, a minister and his wife in Memphis, who desperately wanted a child and couldn't have one. She convinced me to go stay with them, have the baby, and give it up for adoption to them. Their names were Louis and Ella May Cross. Jim never knew about the baby until forty years later when we got together again after losing our spouses. We would like to find our daughter and see how she is doing, how her life went, and see if she would like to know her birth parents. We were told they might have moved to Michigan."

William was on his feet and seemingly weak and shaking. "Excuse me a minute…" He almost ran out of the room.

Margaret and Jim looked at each other and shrugged.

In the bathroom, William washed his face and tried to get control of his emotions. These two people were Marion's parents. She wondered all these years about them, had even known Jim, not imagining he was her father. How would she take this? He had to talk to her before he went any further with this. Taking a deep breath, he went back into the office.

"I'm sorry! I'm not feeling well, Jim. I have everything down that you told me. I promise I will get back to you soon with some ideas." He offered his hand and they left.

Two days later, they received a call from William asking them to come back to his office for another appointment.

"Maybe he has some news for us," Margaret speculated.

"Well, it's kinda soon for that, but he might have some ideas for us like he promised."

They sat down in William's office again and waited as he sat for a while with his chin resting on his clasped hands.

"Jim, Margaret, I don't know how to say this except just to say it."

Margaret's heart jumped. This didn't sound like good news.

"I'm pretty sure my wife is your daughter."

The words hung in the air. Jim and Margaret tried to take in what he said but it refused to register in their consciousness. They were paralyzed.

"I didn't want to tell you that when you were here before. For one, I was in shock, and for another, I wanted to talk to her first. She has wanted to know about her birth parents for a long time. She wants to meet you. In fact, she is here in the next room if you are ready to see her."

Both Jim and Margaret were still glued to their seats not believing what they were hearing. They had seen her on TV. They had seen their daughter and had admired her already. Jim finally got to his feet.

"Yes, of course that is what we've wanted for a long time." He looked at his wife. "Okay, honey?" She nodded still unable to speak.

The reunion was glorious. Margaret held her and held her and couldn't let go.

Finally, Marion held her mother at arm's length and said, "I have just one question to make sure you're my mother. What is my middle name?"

"Angel, Angel." Margaret whispered. They all laughed with joy.

"I told my mother that I was meeting you today. She wants to see you," Marion said.

"Oh, dear, dear Ella May," Margaret cried. "She's still alive. I want to see her too. I want to introduce her to Jim. I want to thank her for so many things."

She stared at Jim and Marion standing with arms around each other and was struck by how much Marion resembled her father.

As the four of them pulled up to the door of Marion and William's home, Margaret spotted the beautiful face of Ella May, peering through the window and waving with excited anticipation.

Inside, Margaret knelt at Ella May's feet and held her wrinkled, shaking hands, pouring out her thanks for all she had done for her so many years ago, and all she and Louis had done in raising Marion.

"No, I need to thank you, Margaret. This beautiful girl is my life, and God sent you to me and Louis so that we could have the privilege of raising her for him. You were obedient to him. Otherwise our lives would have been empty, without the amazing love Marion brought to us. No, I'm the one who needs to thank you."

Jim enfolded the small aging woman in his arms and kissed her on her soft cheek, unable to speak of the joy and gratitude he felt. His mind drew him back to the moment of impact when he was jolted from a burning plane and landed in a huge oak tree, and God grabbed hold of his life, bringing him to this joyous moment.

> And we know that all things work together for good to them that love God, to them who are called according to his purpose.
>
> —Romans 8:28 (King James Version)

# BOOK CLUB QUESTIONS

1. What might have happened to Jim if the men who broke into the house had found him?

2. How would you describe Margaret? Did she change or stay the same?

3. How did the war affect Carl? Was it different then than for those who returned home from Iraq and Afghanistan now?

4. What had changed between the 1940's and the 1980's concerning mixed race marriages? Compare to today.

5. What do you know about the role of the Tuskegee Airmen in WWII?

6. Do you think Margaret made the right choice in giving Jim's baby up for adoption? Was it right to keep this secret from everyone? Do you feel it was God's leading?

7. Should she have told Jim about the baby from the beginning?

8. Who does Marion remind you of? Is she more like her mother or her father or her adoptive parents?

9. What role did William play in Marion's development as a person?

10. Is the ending believable? Would you change it in any way?

11. Do you think Margaret married Carl because she loved him or because it was expected?